THE GUILD TRILOGY

BOOK II

OPERATION
TYPHOON SHORE

J O S H U A   M O W L L

WALKER BOOKS
AND SUBSIDIARIES

LONDON · BOSTON · SYDNEY · AUCKLAND

For my mother and father

INTRODUCTION

HONOURABLE
GUILD OF
SPECIALISTS

A Note to the Reader

In February 2002 Joshua Mowll inherited an extraordinary legacy from his great-aunt Rebecca MacKenzie: a vast archive of documents and artefacts that had been sealed for decades in a vault deep below his great-aunt's Devon cottage. The MacKenzie Archive was the starting point of the book *Operation Red Jericho*, published by Walker Books in September 2005 after years of painstaking research by the author.

In the book Mr Mowll reconstructed the 1920 adventures of the young Rebecca MacKenzie and her brother Douglas as they set sail on their uncle's research ship *Expedient* and became involved in the activities of a mysterious secret society, the Honourable Guild of Specialists. Following publication, Walker Books received many reader enquiries as to the further history of Doug and Becca – as well as several requests to see more documentary evidence to substantiate what have been referred to by some as the "slightly far-fetched" events recounted.

Although Mr Mowll originally proposed to retell the history of his ancestors in three volumes, we were uncertain if further archive material existed on which to base a second instalment of Doug and Becca's adventures. We therefore contacted the author regarding this matter; Mr Mowll's response is shown overleaf.

Dear Walker Books,

Your letter could not have enjoyed a more timely arrival! You will recall from our work on Operation Red Jericho *that, at the time of writing, only three of the five archive chambers beneath Aunt Becca's cottage had been fully explored. Although chamber five is proving difficult to crack, I have at last managed to open the fourth chamber using nothing more delicate than a sledgehammer.*

I cannot describe my elation at the wealth of archive material within, much of it purporting to the events that befell Becca, Doug and the crew of the Expedient *immediately after the battle at Wenzi Island in May 1920. More of Doug's sketchbooks bring life to the pages of Becca's journals; period sea charts and maps crackle with the excitement of untold journeys; MacKenzie family correspondence whispers dustily to be read once again; antique publications and Aunt Becca's research files bulge with the promise of further Guild secrets and lost scientific wonders; and meticulously labelled artefacts jostle on shelves, eager to be restored to the sceptical eye of history.*

Whilst I am inclined to resent your readers' insinuations as to the authenticity of my account – do they really think I could make all this up? – I am bound by my hereditary allegiance to the Guild to continue with my reconstruction work.

And so to volume two. Where do we begin? If I am not mistaken, Captain MacKenzie had just sighted a storm on the horizon…

Yours sincerely,

Joshua Mowll

President, Honourable Guild of Specialists

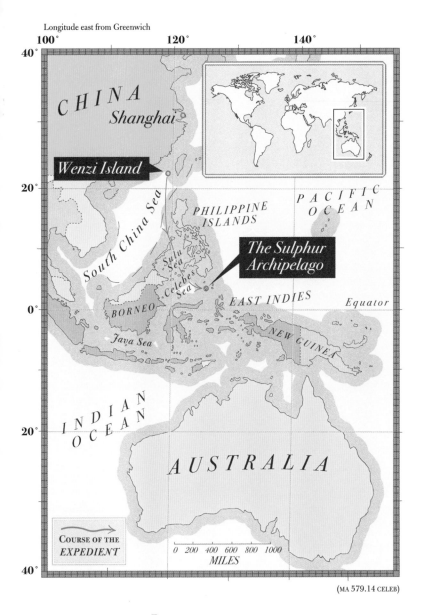

LOCATOR MAP

THEATRE OF OPERATIONS – CELEBES SEA

OPERATION TYPHOON SHORE

Not only is the universe stranger than we imagine,
it is stranger than we can imagine.

Sir Arthur Eddington (1882-1944)

CHAPTER ONE

Cutting from the 6th May 1920 edition of the *Shanghai Post*.

SAVAGE TYPHOON HITS SOUTH CHINA SEAS

UNSEASONABLE CONDITIONS

◆

NUMEROUS DISTRESS CALLS

◆

FIVE SHIPS FEARED LOST

The storm that devastated the coast of Amoy yesterday has strengthened to a full typhoon and turned southwards. The tempest is now believed to be savaging the heart of the South China Sea, from which five ships have already sent desperate distress calls.

The freak weather conditions have been described by experts as 'unseasonably early in the year'.
Captain MacWhirr ... the Nan

THE TYPHOON HAD CHOSEN ITS QUARRY THAT NIGHT AND WAS chasing hard: an injured ship, a straggler showing signs of battle damage, hounded to exhaustion across the Celebes Sea.

STEERING WITH PROPELLERS

On a twin-propellered ship, one propeller (or screw) is positioned on the starboard side of the rudder and the other on the port. A ship can be made to turn without use of its rudder by rotating one propeller faster than the other.

Her name could be picked out on her stern in the momentary brilliance of a lightning flash – RESEARCH SHIP EXPEDIENT. The vessel pitched and yawed, corkscrewing through crazy angles. And the typhoon was winning; for the last day, the course of the ship had been uncertain. The stern gear, damaged during the secret mission to Wenzi Island, had finally given out. She was now steering with propellers, a perilous prospect in such wild conditions.

As the *Expedient* crested a thirty-foot wave, Douglas MacKenzie, wearing oilskins and a sou'wester that made him look older than his thirteen years, clutched the binnacle, checked his lifeline, and gritted his teeth. He'd been in storms at sea before, but never anything like this. The ship seemed to hang on the crest for a moment then tip forward, her engine note rising as the propellers lost grip. The hull pivoted and slid down the wave trough like some hellish fairground ride. A relentless wind snatched words from the mouths of anyone who dared speak.

"Get below … hot drink … end of watch…" bawled Ives, the coxswain.

Doug tapped Xu, his watch mate, on the shoulder.

"Sujing Cha!" shouted Xu, pushing Doug back as a wave burst against the ship.

"What … does … that actually mean?" yelled Doug, laughing and wiping the stinging salt water from his eyes.

Xu cupped his hand to Doug's ear and bellowed, "It means: *this is a very dangerous enterprise!*"

They made their way aft, almost dancing over the pitching bridge deck. The ladders led them down to the shelter deck, which Doug had learnt was the most treacherous place to be. As each wave broke over the bow a deluge of foaming white water swept along the length of the deck. Overhead lifelines had been rigged along the port and starboard alleyways; Xu and Doug timed it carefully, jumping and swinging up on the

From Doug's sketchbook.[1] (DMS 2/99)   *Typhoon! DMC. May 1920*

lifeline as the cataract surged beneath them. As the water swirled through the scuppers, they dropped down and made a final dash for the galley.

"Close that door, for heaven's sake!" called Mrs Ives.

The sudden rush of air as they entered sent up a genie-like cloud of smoke from the stove.

"Evening, Mrs Ives," chimed Doug and Xu.

1 The picture above is from one of Doug MacKenzie's sketchbooks. Most of Doug's sketches were drawn from memory (or, as in this case, partly imagined), and may not be accurate representations of the people and events in this account.

"Oh, it's you two. It's tinned herring and biscuits. Cold."

Cold, hot – Doug didn't care. He'd eat anything.

"Can't cook with the *'Pedie* buckin' about like this. Hang your sou'westers on the door; I'm just tryin' to draw the range proper, and we might manage a nice cup of cocoa."

They wedged themselves on the bench between the rough wooden table and the bulkhead, the best place to be in a storm.

"Captain says we're nearly there," continued Mrs Ives as she emptied a coal scuttle into the stove. "He's about to ditch the submarine over the side. Seems a bit of a waste, but Captain knows best."

"He's doing what?"

"Something about gettin' us over a reef and the steering being broken… There's flooding in the after compartments too, that's why we're wallowin' so. Now, just pass me that tea kettle…"

Another cloud of smoke ballooned up as Doug and Xu bolted out of the galley and ran aft, narrowly dodging another rush of sea water.

The submarine hangar was a collapsible deckhouse tucked between the main island of the ship's upper works and the poop deck. The panels of the deckhouse had been removed to expose the rounded metallic side of the small research submarine, the *Galacia*. She was mounted on a wheeled cradle that slid on rails to allow her to be launched. Nine of the crew were battling with securing lines to steady the sub, which seemed ready to break free.

Another torrent crashed aft; the stern of the *Expedient* was swamped. Doug clutched at a rope and waited as the broiling water surged to knee height. The ship wavered, then steadied and broke free. The submarine cradle creaked and moaned as its huge load shifted with the erratic motion of the ship.

Doug saw his uncle, Captain Fitzroy MacKenzie, teeth gritted against the gale and lashing rain. Normally he carried a walking stick, but now he gripped a deck hydrant with one hand and gesticulated with the other. "Doug! Xu! Clap a hand on that line. There, behind Ten Dinners."

"It's no good, Captain," shouted Ten Dinners. "The third bolt's sheared. We can't hold her!"

"Chambois. Monsieur Chambois! Get out of there!" the captain bellowed.

The ship lurched to starboard, causing the mounting cradle to squeal and shudder. Luc Chambois's head emerged from the top hatch of the sub. "I have it! I have the molecule invigorator, Captain!" The Frenchman ducked down, then carefully lifted his invention through the hatch. With help from Posh Charlie, he soon had the steel-strengthening apparatus on deck. He wiped salt water from the dials with his sleeve. "I have saved it."

"I wish I could say the same for my submarine. Are the buoy and anchor attached?"

"Aye, Captain."

"Ten Dinners, pull the pin on the next starboard roll. The yaw of the ship will take her."

Expedient began to roll to starboard. The *Galacia* followed, shifting back with a screech as metal ground against metal. Charlie jumped clear, but slipped on the

THE MOLECULE INVIGORATOR

A machine invented by Luc Chambois to reinforce metal by strengthening its molecular bonds. It enabled the captain's submarine to dive to much greater depths than a normal vessel of its kind.

(See also Book I, Chapter 3.)

From Doug's sketchbook: The Galacia *goes overboard.* (DMS 3/06)

wet deck as he landed. The moment was right to release the sub.

"Let go securing lines!"

The submarine glided across the deck, building to an astonishing speed within seconds. She crashed over the side, and was immediately swallowed up by the angry waters of the Celebes Sea. Charlie was still sliding about, grasping for a handhold, as the tide of foam swelled and filled the submarine hangar again.

"Here's a line!" Doug called out, grabbing a rope beside him. He threw it, but found himself also slithering on the pitching deck. He bundled into Charlie, causing them both to roll towards the scuppers.

"Not that line, Douglas!" shouted the captain. "That's *Galacia*'s buoyed line. Let go and stand clear. *Stand clear*, I say!"

The *Expedient* levelled, allowing Charlie to stagger to his feet. But Doug was lying on the rope, which tugged backwards and whipped over the side, pulling him with it. Arms and legs flying, he shot clean past the gunwale and into the hungry sea.

The furious row of the typhoon was silenced as he went under. Doug kicked hard, striking out for the surface, his clothes dragging at him. He could hear and feel the propellers thrashing the water near by. Xu's words flashed through his mind as he broke the surface, gasping for air. *This is a very dangerous enterprise.*

The lightning was incessant, illuminating the clouds like Chinese lanterns, and the typhoon winds howled. Doug wondered, in a detached way, if he might die. After his recent experiences at the hands of the ruthless warlord Sheng-Fat, it was surprising that something as simple as lying on a rope might be the thing that actually did for him.

For a few tantalizing seconds, as the waves lifted him, Doug could see the *Expedient* framed in a flash of light. He'd always thought of her as a large ship, but she looked small and vulnerable as the typhoon attacked her, tearing at the wounds she'd suffered during the recent assault on Sheng-Fat's fortress.

Would they try to rescue him? There were no lifeboats left – they'd been destroyed on their davits by the zoridium explosion at Wenzi Island. The ship's dinghy had survived, but Doug knew it would be swamped within seconds of launching on a sea like this.

Then, in the eerie glow of rolling

ZORIDIUM

A highly explosive chemical which emits a characteristic blue smoke when detonated. Discovered before the splitting of the atom, its power was greater than any other known explosive in the early twentieth century. Sheng-Fat had forced Chambois to design and create zoridium-powered torpedoes at his fortress on Wenzi Island. Also known as Daughter of the Sun.

STORM APPAREL

Standard storm gear consisted of boots, oilskins and sou'wester.

sheet lightning, he saw a figure wrap a line around itself and dive in. It surfaced moments later, rearing up on a magnificent white horse of breaking water. Doug tried to wave but he swallowed water and struggled to keep afloat. But his rescuer had seen him; he approached at a steady crawl, sometimes visible as the sea peaked and troughed. Choking and half blinded by spindrift, Doug kicked off his boots and started to swim as hard as he could, fighting the current at every stroke. Little by little his rescuer bobbed towards him.

It was Charlie. Doug struck out with his last reserves of energy, clawing and kicking the water. Charlie grabbed his shoulder with one hand, and cupped the other over his ear.

"N-n-not … like you to … go in at the deep end, Doug," he bellowed. "Here, tie a bowline around you, and they'll pull us back in."

"Wait. Just run this by me again. You're plannin' to crash this rusty tub onto *that* island?"

"Those were not my exact words. Do you have a better idea, Miss da Vine?"

During her five days aboard *Expedient*, Liberty da Vine had managed to clash with the captain daily. Liberty was a

Nautical terms and expressions[2]

BEAM: *widest part of ship*

BILGE PUMP: *pump to remove water from bilges (lowest part of ship's hull)*

BINNACLE: *casing for ship's compass*

BOOM: *spar or pole to which foot of sail is attached*

BUOYED LINE: *rope used to attach float to anchored object it is marking*

CAPSTAN: *revolving cylinder used to wind heavy ropes or cables*

CENTREBOARD: *pivoted board that can be lowered through sailing boat keel to reduce sideways movement*

CENTREPLATE: *metal centreboard*

CLINKER-BUILT: *(of a boat) made of planks which overlap those below and are secured with clinched nails*

DECKHEAD: *underside of deck*

DECKHOUSE: *cabin constructed on top deck*

FLUKE: *barb of an anchor*

FORE AND AFT: *(of sail or rigging) set lengthwise from bow to stern*

GAFF: *vertical spar to which tops of certain sails are attached*

GALLEY: *ship's kitchen*

JIB: *triangular staysail set forward of mast*

KNOT: *unit of speed equal to one nautical mile an hour*

MAINSAIL: *principal sail of ship*

MAINSHEET: *sheet used to control and trim mainsail*

NEAP TIDE: *tide just after first or third quarters of moon, when least difference between high and low water*

OILSKINS: *set of garments made of oilskin (cloth waterproofed with oil)*

PINTLE: *pin or bolt on which rudder turns*

PITCH: *the rise and fall of ship's bow when moving forward*

ROWLOCK: *(pronounced* rollock*) fitting on boat's gunwale that supports oar while enabling it to pivot*

SCUPPERS: *holes in ship's side allowing water to drain from deck*

SHEET: *rope attached to lower corner of sail*

SHEETS: *space at bow or stern of an open boat*

SHIP'S BOATS: *small boats kept on board ship*

SHROUDS: *ropes running from mast-head to ship's sides to support mast*

SNOTTER: *fitting which holds sprit close to mast in a sailing boat*

SOU'WESTER: *waterproof hat with large flap covering neck*

SPAR: *strong pole used for mast or yard*

SPINDRIFT: *spray blown from crests of waves*

SPRING TIDE: *tide just after new or full moon, when greatest difference between high and low water*

SPRIT: *spar crossing a fore-and-aft sail diagonally*

SPRITSAIL: *sail extended by a sprit*

STAY: *large rope, wire or rod used to support mast*

STAYSAIL: *triangular fore-and-aft sail extended on a stay*

STERN GEAR: *general term for propeller, propeller shaft and steering system*

SUPERSTRUCTURE: *(of a ship) the parts, other than masts and rigging, above hull and main deck*

THWART: *crosspiece forming seat for rower in boat*

TILLER: *horizontal bar used to turn rudder*

WARDROOM: *officers' quarters on board a warship*

WARP: *heavy rope used for towing or mooring a ship*

YAW: *to swerve or steer off course*

2 See also Book I, Chapter 2.

pilot and a Texan, although not necessarily in that order. She was also an escaped ransom hostage from Sheng-Fat's fortress, and had helped Doug and Becca survive their short stay on Wenzi Island. Her bandaged left hand marked a recent injury – her little finger had been sliced off by Sheng as a memento to add to the ghastly finger-bone necklace he wore.

Captain MacKenzie was comparing a nautical chart taken from Sheng's junk with his own chart of the Celebes Sea; he'd been obliged to pin it to the chart table because the aft section of the wheelhouse was open to the elements after taking a direct hit from an artillery battery at Wenzi Island. A tiny archipelago had been circled, and it was clear that this small scattering of islands was their destination.

"Sure I have a better idea. We can run with the storm."

"The storm has almost blown itself out. I must make urgent repairs to my ship. The starboard propeller shaft was put out of alignment and has burnt out four bearings. The main condenser is failing. The steering gear is damaged. The bilge pump is broken. We have flooding in the engine room, flooding in the forward hold, and four feet of water in the aft compartments. What's more, the capstan winch is smashed beyond repair, we have no wireless to call for help and the ship's boats are gone. I am therefore planning to beach, unless you would prefer a long swim to Borneo, or perhaps Mindanao."

"I'll swim to Monaco if I have to. I'm

SHENG-FAT

Notorious for his gruesome taste in human-bone jewellery, this brutal pirate warlord terrorized the South China Sea until he was murdered by his former partner Julius Pembleton-Crozier at Wenzi Island.

never, ever, gonna sail on this decrepit jalopy again."

"Ship, madam. We are aboard a ship."

"You should've taken us straight to civilization, darn it! Those hostages you rescued from Sheng-Fat oughta be in hospital. Half of them are a bunch of old women, and they've been shaken about like Annie Taylor down there. They need medical assistance! *I* need medical assistance!"

"Mrs Ives has been attending to them. I resent your accusations, madam, especially when they are delivered on the bridge of my own ship."

Rebecca MacKenzie, Doug's elder sister, lurched into the wheelhouse as Liberty stormed out. She steadied her binoculars from swinging on their neck strap, and gripped the edge of the chart table. She felt more tired than she'd ever been in her life, but her keen eyes glinted in the half-light. For the last day or so she'd dug deep

ANNIE EDSON TAYLOR

On 24 October 1901, schoolteacher Annie Edson Taylor became the first person to go over the Niagara Falls and survive. She made the daredevil attempt in a pickle barrel in which the air pressure had been increased to 30 p.s.i. by a bicycle pump so that she could breathe. On surfacing she is quoted as saying, "No one ought ever do that again."

Photograph used by permission of the Niagara Falls (Ontario) Public Library

into her reserves of resilience, determined not to be beaten by lack of sleep. She untied her sou'wester, pushed the dark mop of sea-tangled hair from her face and tapped her uncle on the shoulder.

He turned. "Rebecca. What news?"

"The auxiliary bilge pump is broken as well as the main. They can't stop the flooding in the engine room; we are taking aboard about a foot of water every ten minutes. We're

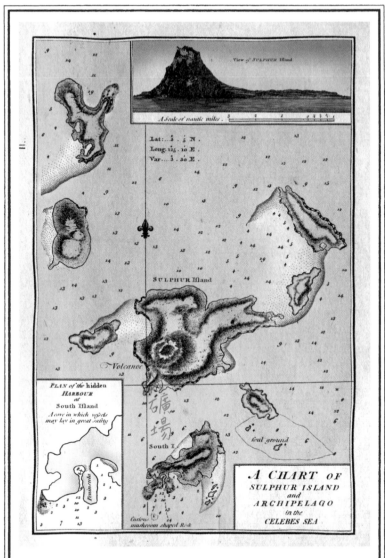

View of SULPHUR Island

A Scale of nautic miles

Lat:..5 . 5 N .
Long.125 . 10 E .
Var...3 . 30 E .

SULPHUR Island

SULPHUR Island

Volcano

PLAN of the hidden
HARBOUR
at
South Island
A cove in which vessels
may lay in great safety

Pirate isle

South I.

foul ground

矿
场

Curious
mushroom shaped Rock

A CHART OF
SULPHUR ISLAND
and
ARCHIPELAGO
in the
CELEBES SEA

SHENG-FAT'S CHART OF THE SULPHUR ARCHIPELAGO

This chart was taken from the pirate warlord's junk at Wenzi Island and shows the location of Julius Pembleton-Crozier's archaeological dig for the ancient ship mentioned in Sheng-Fat's dying gasps. The inset peninsula map details the narrow tidal creek negotiated by the crew to secure Expedient *in the hidden bay of South Island. Depths are marked in fathoms.*

sinking, Captain. Oh, and Doug says he's sorry for going over-board last night."

"I'm sure he is, niece. His seamanship leaves something to be desired."

"Captain, mushroom-shaped rock bearing Red 25," called out Vasto.

"Excellent. We've made the channel. It should lead us to a hidden bay which will answer our needs perfectly. The *Expedient* will hold out until we get there. Sheng-Fat's chart marks Pembleton-Crozier's base on the next island, three sea miles distant."

To starboard Becca could see the seas breaking as they hit shoal water and a reef half a mile off.

"Herr Schmidt?" the captain called down the speaking tube.

"Ja, Captain!"

"We're lying just off the island. Dead slow ahead both, if you please."

"Dead slow ahead both!" Schmidt's voice echoed back. "Captain, we have half an hour before we sink."

"That will be enough. Will the starboard propeller shaft hold out?"

"It's a mess down here. But the flooding is good for one thing – cooling the bearings."

In the gathering light, Becca saw an island covered with thick, lush vegetation. As they moved into the lee of the island the sea settled and the motion of the ship eased.

WOLFGANG SCHMIDT

The Chief's vast knowledge of and passion for machinery was exceeded only by his love of music, particularly the great composer Wolfgang Amadeus Mozart (1756–91), after whom his parents had named him. He often described Expedient's *engines as "a mechanical orchestra, of which I am the conductor".*

"Sam? Forward to swing the lead."

The narrow channel between the headlands was indistinct in the rain. Sheer cliffs rose straight up to a height of sixty feet, fringed with jungle. The ship was on course towards a small creek.

"Is the river going to be wide enough?" Becca asked, checking ahead with her binoculars.

"It's a tidal creek, not a river. According to the chart there's a cove beyond. The *Expedient* will be well hidden."

The headlands loomed larger and larger. They adjusted course again, but Becca could see it was going to be tight. They were becoming hemmed in on either side by outlying rocks and reefs.

The captain stepped out of the wheelhouse and shouted down to Slippery Sam on the fo'c'sle. "What's the depth?"

"By the mark, ten fathoms, Captain!"

The opening in the coastline seemed to swallow them up; there was little more than thirty feet of clear water on either side of the ship. Becca felt she could have leant out and touched the rocks that darkened and towered overhead as they steamed slowly down the channel, which began to widen into a large, circular cove. The land to starboard proved to be a peninsula connected to the main island by an hourglass-shaped beach of fine volcanic sand.

TIDAL CREEKS

Tidal creeks are coastal waterways affected by tides. At low tide there is frequently little or no water left in the channel; at high tide there is often significant depth.

"Starboard engine dead slow astern. Port engine dead slow ahead."

The *Expedient* began to pivot. The captain strode out onto the far end of the boat deck to get a better view.

"Port engine dead slow astern."

Doug appeared at Becca's shoulder. "He's reversing the ship!"

The propellers thrashed the shallow water as the vessel's stern ran aground on the hourglass beach.

"That'll do it. Engines stop," commanded the captain.

Ever so gently the *Expedient* glided ashore. She shuddered to a stop and, as the dying wind rattled through her shattered wheelhouse, seemed to give one last mournful sigh.

THE EXPEDIENT BEACHED ON SOUTH ISLAND

Painted by Doug in 1927. The back is inscribed in Becca's handwriting: Matched against my memories, this seems a fairly accurate rendering, although I fear that my dear brother has moved the *Expedient* somewhat in order to improve his composition. R.M. 1929.

CHAPTER TWO

Finally it's quiet after days of storm. We've reached dry land! The ship has stopped rolling and pitching! I've had some sleep! Outside is a whole tropical island to explore. The rich smell of land – of luxuriant jungle flora – wafts in through the scuttle.

Sea water has penetrated every deck of the ship. During the typhoon it sloshed downwards through hatches, ducts and companionways, and finally to my cabin. It's still here – a moat three inches deep around my bunk.

Down in my cabin, I spotted Mother's correspondence box floating beside my desk. I remembered that I'd forgotten to pack it when we were sent back to Shanghai some three weeks ago. (Three weeks? It feels like ten years!) As I picked it up the whole ship shuddered. I thought perhaps it was the hull settling on the beach, but I think it was more likely an earth tremor like the ones I felt when we lived in India. I wiped the box dry and put it on the shelf for safe keeping.

I realized with a pang of sadness that, since our recent stay on Wenzi Island, the cherrywood box is near enough my sole possession in all the world. My suitcases and the few items I brought from our old home in Lucknow are gathering dust at Madame Zing Zing's in Shanghai. Still, I'm glad I own at least one thing on board this ship.

This is my first diary entry since we left Wenzi Island. Writing

– in fact almost every normal activity – is just about impossible on board a ship during a force twelve typhoon; I was too busy clinging on to something solid to do anything else. Although the Expedient's stopped moving now and is resting on solid ground, I've that strange sensation you get when you've been on a ship of still being afloat. It's as if my brain is replaying the whole terrible journey.

As we left Wenzi Island, Doug and I swore a secret pact to mount our own expedition to the Sinkiang desert to look for our parents, who are still missing. Xu and Xi promised to come with us. Moments later, we were summoned on deck as the captain and Master Aa mustered the ship's complement and the Sujing fighters. The captain said he knew where the renegade Pembleton-Crozier was heading and declared his intention to pursue him without delay.

In the final desperate minutes before Sheng-Fat's fortress exploded, we'd followed our uncle on board the pirate warlord's junk, where he discovered a hoard of papers – reports from the network of spies and informants run by Sheng throughout Asia. They revealed that P-C is on an island somewhere in this archipelago where we are beached, searching for an ancient ship containing what they describe as a "Sujing clockwork compass". The captain and Master Aa think that this is the missing southern gyrolabe.

The captain's plan was simple: search these islands and arrest Pembleton-Crozier. The crew seemed in agreement and even managed a light-hearted cheer.

So we've steamed here as fast as the typhoon would allow. During the passage, our uncle has rarely left the wheelhouse. His determination to pursue P-C through the savage heart of a full typhoon – to cast the submarine Galacia overboard even – has been

the most extraordinary display of tenacity and seamanship. Nothing has swayed his resolve.

A thought has occurred to me. Is it really Pembleton-Crozier, or the chance of finding the lost gyrolabe that has fired our uncle to drag his crippled ship through one hundred and forty mile an hour winds? This missing artefact, sought by the Honourable Guild of Specialists for four hundred years, seems tantalizingly close.

I feel these gyrolabes must be connected to the mystery of Mother and Father's disappearance. Our uncle does not know – or refuses to say – if this is the case. And yet I realize that we are now on the trail of the missing southern gyrolabe. Does this mean that Mother and Father were sent on a wild goose chase? Or was there another reason for their ill-fated mission to the Sinkiang?

GYROLABES

A set of four strange and ancient gravity devices powered by zoridium. Becca and Doug first saw one demonstrated by Captain MacKenzie in his cabin.

(See also Book I, Chapter 21.)

As Becca wrote her diary, the captain waded ashore with a survey party to gauge the lie of the land. Doug and Xi had managed to tag along, although they hadn't been invited. Liberty wasn't to be left behind either, bounding down the companion ladder and joining the group just as they reached the jungle's edge.

For twenty minutes they climbed through thick vegetation. Doug had never seen such an active natural environment. All about him were palm trees covered by the tangle of rattans, fast-growing creepers, ferns, rare flowers and exquisitely coloured orchids. The smells of the plant life had been freshened by the recent rain. The stark call of parrots and the *zig-zig-zig* of insects seemed to him delicate after the fury of the typhoon. For a moment Doug thought he saw a sad-eyed, long-faced monkey peeping at him from high in the leaf canopy, but it was no sooner seen than gone.

Much of the way they followed a small stream which smelt sulphurous and foul. The climb was steep and unrelenting, sapping the little energy they had left. Gasping for breath, they reached the barren rock leading to the jagged ridge that ran like a spine across the island.

Just before the crest, Doug turned to get a better view of *Expedient* lying on the hourglass spit of sand far below. The hidden bay was almost perfectly bowl shaped and filled with turquoise water of startling clarity; the narrow entrance beside the peninsula and the mist rising from the storm-drenched jungle imbued the cove with a mystical atmosphere. This secret place was an ideal spot to hide the ship. Master Aa had set picket guards to protect her, and the crew who remained behind were already consolidating her position, using the dinghy to tow mooring warps from the bow.

Xi scrambled up and handed Doug a water bottle. He hadn't even broken into a sweat. "Not tired, are you?"

"No," lied Doug, swigging down a mouthful of water.

"Your cheeks are red. You wheezed up that hill like a fat old woman!"

Doug knew that Xi was always looking to prove himself the strongest, the fastest, the best. He glanced over his shoulder at the ridge. "Race you, Xi. First to the ridge."

Xi took up the challenge immediately, bounding off before

Doug had time to turn. He chose the most direct and ambitious route, which meant he would have to negotiate a short, near vertical ascent. Doug ran left where the route was easier but longer, following a sloping outcrop to where Chambois was nearing the crest.

Doug jinked and leapt, darting up the path. Xi was trying to climb, but lost his foothold and slid back down. Doug raced up the last section, sidestepping Chambois. The vista beyond the ridge opened up before him: first the tangled storm sky; then the white caps of the Celebes Sea; and finally the rest of the islands of the archipelago.

Chambois stepped up and saw the same dreadful sight at the same moment. His face dropped, his mouth opening in shock. "*Mon Dieu!* What nature of catastrophe…"

A horseshoe of islands fanned out towards the horizon. Four out of seven were devastated, levelled almost flat and devoid of all vegetation. They appeared as little more than muddy streaks just above sea level. The nearest island, whose dominant feature was a volcanic cone at its western end, lay some three sea miles away and seemed to be at the centre of a massive mining operation. A tongue of land four or five miles long stretched away to the east of the dormant caldera. Half of this was still vivid green jungle; the other half was the same sludgy orange as the other decimated islands.

Then, with a shock, Doug saw that their own island was also being ripped apart. The work seemed to have only just started and was confined to the opposite end of the island, but on a distant headland a vast excavator tore into the jungle landscape, cutting its contours to sea level. Further inland a huge explosion cracked out and a curtain of rock was dynamited from a hillside in a rolling cloud of dust.

"These islands – they have been flattened. Obliterated!" exclaimed Chambois.

Xi crashed into Doug, but the race was forgotten in the dying boom of the explosion.

"Everyone down! Keep low," ordered the captain. He hurried towards Chambois and Doug, pulled a telescope from his pocket and steadied it against a rock. Doug crunched up by a boulder and dug out a pair of binoculars from Charlie's haversack.

"Hey, give those b-b-back."

Doug batted his friend's hand away and focused on the mining activity on the next island. In the shadow of the volcanic cone, a truck skidded along a muddy track. He watched it pull up to the gate of a mining compound packed with towering buildings, railway tracks, a tall lattice mast, conveyor belts and workshops. "K-a-l… Kal-axx. The truck says *Kalaxx*, Captain!"

"The Kalaxx? A thousand curses," muttered the captain. "Sheng-Fat's papers made no mention of them, Master Aa. I had no idea."

Master Aa lifted a pair of binoculars and began to scan the island.

"Oh, brother," sighed Liberty. "Those crap kickers."

"Do you know them?" asked Doug.

"I know *of* them. They're so dirty not even my dear ol' daddy would use them. They're an exploration and minin' corporation. I thought they'd been outlawed by civilization."

Doug recalled Sheng-Fat's dying words. "It's just as Sheng said. Pembleton-Crozier must be digging for the ancient ship—"

Master Aa's booming voice interrupted him. "Captain, we are in mortal danger. We must leave these islands immediately."

"Master Aa?"

"Your plan was to arrest Pembleton-Crozier. I agreed to assist you in this simple matter. There was no mention of Kalaxx involvement. If there had been, I would not have come within a hundred miles of this archipelago with so few Sujing Quantou warriors. We must leave. Now."

Doug was astonished. The Sujing Quantou, the fiercest fighters in all China, had just suggested unqualified retreat from a bunch of miners.

"My apologies, Master Aa," said the captain. "I'd imagined a few modest excavation trenches, not this. Not the Kalaxx."

"How long will it take you to repair the ship?"

From Doug's sketchbook: The devastated archipelago. (DMS 3/10)

THE ORDER OF THE SUJING QUANTOU

An ancient fighting order dating back to 326 BC, divided into four chapters. The northern chapter had become the bitter enemy of the eastern and western chapters since its expulsion from the Sujing brotherhood in 1720. Its supplies of Daughter of the Sun (zoridium) were confiscated at this time, but the northern chapter (the Kalaxx) had since embraced contemporary weaponry and earned a reputation as soulless mercenaries.

(See also Book I, Sujing panel.)

"Four days, perhaps."

Doug tapped Xi on the arm. "Why's Master Aa so scared?"

"The Kalaxx are clearly in league with Pembleton-Crozier," whispered Xi.

"So what?"

"The Kalaxx are the recreant northern chapter of the Sujing Quantou. They have earned their living mining precious metals and gems since they were excommunicated from the Order of the Sujing. If we are found here they will kill us all. They will show no mercy."

"What's their strength?" asked Captain MacKenzie.

"Our latest intelligence report put their numbers at five hundred. They always work together. If one is here, they will all be here," stated Master Aa.

"By Jove, as many as that? Do they have Daughter of the Sun weaponry?"

"No," sighed Master Aa. "But had I expected to encounter the Kalaxx, I would first have sought the help of the western chapter of the Sujing. We must act. We need a plan of defence in case of discovery before the *Expedient* is ready to sail."

"I concur," said the captain. "The bay offers natural protection. We cannot be seen by passing vessels."

Калакс
Горная Компания

The Kalaxx Mining Company

The Kalaxx fought for the Imperial Russian Army as reconnaissance troops for 140 years, supplementing their income by mining mineral-rich lands in the Caucasus awarded to them by Catherine II after their service in the battle at Balta (first Russo-Turkish War, 1768–74). A hundred years later they fell out of favour with the court of Alexander II, and were finally expelled from Russia in 1861. They joined the gold rushes in America, amassing a colossal mining fortune in Idaho and Montana. Their trademark blend of brutality and greed won them notoriety the world over. The Kalaxx left America for Africa following rumoured involvement in the murder of a state official who had denied them a mining claim. Nothing was proved, but the murder weapon was a Kindjal dagger of a type found only in the Caucasus region of Russia. A newspaper article written in 1911 estimated the Kalaxx's fortune at thirty million dollars.

Photograph of a derailed Kalaxx Mining Company train carriage in Southern Africa, 1913.

"If your crew repair the ship, we Sujing Quantou will build defences to protect our position."

"Very good, Master Aa. We'll set up an observation post just here."

"And what do the passengers get to do?" enquired Liberty.

"The ransom hostages are in no fit state to do anything. But if you are seeking employment, Miss da Vine, you could assist Mrs Ives with their welfare," suggested the captain.

Xi sniggered and whispered to Doug, "I don't think Mrs Ives is going to like that idea any more than Liberty!"

For a moment, Liberty was speechless. But many of the captives rescued from Wenzi Island had become her friends, and reluctantly she nodded, her face twisting into a scowl. She punched the ground with her good hand. "Boats! Thrown about the ocean, makin' less than ten miles an hour, only to end up marooned on a pathetic excuse for an island nursemaidin' Sheng-Fat's victims! How did I get into this? Give me air travel any day. All I wanna do is fly my plane."

"Madam, if you would care to look through this telescope, I think you might see something of interest."

Liberty crawled over, muttering.

"There. Look to the side of that pier in the bay."

"Where?" She adjusted the telescope. "Well, I'll be … that's *Lola*. My plane! You've found my plane!"

That first day on the island was one of organization and preparation. The observation post kept an eye on Kalaxx activity, while the Sujing set about building a defensive line of trenches and sharpened bamboo on a saddle of land just above the

beach, allowing them to defend the *Expedient* and the peninsula from an overland attack. More bamboo had been cut to
create a scaffold at the *Expedient*'s stern so the rudder could be
repaired.

Posh Charlie surveys the Expedient*'s damaged rudder.*   (MA 556.214 EXP)

(See also Appendix 1.)

As they were so near the equator the sun sank quickly, and by
seven o'clock it was completely dark. Many of the ship's complement were seated around the captain's elegant mahogany
dining table, which had been unbolted from the deck and
carried to a position above the high-water line of the beach. On
a white linen cloth, pegged against a lazy onshore wind, the
ship's fine silverware and china glinted in the flickering light of
three Georgian candelabra. The Duchess circled the table, nudging people's chairs and scaring them into feeding her titbits.

The meal had been a rather curious selection of courses:

a coconut starter, a thin meat stew for the main course, and a banana crumble pudding. As the decanter of port returned from its clockwise circuit of the table, the captain stood and tapped his knife against his heavy crystal wine glass. A hush fell across the table.

"Ladies and gentlemen, as you know we are unable to request assistance, as we have no radio, nor ship's boats other than the dinghy. However, it is my belief that we are safe here, and that the ship's refurbishments are within our capacity; we should complete the repairs within the next three days. Our observation post is established and we can keep a constant watch on the other islands for signs of trouble. Once the *Expedient* is overhauled, we will float her off and return to China with all possible haste. It is with regret that I am forced to announce the abandonment of my original aim in coming here. It was my intention to arrest Julius Pembleton-Crozier, but his alliance with the Kalaxx makes this impossible."

From Doug's sketchbook. (DMS 3/15)

Liberty gave a slow handclap. "First sensible thing you've coughed out since Wenzi Island."

"Good. Which brings me to my next point. It gives me great pleasure to welcome you to this dinner in honour of my niece and nephew, Rebecca and Douglas. After their recent exploits in the South China Sea, where they showed great initiative and fortitude in the face of enormous odds, I am delighted to induct them into the Honourable Guild of Specialists as associate members—"

"Whoa, just rein in your horses there, Skip!" interrupted Liberty with surprising vehemence. "Have you given these two a choice in the matter?"

"Whatever do you mean, Miss da Vine?"

"Now I'm just a passer-by at this sideshow, an inconvenienced traveller as it were, and my view of your secret club here is by no means full or complete, but the way I see it, this HGS is no breeze ... no darn stroll in the park." Liberty turned to Becca. "Y'all sure you know what you're gettin' into, coz?"[3]

"Miss da Vine, this is a solemn occasion. I have absolutely no doubt that it is what their parents wanted."

"And where exactly are their parents, Captain? I heard they were lost on some secret expedition to the backside of China. We're in the same fix ourselves – only we're shipwrecked to boot. Our closest neighbours are that mad English guy who stole my plane in Foochow – also a one-time member of your so-called Guild – and a bunch of cut-throat miners wanted for mass murder by the civilized world. Cousins, I'd think *lonnng* and hard before you swear an oath to this crazy gang."

"Thank you for that succinct and interesting point of view," snapped the captain.

---

3 Liberty often referred to Becca and Doug as her cousins just for fun, as Doug had claimed to belong to the oil-rich da Vine family when forced into a tight corner by Sheng-Fat on Wenzi Island.

"As my dear ol' daddy always says, make sure you know what's in it for the other guy before you spit and shake on a deal."

"If you'll raise a glass, Rebecca and Douglas, we will complete your induction into the Honourable Guild of Specialists. Without the need for spit."

Becca and Doug stood, raising their glasses.

"Douglas and Rebecca MacKenzie, I welcome you to the Guild. Do you swear to uphold its high ideals and honour its ancient purposes? If so, drink and declare: honour, duty or death!"

Doug slugged the port down in a single gulp, spluttering, "Honour, duty or death!" He wiped his mouth on his sleeve and grinned.

Becca lifted the glass to her lips, wavered for a moment, then suddenly threw the port away, splattering it on the sand behind her.

"Rebecca! What manner of rudeness is this?"

"No. Liberty's right. Not until we've discovered the fate of the Sinkiang expedition. Not until I've found my parents."

Liberty arched an eyebrow, flashing a smile of vindication first at Becca and then the captain.

"Impossible child!"

Becca crashed the glass down and stormed off towards the dark shadow of *Expedient*'s stranded hull.

Becca slammed her cabin door, turned up the oil lamp's wick and took out her diary. But her mind was too agitated to write, so she sat staring at the bulkhead rivets, face fixed in

From Doug's sketchbook: Becca slams down the glass. (DMS 3/17)

unhappy contemplation of the Guild and how it controlled every aspect of her life. She was there some time before her annoyance at her uncle's attitude was replaced by annoyance at the slow drip, drip of water splashing onto her desk.

A brief investigation pointed to her mother's correspondence box. It appeared to be dry inside and out, but when she lifted it to her ear and listened closely, she could hear a faint gurgle as she tipped it from side to side. Opening it, she noticed that a small hidden compartment in the lid was weeping sea water. She saw an indent for a fingernail to push. Silently she chided herself for never having examined the box more closely.

The panel was difficult to open because the wood had swelled with soaking. She got it open after a minute or so, releasing the remaining salt water onto her desk.

Fitted neatly inside were two waterlogged envelopes. The first was addressed to Mr and Mrs A. K. Jukes, Srinagar. The envelope was so saturated that the gum seal had dissolved, but Becca recognized her mother's handwriting. She turned over the second envelope: *To Rebecca and Douglas.*

Elena MacKenzie's correspondence box

This box was one of Becca's most treasured possessions, and she always kept it on her desk at Cove Cottage. The photograph below shows the slim false compartment where her mother's letters were hidden.

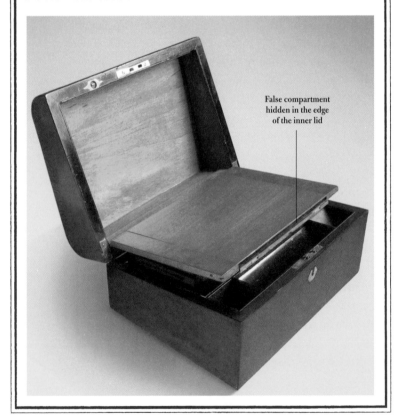

False compartment
hidden in the edge
of the inner lid

Her hands started to shake. Her mouth went dry. Her heart began to pump so fast she could hear it.

For a moment she felt quite light-headed. Questions flooded her brain. Would this tell them about their parents' expedition? Give them an explanation, perhaps, as to why they'd left her and Doug? Might it even reveal a destination: a clue that a search party could follow? Would the mystery of their parents' disappearance finally be solved?

Her mind screamed to tear open the note, but she calmed herself and very carefully removed the envelope. She scanned through the letter, tripping over the words, all the time hoping to see a name, a place, anything that would indicate where her mother and father had been bound. Some of the characters were blurred but she could make out every word.

She reread it three times, then slumped back in her seat. There had been a single mention of Sinkiang, but not even the vaguest indication of a route or a specific destination. There was a second sheet but this was in code, and indecipherable. She read that three times too, in the hope that something might leap out. It didn't.

Becca skimmed the letter to the Jukeses. It merely confirmed the contents of the first letter.

The palpitations calmed. She opened her desk drawer and laid the damp pages flat against some sheets of blotting paper to dry out, then closed it firmly and locked it.

For some time Becca lay on her bunk, staring at the drawer, spinning the key idly in her fingers. She was too exhausted to cry, too confused by the letter to know what to do. It had answered none of her questions.

But something about the letter was troubling her, something she couldn't quite put her finger on. Her mind was wrestling with the problem when Doug crashed into his cabin next door, his normal clumsiness enlivened by the glass of port. Becca considered telling him of her discovery, then remembered that he was now a sworn member of the Guild. Could she trust her brother with secrets like this? Did his oath mean that he had to divulge everything to the captain? She didn't know.

Becca suddenly felt much older. She was even more certain now that she'd been right not to join the Guild.

CHAPTER THREE

Becca's diary: 8th May 1920

I have just helped move the patients up on deck from their berths in the fo'c'sle. There was something of a showdown as Liberty reported to Mrs Ives for duty. It was plain from the start that Mrs Ives didn't want Liberty anywhere near the hostages. It's also abundantly clear that Liberty can't stand Mrs Ives.

The patients, bandaged from the horrific injuries inflicted by Sheng-Fat, are weak after the typhoon. But as we passed around glasses of water some of them started to sing – of the twenty rescued, there are nine members of a ladies' choral society, who are intent on singing despite their condition. Liberty put her fingers in her ears, shouting, "Stop! Locked up with that caterwaulin' was just about more than I could stand on Sheng's island!"

I rather like the singing; I can hear them now, as I write this in my cabin. Their leader is a Mrs Cuthbert, who's a widow. In fact, they are all widows. They explained that they were on a world tour in honour of Mrs Cuthbert's late husband, a famous banker from Long Island, when they were kidnapped by Sheng-Fat in the

Mrs Cuthbert

From Doug's sketchbook: Studies of Mrs Cuthbert. (DMS 3/22)

Formosa Strait. They are keen on requiems, particularly, she said, *as they are all grieving. Mrs Ives said not to tell the crew that they're widows, as it's considered unlucky to carry one widow on board, let alone nine.*

"…well, I c-c-can't h-help you, Captain," stuttered Posh Charlie.

"But you were prepared to storm the fortress at Wenzi Island, Charles."

"I know, and very exhilarating it was too, b-b-but that c-c-changed everything. I had no idea Julius would be there and that we'd pursue him here. I just can't be p-part of this m-m-mission any more."

"Do you wish to leave the ship? Is that what you want?"

"Well, in a way, I … I do. I would like to return to F-F-Firenze and if p-p-possible continue my research."

"There's no way off this island. The *Expedient* isn't fit to sail."

"I know."

"Puts us in a rather difficult position, doesn't it?"

"I'm prepared to work light duties, but I'll take no further p-part in the pursuit of J-J-Julius. I can't be involved."

Doug knocked very hard, although the door was ajar.

"Enter. Ah, Douglas. Come in. Where's your sister? I sent for her too."

"Here, Uncle," Becca said running in, eyeing the Duchess. The tiger stretched and yawned noisily. "Sorry I'm late. I was helping with the patients."

"Good morning, niece." The captain smiled, her outburst of the night before apparently forgotten. "I've promised Mrs Ives we'll replenish our food stores. I've spoken to

Master Aa, and Xu and Xi are to help you scavenge for food on the peninsula. Douglas, what do you know about sailing? Do you know your sheets from your shrouds?"

"I sailed with my father in Chesapeake Bay."

"Well, I'd like you to go with Charles in the *Powder Monkey*, and see what victuals you can find in the cove. The water looks to be teeming with fish, many of which are damned fine eating, I'll be bound. Charles is an excellent fisherman. Is that all right for you, Charles?"

"Q-quite all right."

Becca wondered whether Doug was getting special treatment because he'd joined the Guild the night before. "So Doug gets to fool about on the water while I'm toiling through hot jungle?"

"I meant nothing by it," Captain MacKenzie answered with irritation. "You can swap after luncheon."

Doug pulled a face at Becca. "You *hate* small boats. When we went out with Father, you complained about the thing wobbling so much he put you ashore."

POSH CHARLIE

From Becca's diary:
Charlie is an enigma.
A refined gentleman, a scholar and an expert shot
– attributes that jar with his current employment as a deckhand. He has the air of an amateur rather than a professional sailor – sometimes he has trouble tying a simple bowline. Enquiries into his career before he joined the *Expedient* are met with scant answers, much garbled by his stammering. A good friend, however.

Becca flushed. "Shut up. I've been through a typhoon since then."

The captain continued. "I've split the crew into work parties, and suspended the watch system. But let Mr Ives know your movements just for courtesy and safety's sake. Mrs Ives will provide you with baskets."

The captain picked up the Duchess's lead and lobbed it towards Becca. "Take the Duchess with you. She's becoming lazy." The huge tiger rolled over, one eyelid flicking open to cast a languid scowl in Becca's direction.

Becca parried her opponent's swords and lunged. But he was too quick, twisting backwards so that she overran and tumbled into the soft scrub grass.

"I told you I was a better swordsman," said Xi arrogantly.

Their blades were lengths of bamboo, which felt clumsy to Becca compared to the real thing. For ten minutes she'd been soundly outclassed by the sinewy Xi. The impromptu contest was a strange mix – Xi with two blades to her one – and she could see that she needed to change tactics.

Xi's Sujing Quantou style – wrought from influences as far afield as Alexander's Greece, ancient Japan and the desert caravans of the Chinese Silk Road – was fast, flexible and improvisational. By comparison Becca's medieval European rapier style seemed too disciplined and tutored. For every combination

THE SILK ROAD

For at least 3,500 years this network of trade routes connecting Asia to Europe carried valuable goods such as silk, jade and spices across deserts, mountains and seas. Some of the most famous routes led across the Sinkiang deserts of western China to Samarkand and the Mediterranean.

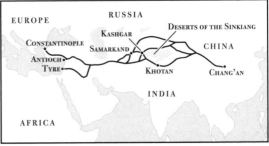

of fast parry and lunge she tried, Xi would answer with a double up-cut or half-twist, backflip or cartwheel.

"The match is unbalanced," said Xu, who was sitting on one of Mrs Ives's baskets, acting as umpire.

"Here, I'll make it easy for you." Xi chucked one of his bamboo sticks away.

"Make it easy for me?" snapped Becca, wiping the sweat from her eyes. She thought back to a fencing lesson with her father, who'd related a tale about "a sword fight with several Chinese gentlemen in Kashgar". Becca had always imagined it as a formal contest. Had it in fact been some sort of street fight? *"To stick rigidly to what one knows in the hope that your opponent may oblige and fight the match by your rules means you will lose. I had to adapt to their methods. I ran at them hard, shouting and screaming. This stampede surprised them as much as it did me. They expected one thing; I gave them another. I won the contest and retired to my hotel for a refreshing gin sling."*

Becca handed Xi his discarded sword. "I don't want any special treatment."

"En garde!" called Xu.

Becca assumed the classic stance, while Xi chuckled. "You know—"

She dropped the stance and charged at him, screaming as loud as she could, wielding the bamboo more like a cutlass or sabre. He staggered backwards, taken by surprise, unable to make a proper counter as he tried not to fall. Becca continued to yell, never letting up the pressure of her attack, as she pushed him twenty or thirty feet back across the flat arena they'd found to the jungle's edge. Xi stumbled over the roots and undergrowth, until she finally dropped the bamboo and just screamed at him.

"All right, all right, you win!" laughed Xi. His laugh changed to a shriek as he turned his head and saw embedded in the grass beside him a headless skeleton, the bones bleached white by the sun. Xi leapt up and readied his bamboo sword, his face drained of blood. "By the Great Iskander[4] himself!"

Becca recoiled too, stepping away but suddenly halting as she put her foot through the brittle ribcage of a second skeleton.

Xu folded up with laughter, first at his brother, who'd jumped like a scalded cat, and then at Becca, who was struggling to disengage herself from the bones.

"Why are they here?" asked Xi.

"It's a graveyard. What else can it be?" replied Xu.

Becca composed herself and picked up her bamboo. "They usually bury people in graveyards."

Xu pushed back the leaves of a fern. "There's a third one here. Have you noticed? None of them has a skull."

Becca shuddered.

"Sorcery?" whispered Xi. "Demons? Cannibals?"

"Frightened of a bunch of old bones, brother?" scoffed Xu. "Scared they might fight better than you?"

"Frightened?" echoed Xi incredulously. "*Frightened?* I am the Sujing prodigy! I fear nothing and no one—"

"Oh, don't start," snapped Becca. "Just get the baskets and we'll report this to the captain."

The fishing expedition was turning out to be rather unsuccessful. They had spent the morning sailing up and down the sheltered cove, improving Doug's boatmanship, but catching little. The sum total of their efforts was a garish reef creature

4 Alexander the Great (356–323 BC), King of Macedonia. His armies conquered Persia, Egypt, Afghanistan and India.

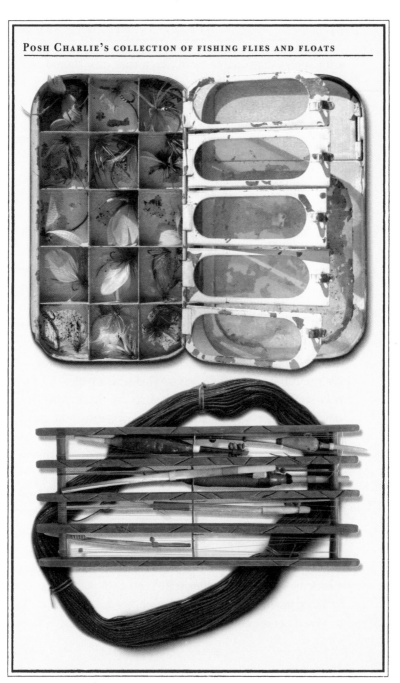

POSH CHARLIE'S COLLECTION OF FISHING FLIES AND FLOATS

with spines that Charlie wasn't even sure they should pick up, let alone eat. After much pestering from Doug, for whom sailing was infinitely preferable to fishing, Charlie baited a spinner and they set a towed line astern.

"I'm going to tack now, Charlie," announced Doug, sitting in the stern sheets of the boat.

"Don't throw the t-t-tiller this time. You're not changing a set of p-points on a railway t-t-track. Smoothly. Let the j-jib do the work and pull her bow round. You'll n-not lose so much way."

"Ready about!" Doug did as Charlie said, and eased the tiller onto a new course. "Lee ho!" He ducked as the red tanned mainsail glided over, then ruffled and filled. He swapped sides and let the mainsheet out a little. Charlie took care of the jib then shifted his weight to the windward side to balance the boat. Waves lapped the bow as the sturdy little dinghy picked up speed and heeled over.

The *Expedient* lay a little more than four hundred yards off their port beam. Her stern was covered with a lattice of bamboo scaffolds as the crew worked to fix the rudder. The damage was far worse than anyone had expected; the metal had been bent as easily as a piece of cardboard by Sheng-Fat's diabolical Dragon's Teeth mechanism, and two long gashes in the plating had caused the flooding.

Xu, Xi and Becca came into view, leading the captain and Master Aa towards the peninsula at a brisk walk. Doug forgot the tiller momentarily, wondering what the excitement might be, and the mainsail flapped and threatened to gybe.

"Fluky winds circle the b-b-bay. Good practice for you. Check the s-spinner. Anything yet?"

Doug tested the fishing line. "Er, no."

"We'd better p-p-put the anchor down and try again with

the rods. Mrs Ives will be expecting a shoal of f-f-fish for the amount of time we've been gone."

"We'll try a little further out. Over there by that rock."

"Very good, s-s-skipper."

Doug set course for a lone rock near the cliffs on the far side of the bay. He'd been eyeing this outcrop for the last hour and curiosity had got the better of him. Charlie dropped the mainsail and jib as Doug clambered forward and let go of the anchor. It gave a satisfying splash, and he watched it sink through the crystal-clear water until it struck the bottom. "Plenty of fish down there. Hundreds. I can see them."

Doug jumped in, doing a perfect running bomb which soaked the bow of the dinghy. He swam underwater for a few strokes, then surfaced on the opposite side of the boat.

"You'll scare the ruddy f-f-fish away if you do that. Now, Mrs Ives said b-big ones. No minnows."

Doug paddled back, relishing the cool water. "This is like a swimming pool. Pass me the net; I'll see what I can catch."

Net in hand, he took a breath and kicked out for the bottom. The visibility was excellent; hundreds of small fish flashed by, their vivid scales picked out in dancing shafts of sunlight that filtered down from the surface. Startled, they darted in a thousand directions as he approached.

Doug surfaced.

"Catch anything?"

"Give me a chance."

Charlie was unravelling an antique fishing rod; he'd donned a crumpled tweed cap with brightly coloured fishing flies pinned to its peak. "Well, g-g-get on with it. Stop m-m-mucking about. Difficult to know what we'll land out here. Salmon and trout's more my bag..."

The Powder Monkey

The Powder Monkey was a thirteen and a half foot clinker sailing dinghy built to a standard Admiralty pattern. She was fitted with a jib and spritsail, as well as a pair of oars. A snotter supported the heel of the sprit when the sail was hoisted. The snotter had to be made of strong rope or wire, since if the sprit broke free in strong winds it had the potential to hole the planking and sink the boat.

POWDER MONKEY

1   Tiller
2   Stern locker
3   Thwart
4   Centreplate box
5   Centreplate lifting gear
6   Mast
7   Anchor
8   Oars
9   Mainsail
10   Main halyard
11   Mainsheet
12   Sprit
13   Snotter
14   Jib
15   Jib halyard
16   Jib sheet
17   Shroud
18   Forestay
19   Rudder
20   Rowlock (shipped when sailing)
21   Centreplate

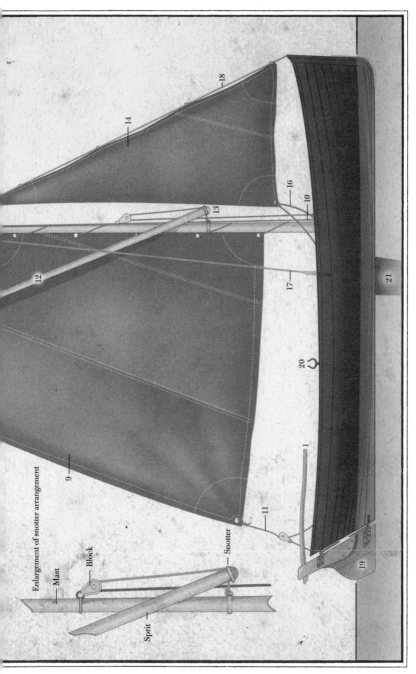

Enlargement of snotter arrangement

Mast

Block

Sprit

Snotter

(MA 556.154 EXP)

For ten minutes Doug wielded the cumbersome net at anything that passed by. But hard as he tried, he could only get the most meagre fish. He chucked the net back aboard and hooked his elbows over the dinghy's transom, defeated and out of breath.

"Becca said I wouldn't catch anything. I have to get at least one fish to shut her up."

"Things n-n-not so good between you?"

"We've fallen out. She's not speaking to me. Hardly a word since I took the oath and joined the Guild last night."

Charlie rummaged around in his wicker fishing box and pulled out a fly case crammed with multicoloured hooks. "That's the trouble with s-s-siblings. They can make you more exasperated than any other p-person alive."

"Strange, isn't it?"

"What's s-s-strange?" said Charlie, spiking his finger by accident.

"Strange that you can be brother and sister and think the absolute opposite of each other. I couldn't wait to join the Guild. I don't know what her problem is."

Charlie didn't answer immediately. He threaded a fly to his line with great concentration and tied it off. "P-p-positive and negative, old sport. Like a compass."

"She wouldn't join the Guild, though. She refused," Doug mused.

"We each have our own paths in life. She thinks s-she's chosen the right way; you think you have t-t-too. Who's to know who's got it right?"

"But which *is* right ... you know, where the Guild's concerned?"

Charlie cast his line. "Why did you j-j-join the Guild, Doug?"

"Because Mother and Father were in it – are in it. And the captain can be a bit tetchy, but he's all right. Besides, what choice did I have?"

"There's always a choice, Doug. Becca made a different choice. It's just a case of finding the p-p-path you're most happy with. Sometimes things change. Sometimes difficult choices have to be made – for the greater g-good, I mean."

Doug turned to look at him. "You sound like you're not sure about the Guild yourself."

"The Guild is an honourable institution. 'Honour, duty or death.' Just remember that. But t-t-try and make friends with her, Doug. I've seen a lot of fighting in my life, and I'm now of the firm opinion that talking is f-far more useful."

Charlie suddenly looked remote and withdrawn. He didn't say any more.

"Four?" yelped Mrs Ives. "*Four?* With that great ocean out there, you managed to catch four fish? Well, let's 'ave a look!" She shrieked as an enormous crab leered out of the basket waving its immense claws at her, pincers open, ready to defend itself from the cooking pot.

"What do you think of him?" beamed Doug. "I believe he's a member of the *Crabius maximus* family." Becca, seated on the bench, watched her brother with detached boredom. Xi tried to grab the crab but got a nip on the wrist.

"Douglas MacKenzie!" squawked Mrs Ives. She tried to get the wicker handle, but the crab went for her, causing the basket to topple off the table onto the deck. The pugnacious crustacean was on the loose.

From Doug's sketchbook: Mrs Ives and the crab. (DMS 3/28)

"He's quite lively, Mrs Ives."

Xi rose to the challenge. "I'll catch him."

The crab scuttled sideways towards the door. Doug tried to block its escape route with his boot, but was beaten back by the snapping claws. Xi nudged him forward and the crab nipped Doug on the knee.

In retaliation, Doug headlocked Xi and tried to wrestle him towards the pincers; all the while Mrs Ives shouted for them to behave. The crab managed to climb the door coaming and scamper across the deck, where it made a desperate jump for the sea through a scupper.

"He's escaped," said Becca calmly, crossing her arms.

Doug and Xi forgot their play fight and ran out onto the deck just in time to see the crab splash into the shallow water below.

"Er, crab appears to be off the menu tonight, Mrs Ives," said Doug.

"Tonight? That was meant to be lunch, God help me! Now, let's see the rest of your catch." She lifted the spines of the ugliest fish with the tip of her knife, and recoiled in horror. "What in the name of all things...? What am I meant to do with *that*? It'll poison the lot of us. These other tiddlers are so small they won't make a single fish cake. Look at 'em!

"Take those 'orrible creatures and put 'em back where you found 'em. Your sister and the Souchong twins at least found us some coconuts."

"Sujing. Not Souchong," corrected Xi, nursing his wound. "We are an ancient fighting order, not tea merchants."

"Well, Master Aa was lookin' for you. He wants you and your brother up at the redoubt."

"Why didn't you tell me sooner?" grumbled Xi, ducking out of the door.

"I'll tell you why!" called Mrs Ives after him. "You were too busy fightin' shellfish and causin' a ruckus with Douglas, that's why!"

"Do I get any marks for artistic merit?" tried Doug, lifting out a tiny rainbow fish.

"Artistic merit? Look on the door, my lad. It says galley, not ruddy gallery!"

Doug picked up the basket.

"Where are you off to now?"

"To take them back, like you said."

In frustration Mrs Ives snatched the basket from him, stood at the door and with a smart swing chucked the entire catch over the side.

"I want you and Becca to take this pitcher of water to the patients. I've spent the whole morning bandagin' little fingers, and now I've got to find a way to feed the five thousand with a bunch of ruddy coconuts!"

Doug read the letter from his mother in the stifling heat of Becca's cabin. His sister sat in silence on her bunk. She knew the contents pretty much by heart.

Dear Becca and Doug,

As you know, your father and I have been working very hard on a research project of great significance, and we have been forced to travel north to the Sinkiang in China. I write in case anything should go wrong and our return is delayed.

Aunt Margaret is here to look after you, but she cannot stay beyond the end of June, as she has pressing engagements in San Francisco. Bhanuprasad[5] will give you this letter if you have not heard from us within four months. If this is the case and you are reading this, I have made arrangements for you to stay with the Jukeses in Srinagar until our return.

5 The MacKenzies' trusted housekeeper at the family home in Lucknow, India.

They will be your guardians and keep you safe until we are all together again.

Although you haven't met them often, I remember you got on well with Anders and Astrid when we holidayed together in the Hindu Kush two summers ago. Do you recall what fun we had staying at their house beside the Dal Lake and picnicking at the ancient Pari Mahal observatory?

Now, you must be kind and polite to them, and Doug, please try to behave.

This expedition is of great importance, otherwise your father and I would not have both gone. I entrust to you a document which you must give only to one person. His name is Alfonso Borelli and he's coming from Italy to collect it. He is a trusted friend. You will know him by his blue eyes and prodigious moustache. He will send a telegram ahead to see if you are at Lucknow or Srinagar. Hide it somewhere clever until he arrives – Doug, you're good at those sorts of things.

Take care, precious children,

Your ever loving mother.

Doug sniffed, and flicked the page over to read it a second time. In the stark tropical light Becca noticed that her brother's silhouette looked identical to their father's; the stance and slope of the shoulder and the line of his nose were almost exactly the same. She noticed too how his clothes no longer fitted. He was now almost as tall as she was, which was quite annoying.

Doug sat down slowly, lost in thought. His first words were distant. "No mention of Captain MacKenzie. No mention of *Expedient*."

"Apparently not."

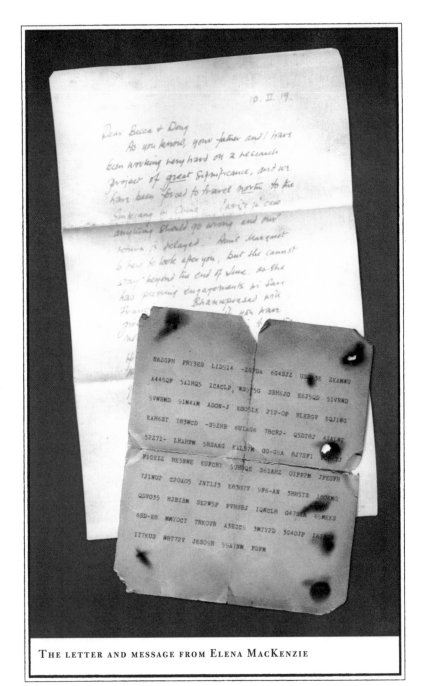

THE LETTER AND MESSAGE FROM ELENA MACKENZIE

"Aunt Margaret sacked Bhanu, that's why the letters stayed in the correspondence box and never reached the Jukeses or us," said Doug. "She must've known about the Jukeses, the old battleaxe."

"If we hadn't wound her up so much, we might have made it to Srinagar."

"D'you think this Borelli has tried to collect his message?"

The question was left hanging. Becca was still considering the implications. Was Alfonso Borelli another member of the Honourable Guild of Specialists?

"Whatever Mother and Father were doing in the Sinkiang must be in this cipher," said Doug, looking at the encoded document. "Doesn't take a genius to work that out."

"Might take a genius to crack it, though. Could Sparkie decipher it?"

Doug studied the code more closely. "Looks like the HGS codes we saw in the wireless telegraphy office. Sparkie would need the code books. Only one problem – the code book safe was blown up at Wenzi Island."

"Do we show this to the captain?"

"Mother's note says to give it to Borelli and no one else. We should hide it until then. Why did you wait to tell me about this?"

"I was thinking," she replied. "I wasn't sure I could…"

"Could what?"

"Well … trust you, now you're a member of the Guild. I was angry with you too."

"Oh, I know that. But why didn't you trust me?" Doug crossed his arms, looking confused and wronged.

"It's not you, it's the Guild. There you were swearing this, that and the other to an organization you know nothing about… And there's a problem with this letter to the Jukeses," said Becca.

"Seems fine to me."

"Something's bothering me – something that doesn't make sense. But I'm not sure what. I need to do some checking." She folded the pages and tucked them back into the envelopes.

"Who are the Jukeses, anyway?" asked Doug, seeing he'd get nothing more out of his sister. The name made him feel uneasy.

"Doug! Don't you remember? You hurled your boot through their front window. You smashed two panes of glass and a pair of Ming vases."

"Oh, *those* Jukeses…" Doug winced as he recalled an impromptu parabolic trajectory experiment that had gone horribly wrong.

Becca handed him the envelopes. "Hide these, will you? You're the expert, apparently. And *not* in those disgusting socks."

CHAPTER FOUR

Mrs Ives had returned to her normal good humour. She'd found a store of tins in one of her cupboards deep in the bowels of the ship, and produced a meal large enough to feed the ship's complement. With a full belly, Doug set off for the peninsula with orders to scavenge for coconuts. Xu and Xi had gone to the redoubt, so he was quite alone as he sauntered across the beach towards the graveyard.

Most of the crew were still hard at work repairing the *Expedient*. They were cutting pieces of steel from the tangled remains of the wireless telegraphy office walls to use as hull patches. These were then welded into position, their new red oxide paint bright against the rusty brown of the old.

The small plateau on the peninsula was not difficult to find. Ten Dinners was working away, hacking back the vegetation. There were now six skeletons, all headless. Captain MacKenzie stood taking notes.

He nodded to Doug. "What do you make of this?"

"I'm not sure."

"Frightened, are you?"

"Not especially. I had a skeleton for a neighbour in Sheng-Fat's tide cages. He was friendly enough."

"So you did. From a scientific point of view, how do you find the scene?"

Doug looked about him. "They all died at the same time?"

"I would think so. Human instinct is to bury the dead."

The skeletons were sprawled haphazardly, arms and legs

stretched out as if they had died in some elaborate primal
dance. Doug could make little sense of it. Then he saw four
cannon pointing in the direction of the hourglass beach and
the saddle. Their carriages had rotted away long ago, but their
purpose seemed obvious.

"Were they killed in battle?"

"Go on," encouraged the captain.

"Defending the peninsula?"

The captain knelt down and pointed at a rusting lump of
metal beside the hand of one of the skeletons. "Look closer,
nephew. What do you see?"

"A musket guard and flintlock." The wooden stock had
long since been eaten by termites. "It *must've* been a battle!"

Ten Dinners

may 1920

From Doug's sketchbook: Exposing the skeletons. (DMS 3/34)

"I should say so."

"But why were they here, and what were they defending?"

"We'll probably never know. Any more skeletons, Lincoln?"

Ten Dinners looked about. "I think that's it, Captain."

"Bury the poor souls. I'll come back up and say a few words at sunset."

TEN DINNERS

Becca's diary: 8th May p.m. 1920

Robert Lincoln's legendary reputation for food capacity was founded when he ate ten plates of steak pie and plum duff in a single sitting. He always carried what he called a "bridging sandwich" in his pocket to lessen the gap between meals.

A Kalaxx boat has landed on the beach below the observation post. For half an hour all work was suspended and we were told to make no noise. It seems to be a survey party of some sort. They have started to clear a patch of jungle and are establishing a camp. They can't see the Expedient *because of the steep ridge line between us, but I can't help feeling that they're very close.*

Our second afternoon on the island has passed in quiet industry. Charlie and I managed a respectable catch fishing in the cove, which Doug has put down to a variation in the choice of fishing flies. We were called back to shore by the captain at about four o'clock, whereupon Doug and I were handed a pitcher of water and told to report to the redoubt.

We climbed to the saddle, and had our first close-up look at Master Aa's defensive line. They have cleared all the scrub and constructed a bamboo wall ten feet high, and are furiously digging earth behind to strengthen it. Monsieur Chambois has been building a trebuchet as a further defensive measure – this sits on its own earth platform, and looks dangerously medieval. Xu and Xi came out to greet us, joking that they'd done all the work while we'd been out gathering supplies. Doug has in fact found and delivered to the galley 52 coconuts, 12 watermelons and 228 bananas. He also claims to have discovered several new species of butterfly, a giant lizard and a python, but wisely decided not to present those to Mrs Ives.

I have asked the captain whether Mother and Father sent any information to the Guild about their expedition. I can't put my finger on it, but there's something not quite right about those letters.

"Enter!" called the captain. Becca pushed open the door to his study. Her uncle was holding a flimsy piece of paper in his hand. Metallic crashes and bangs could be heard in the steering gear compartment next door.

"You sent for me, Uncle?"

"You asked earlier if your parents had sent any information to the Guild about their expedition, prior to their departure. You understand that your parents never revealed the purpose of their mission to the Sinkiang?"

"I understand."

He handed the paper to Becca. "This is their last communiqué. Take it. Read it… I've been over it a hundred times myself to check for some clue. There's none that I can see. I … I also wanted to talk about your induction into the Guild."

"I told you, I'm not joining."

The captain ushered Becca to an easy chair beside his desk. This was the best cabin aboard. The leather-topped desk faced a broad window that opened onto the gallery, a sort of private veranda at the stern of the ship. As the captain sat down and pulled a pipe from its holder on the wall, a breeze ruffled the papers on his desk. Becca noticed a large map of China laid out with sheets of handwritten notes beside it.

"I can understand your position." The captain paused for a second. "It's exactly what I told *my* uncle when he asked me to join the HGS. I was a little older than you."

"Why didn't you want to join?" Becca asked curiously.

"My father – your grandfather – had been killed. He was a scientist working at the very edge of our understanding of *The 99 Elements*. An experiment went wrong. He and several others..." The captain turned and looked towards the island. "In many ways Liberty is right. The Guild is a dangerous cabal. But our intentions are true. You have to believe that the cause is just. It is an honour to protect these secrets."

"A dubious honour."

"It is our duty. *The 99 Elements* warns of an astonishing power which can both create and destroy. To mishandle such science would spell disaster. It isn't the Guild's intention to harbour these secrets for ever, but to keep and protect them until we fully understand them."

THE 99 ELEMENTS

A collection of texts believed to have been written by the Tembla civilization circa 4,000 BC recording the Tembla's knowledge and understanding of science and philosophy. The writings are still not entirely understood, though generations of scholars have laboured to translate their meaning.

Rebecca jumped up. "All *I* understand, Uncle, is that my parents are lost somewhere in China, and if the Guild is responsible for this, I think you're asking a lot for me to join you in your scientific crusade. I'd like to ask my mother and father's advice about joining the Guild and let them explain

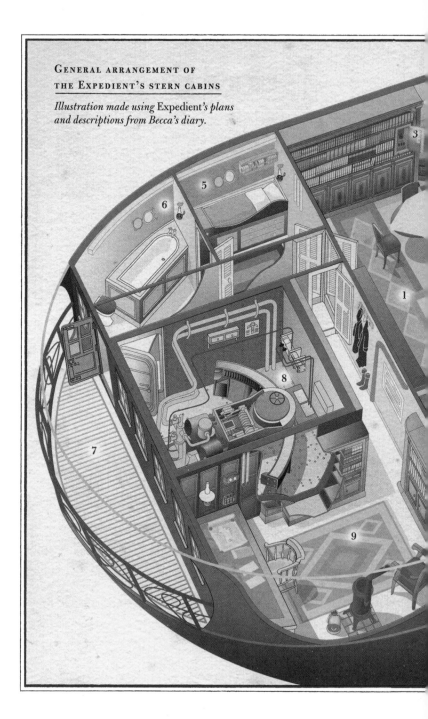

GENERAL ARRANGEMENT OF THE EXPEDIENT'S STERN CABINS

Illustration made using Expedient's *plans and descriptions from Becca's diary.*

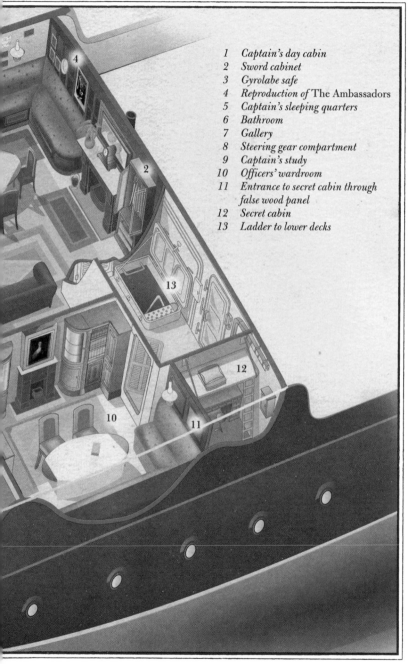

1 *Captain's day cabin*
2 *Sword cabinet*
3 *Gyrolabe safe*
4 *Reproduction of* The Ambassadors
5 *Captain's sleeping quarters*
6 *Bathroom*
7 *Gallery*
8 *Steering gear compartment*
9 *Captain's study*
10 *Officers' wardroom*
11 *Entrance to secret cabin through false wood panel*
12 *Secret cabin*
13 *Ladder to lower decks*

what it's all about. If they are dead, and their connection to the Guild is what killed them, I may well take Liberty's view."

"My dear Rebecca, I'm sorry, but they probably *are* dead. Don't you see that?"

"Then I must find out what happened to them. Don't you see *that*, Uncle?"

Xu and Xi arrived at Doug's cabin a little after ten o'clock, and in the glow of the oil lamp, a late-night party developed. They sat around the remains of a coconut duff, telling ghost stories inspired by the peninsula's skeletons. The conversation swung to their various upbringings. Xu and Xi were fascinated by Becca and Doug's stories of Lucknow, New York and London. These cosmopolitan cities seemed a million miles away from the equatorial jungle island they now found themselves on.

"Have you always lived in Shanghai?" asked Doug.

Xu laughed, and nudged his brother.

"We're not Chinese," said Xi.

"No, you're Greek," said Becca.

"We're not Greek!"

"I don't understand. Your father's Master Aa," insisted Becca.

"When did you ever hear us call Master Aa father?" laughed Xu.

"Our father was a merchant from Osaka," added Xi. "We're Japanese."

"But you're Sujing Quantou!"

"The Sujing Quantou adopted us. It was a great honour.

Our family fought alongside them many centuries ago in the Epoch of the Warring Country. The bond has remained strong. Our parents were killed shortly after we were born."

"I ... I'm sorry."

"The Sujing way is all we have ever known."

"The Epoch of the Warring Country ... was that the Ha-Mi Wars?" asked Doug.

"No," guffawed Xi. "You should know about the Ha-Mi Wars. Doesn't your uncle teach you anything?"

"We're – I mean *I'm* a bit behind with my Guild lessons."

"The Ha-Mi Wars were fought in China two hundred years ago, between the Sujing Quantou and the Ha-Mi. The Guild were there, fighting on our side. An alliance of the northern chapter of the Sujing, ancestors of those Kalaxx dogs on the other island, and the Ha-Mi wanted to take control of the Daughter of the Sun mine and refinery beneath the Sujing Quantou temple at Khotan."

Xu took over the story. "They almost succeeded, but the northern chapter's treachery was discovered by two Scottish MacKenzie ancestors of yours – Doon-carn and Kar-mer-oon."

"Doon-carn? Duncan and Cameron?"

"Heard of them?" Xi asked.

Becca and Doug nodded. There was an old oil painting of the pair above the fireplace in their dining room at Lucknow. Doug felt slightly miffed that Xu and Xi seemed to know more about his ancestry than he did.

Xi picked up the story again. "They were great travellers, explorers... It was they who frustrated the attack on the Khotan temple. Your forebears joined the eastern and western brotherhoods of the Sujing Quantou to defeat the northern Sujing and Ha-Mi alliance."

1718 *October:* Master Da'ar, leader of the northern Sujing (later the Kalaxx), poisons Tal, the Sujing Quantou Grand Master, in a conspiracy to seize power and take control of the Daughter of the Sun mine and refining facility at Khotan. The plot is discovered and the northern chapter are expelled from the brotherhood. Their supplies of refined Daughter of the Sun are confiscated and they are banished to the Gobi Desert. Master Da'ar escapes and rejoins his forces at Turfan.

1719 *February:* With the intention of capturing the Khotan temple by force, the northern chapter forge an alliance with the Ha-Mi, a Mongol fighting order.

April: The northern chapter and the Ha-Mi cross the Takla Makan Desert and approach Khotan. Their attack almost succeeds, but for the intervention of the travelling HGS explorers Duncan and Cameron MacKenzie, who warn the Sujing Quantou just in time. The attack is foiled and Master Da'ar's forces retreat. The MacKenzies join the eastern and western Sujing to defeat the northern Sujing/Ha-Mi alliance.

June – October: Many patrols are lost in skirmishes.

November: A secret mission to infiltrate the northern chapter's headquarters at Turfan finds maps showing the location of the northern Sujing and Ha-Mi secret base where they are rearming and training for a spring attack.

1720 *February:* In a pre-emptive move, the Sujing Quantou attack. The rival armies clash in the Celestial Mountains north of Kucha. Fighting lasts for three days, but the outcome is indecisive. Victory is claimed by both parties; however, such are the losses – over a thousand men on each side – that both camps fall back to regroup.

August: Information from Silk Road spies reveals that the Ha-Mi and the northern chapter are camped outside Kurghan and preparing to march on Khotan.

September 22nd: The Sujing Quantou set an ambush outside Kopa. This is a spectacular success and Master Da'ar is captured. Da'ar's son and three hundred fighters escape and make for Ayor-Nor.

October 1st: The Treaty of Khotan is signed, in which the Sujing reward Duncan and Cameron for their help by giving them the eastern gyrolabe. They will not allow their chapters of *The 99 Elements* to be removed, but grant members of the HGS access to them. In return Duncan and Cameron promise on behalf of the HGS and in perpetuity to inform the Sujing of any discoveries made concerning Daughter of the Sun.

October 2nd: Cameron leaves for Firenze with the eastern gyrolabe.

December: Duncan and the western Sujing subdue the northern chapter, who flee from Ayor-Nor to Russia. The Ha-Mi Wars end. Duncan disappears.

"The victory is honoured every year at Khotan," added Xu.

"We have a firework that fires into the sky with a tar-tan pattern! It was the desire of Kameroon to see such a thing at the celebration feast. And" – Xi fell about laughing until tears filled his eyes – "they danced over crossed swords ... in skirts!"

"A tartan firework?" exclaimed Doug. "Lethal!"

"Absolute nonsense," Becca scoffed.

"It's true! And those two MacKenzies signed the Treaty of Khotan with our ancestors. We gave them our eastern gyrolabe and in return they promised that the Guild would tell the Sujing of any discoveries of Daughter of the Sun," Xu explained. "After the celebration they parted. Kameroon rode west for Europe with our gyrolabe. Dooncarn stayed in China helping to hunt down the Ha-Mi."

"What happened to Duncan?"

"He disappeared."

"He can't have just vanished."

"Yes, with his horse! It is said that the Ha-Mi may have captured him one night after poisoning him with a sleeping draught. It is the sort of underhand trick they would have played."

"So Duncan just disappeared?"

DUNCAN & CAMERON MACKENZIE

Scottish brothers with a taste for exploration and adventure, they were the first MacKenzies to join the Guild. Fugitives of the failed 1715 Jacobite rebellion, they fled to Italy, where they joined an HGS expedition to the Sinkiang. Taking their horses Little Mountain Barb and Lister Turk with them, they set out to discover more about the gyrolabes and The 99 Elements. *In 1720 they signed the Treaty of Khotan, and Cameron raced to Firenze on Lister Turk with the eastern gyrolabe. Duncan and Little Mountain Barb stayed in the Far East trying to locate the southern gyrolabe. Although Cameron returned to search for his brother, Duncan and his horse were never heard of again.*

"Yes. In the deserts of the Sinkiang. It is not a lucky place for MacKenzies."

"No, it's not," said Doug, picturing his mother and father. Becca caught his eye and smiled sadly.

CHAPTER FIVE

At eight o'clock the next morning, high on the ridge that sheltered the observation post, Doug replaced the field telephone receiver and smiled: Sparkie had reported that Captain MacKenzie was on his way.

The Sujing guard had been doubled, on the instruction of Master Aa, and a small defensive wall of trenches had been constructed overnight with booby traps set on the boundaries and approaches. A little before dawn some kind of tunnel-boring machine had broken through the side of the ridge and now lay in the clearing beside the newly established Kalaxx encampment.

The captain had asked Chambois to accompany Becca and Doug to the observation post, in order to take detailed notes on the machine.

"This is a most exceptional contraption," marvelled Chambois, squinting into the captain's best telescope. "If only we knew how many of these machines Pembleton-Crozier has … their speed … their rate of excavation."

Doug rolled over onto his back and imagined the rotation of the earth beneath him and how gravity was holding him from flying off into space.

Becca observed the two female Sujing warriors. Neither had spoken for the entire time they'd been there. They sat with their swords at the ready, watching the Kalaxx servicing the machine below. One of the women looked about the same age as Captain MacKenzie, her hair streaked with grey;

the other was younger and had a wound on her cheek received in the fighting at Wenzi Island.

Becca said in a firm voice, "I'm Rebecca. What's your name?"

The elder Sujing fighter turned very slowly and smiled, nodding her head with great serenity. "My name is Ba'd Ak."

Becca shrank back. The words were said with such intensity and the woman's gaze was so focused that she was almost a little frightening. The Sujing turned back to continue her watch. It was clear she would say no more.

"Not great conversationalists," said Doug, settling down at his post. "The other one is called Tak'a Chi."

"How d'you know that, Doug?"

"I asked Xi when we were standing watch." He leant closer and whispered, "Ba'd Ak is married to Master Aa."

Becca was irritated that Doug had ingratiated himself into the Sujing Quantou world with the same ease with which he'd befriended *Expedient*'s crew. "Do you know all their names?"

"Yeah, most. Each has a specialist skill. Ba'd Ak's is using throwing stars. Tak'a Chi's is three-sword technique."

"She fights with three swords?"

"That's what Xi said – although he specializes in talking a lot of rot most of the time. Says it looks a bit like juggling, but deadlier, obviously." Doug lay flat on the trampled grass, taking up his binoculars and finding his target: a V-shaped nick on

THROWING STARS

Ba'd Ak carried four throwing stars embellished with the traditional stylized ram's horn motif. On contact with an opponent, the mechanism at the centre injected lethal snake venom from the blade's tips.

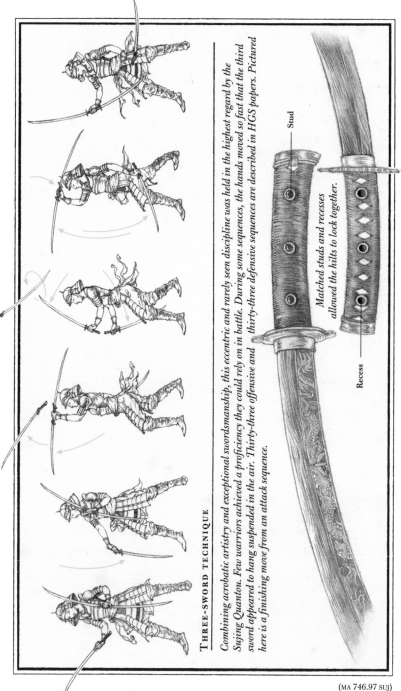

THREE-SWORD TECHNIQUE

Combining acrobatic artistry and exceptional swordsmanship, this eccentric and rarely seen discipline was held in the highest regard by the Sujing Quantou. Few warriors achieved a proficiency they could rely on in battle. During some sequences, the hands moved so fast that the third sword appeared to hang suspended in the air. Thirty-three offensive and thirty-three defensive sequences are described in HGS papers. Pictured here is a finishing move from an attack sequence.

Stud

Matched studs and recesses allowed the hilts to lock together.

Recess

(MA 746.97 SUJ)

From Doug's sketchbook: Ba'd Ak and Tak'a Chi. (DMS 3/39)

the calm surface of the sea. "The periscope's still making for the mining compound."

He sat up and continued work on a detailed map he'd begun to make of Sulphur Island and the Kalaxx compound, using the theodolite to get it as accurate as he could. Several things intrigued him, most of all a star-shaped building inside the compound. The tall lattice mast also required an explanation. Chambois was convinced it was for transmitting and receiving radio signals, but Doug wasn't so sure. He marked it *possible oil well* in very light pencil, as that seemed just as likely.

The captain strode towards the observation post as fast as his gammy leg allowed. "Where's this periscope?"

"It came into view about twenty minutes ago. We thought

A surveying instrument for measuring horizontal and vertical angles. Set on a tripod, it consists of a telescope which can be rotated within two perpendicular axes. A landmark is plotted from two separate standpoints; the two points are super-imposed; and simple math-ematical triangulation is used to plot an accurate position for the landmark on a map.

(See Appendix 4.)

it might be a shark or a whale, but it was moving in too straight a line. It's nearly at Pembleton-Crozier's island."

Chambois handed him the telescope.

"I have it. Well done."

"I have almost completed my report on the tunnel-boring machines, Captain," Chambois informed him. "I believe that the machines are tunnelling beneath the sea, and that these islands are all inter-linked by mine galleries. The machines can move from one island to another with ease."

"How do you think they're powered?"

"Quite simple: electricity. It cannot be petroleum or diesel; the miners would be poisoned by the exhaust fumes. There is a problem for which I have no solution, however."

"Why so?"

"It is a matter of supply. The machines are drawing their power from the compound, where all those cables lead into the substation. But where is the power station that supplies the electricity? It is not in the compound – there are no cooling towers, no smoke, no evidence at all for the generation of the quantities of electricity needed to run such large machines."

"Could the power station be beyond that low hill? You can just see the edge of a domed roof."

"But where is the smoke and the steam? You cannot have power without them. I don't think it can be there."

Over at Sulphur Island a patch of water in the harbour suddenly boiled, and the menacing superstructure of a sub-marine broke the surface. The captain fixed his telescope on the conning tower as a figure climbed up through a water-tight hatch and put on his hat.

"By Jove, that's Borelli! What on earth's he doing here? And Pembleton-Crozier's wife, Lucretia. This is a most peculiar turn of events."

Becca grabbed her binoculars and found the distant figures as they walked along the submarine's hull. Lucretia wore an elegant black dress totally unsuited to the climate. Then she turned her attention to the figure that interested her most.

"Who is Borelli, Uncle?"

From Doug's sketchbook: Figures on the conning tower. (DMS 3/45)

"Why, Borelli is the head of scientific research at Firenze … a director of the board. A guildsman, damn it. And he's shaking hands with Pembleton-Crozier!"

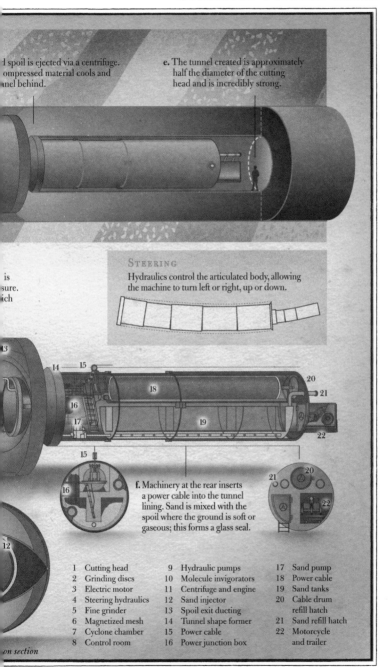

l spoil is ejected via a centrifuge.
ompressed material cools and
nel behind.

e. The tunnel created is approximately
half the diameter of the cutting
head and is incredibly strong.

STEERING

Hydraulics control the articulated body, allowing
the machine to turn left or right, up or down.

f. Machinery at the rear inserts
a power cable into the tunnel
lining. Sand is mixed with the
spoil where the ground is soft or
gaseous; this forms a glass seal.

1	Cutting head	9	Hydraulic pumps	17	Sand pump
2	Grinding discs	10	Molecule invigorators	18	Power cable
3	Electric motor	11	Centrifuge and engine	19	Sand tanks
4	Steering hydraulics	12	Sand injector	20	Cable drum
5	Fine grinder	13	Spoil exit ducting		refill hatch
6	Magnetized mesh	14	Tunnel shape former	21	Sand refill hatch
7	Cyclone chamber	15	Power cable	22	Motorcycle
8	Control room	16	Power junction box		and trailer

on section

(MA 748.31 KAL)

KALAXX MINER'S SUIT

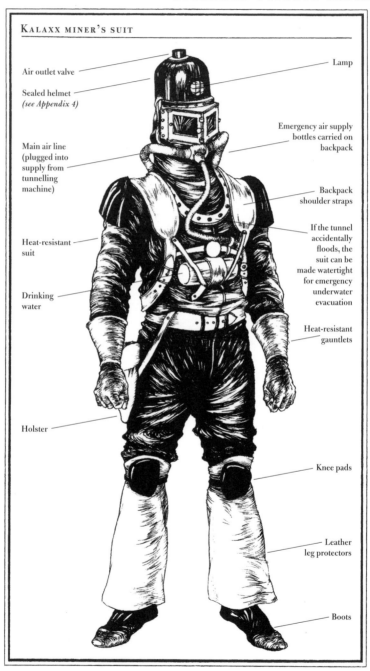

Air outlet valve

Sealed helmet
(see Appendix 4)

Main air line
(plugged into
supply from
tunnelling
machine)

Heat-resistant
suit

Drinking
water

Holster

Lamp

Emergency air supply
bottles carried on
backpack

Backpack
shoulder straps

If the tunnel
accidentally
floods, the
suit can be
made watertight
for emergency
underwater
evacuation

Heat-resistant
gauntlets

Knee pads

Leather
leg protectors

Boots

(MA 748.35 KAL)

Becca's diary: 9th May 1920

The words of Mother's letter raced through my head. I entrust to you a document which you must give only to one person... He is a trusted friend. You will know him by his blue eyes and prodigious moustache.

But Borelli was there, talking to our sworn enemy, not three miles away. I could see the same question twisting at Doug. If Borelli was Mother and Father's friend, were we on the wrong island? Was Captain MacKenzie our real enemy and Pembleton-Crozier our ally?

At around 10 a.m. we were relieved from our stint at the observation post by Slippery Sam and Sparkie. Doug and I climbed back down from the ridge with Chambois, stopping at the redoubt on the way to inspect his trebuchet. Chambois demonstrated its features with great pride, explaining its many refinements, particularly the trigger, which is apparently of ingenious design. But even Doug was too distracted to pay attention as he wrestled with the implications of Borelli's arrival. Poor Chambois looked a little hurt at his lack of enthusiasm.

On our return, Mrs Ives gave us our baskets again, and we were dispatched to search for more food on the peninsula. The last thing I want to do at the moment is look for coconuts.

"Maybe it's a different Borelli?" suggested Doug as they entered the thick jungle beyond the burial ground.

Becca pushed a large fern from their path with her empty basket. "Wishful thinking. It must be him. Doug, I managed to get Mother and Father's last communiqué from the captain."

"What?"

"You know I was uncertain about the Jukeses' letter? Well, I was right."

She pulled out the communiqué. Doug snatched it from her and read it aloud:

"*To HGS Board, Firenze. Mounting expedition north to Sinkiang via Mintaka Pass. Expect return Lucknow 4 months. H. and E. MacK.* Not much to go on, Becca."

"Don't you see?"

"See what?" Doug read it again, and shrugged.

"Think about it. Where do the Jukeses live?"

"Srinagar."

"Correct. Now, where is the Mintaka Pass?" Doug thought for a moment. "Come on, we walked up it when we went to the Hindu Kush."

"North of Hunza."

"Blimey, Doug, must I spell it out for you? What is south of Hunza?"

Doug thought for a moment. "Srinagar. Where's all this leading?"

"Mother wrote a letter to the Jukeses, who live in Srinagar, but she left it in her correspondence box. The thing is, if this communiqué is to be believed, Mother and Father must have walked right past the Jukeses' front door on their way to the Mintaka Pass. It's the fastest route to China. That's what's been bothering me ever since I read the letters. Why didn't she take the Jukeses' letter to them herself? It makes no sense."

Doug began to cotton on. "So Mother and Father must have gone to Sinkiang via a different route. But why did they tell the HGS the wrong route?"

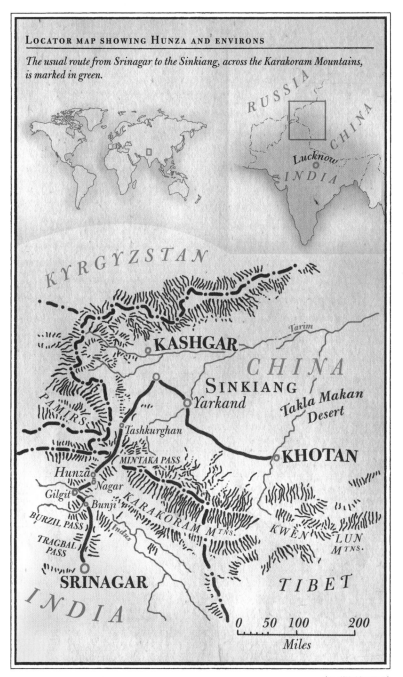

LOCATOR MAP SHOWING HUNZA AND ENVIRONS

The usual route from Srinagar to the Sinkiang, across the Karakoram Mountains, is marked in green.

RUSSIA

CHINA

Lucknow

INDIA

KYRGYZSTAN

KASHGAR

Tarim

CHINA

SINKIANG

Yarkand

Takla Makan Desert

PAMIRS

Tashkurghan

KHOTAN

MINTAKA PASS

Hunza

Nagar

Gilgit

Bunji

KARAKORAM

BURZIL PASS

Indus

MTNS.

KWEN LUN MTNS.

TRAGBAL PASS

SRINAGAR

TIBET

INDIA

0   50   100   200

Miles

(MA 479.18 HUNZA)

"To throw them off the scent. They didn't trust the Guild. It's the only logical answer."

"Does that put Borelli on our side or not? Should we go and give him Mother's letter? I mean, what do we do?"

Becca gave a frustrated sigh. "We have to ask: what do we know ourselves? What have we found out that we're certain of, that we've seen with our own eyes? These are the only things we can trust."

"We know Julius Pembleton-Crozier is a lunatic. That's a start," said Doug with absolute certainty. "Mother and Father were friends with Borelli, according to the letter. Borelli is friends with Pembleton-Crozier – we saw them shake hands. The bit I can't understand is that Pembleton-Crozier was friends with Sheng-Fat, and I can't believe Mother and Father were friends with Sheng – or P-C. Least, I hope not."

"Sheng-Fat had never heard the name MacKenzie, so we're safe there. He can't have known Mother and Father."

"The captain *must* be on the right side. He's been good to his word so far," reasoned Doug.

"Why don't we say we don't trust any of them?" suggested Becca. "Not until we find out what the coded letter says."

"I've sworn an oath to the Guild," protested Doug. "I can't go back on my word. I like the captain; I like the *Expedient*; I like the crew. Charlie saved my life."

"But Mother's letter – it said Borelli was a friend, Doug."

"She wrote that over a year ago," he said with exasperation. "A year's a long time."

"Then the only way to settle it is to get hold of some code books to crack the message."

"Code books!" he scoffed. "From where?"

"Borelli must have a set. We'll have to get them from his submarine."

"No, Becca. It goes against all I've promised to the captain and the Guild." Doug glared at his sister. "I'm *sure* he's on the right side of all this—"

They heard a tumble of rocks, and froze. It had sounded close. His heart racing, Doug pushed the undergrowth away.

"Liberty!"

She was standing on a ledge of rock above them.

"Hey, cousins!"

"What are you doing?" asked Becca.

"That's no way to greet your old partner. Tell me, when did y'all see me comin' up the path there? Could you see me through all that greenery?"

"No."

"Good." Liberty stooped down and chalked a cross on the rock. Becca and Doug climbed up to her position.

"Whatever are you doing?"

"A bit of tactical appraisal. See, I was contemplatin' those bones y'all found yesterday and it set my mind to thinkin'. I like to consider myself a naturally optimistic gal, but I don't see anythin' on this here island that gives me hope I'll be alive come this time next week."

"The ship's being repaired," said Doug with injured pride. "She'll float. The captain says so."

"That captain says a lotta things. Any minute now one of those diggin' machines is gonna break through and find us. Who's to say that ship's rudder's ever gonna work again ... and then your uncle's still gotta relaunch the rustin' hulk. So excuse me if I start to make a few contingency plans." Liberty picked up her blunderbuss and climbed the path a little further.

"But the Sujing have built a defensive wall," called out Doug.

"The Kalaxx have boats. Master Aa knows he can't hold the beach with ten fighters."

"Monsieur Chambois is digging a flooding channel to refloat the ship. I saw his plan yesterday."

"And I heard they hit bedrock this mornin'. Hard against the hull too. Makes me twitchy to think we might be stayin' as long as those guys." Liberty nodded back in the direction of the graveyard. "Can y'all see me now?"

"No."

A few seconds later Liberty appeared on top of a rock overlooking them. "This is a fine spot." She marked it with the chalk and disappeared. They could still hear her voice. "See, I think those headless stiffs that died fightin' had a point about this peninsula. The pinnacle we're climbin' here is like a castle. Easy to defend, hard to attack." She appeared unexpectedly from the gully behind them. "If we're attacked we can pull back here, but that means abandonin' the ship."

"But the *Expedient* is our way off the island!"

"You sure about that, Doug? That boat looks beaten like a hired mule to me. There's every chance it'll never sail again. And if it comes to a last stand, I'm sure gonna take as many Kalaxx with me as I can. Now follow me, cousins; this is the easiest climb up."

The top of the pinnacle offered an excellent view of the *Expedient*'s bay and the vista towards the east of the island. The sky was cloudless and the sun beat down with a ferocious heat, forcing them to stop and catch their breath.

Doug was still unsettled by Liberty's assessment of the

situation. "There's the crew of the *Expedient* as well," he argued. "It's not just the Sujing Quantou defending us."

"Are they refloatin' the ship at this point or fightin' five hundred bloodthirsty miners at the bamboo wall?"

"There are the ex-ransom hostages," added Becca. "Some of them will fight, I'm sure of it."

"What, the singin' widows? Scariest thing about those girls is when they hit top C."

Liberty's argument was gaining strength. Doug slid down the smooth face of the rock and strode over to a boulder marked LAST STAND, the spot Liberty had chosen for her final defence. He peered down at the route of their ascent. The vegetation was thin here, with few places for an attacker to hide.

Doug turned and heard a crack. The earth gave way beneath his left foot, and he tumbled forward, sprawling his arms out to stop himself. "Becca!" he called out, scrabbling and clutching at the scrub grass as he fell waist deep into a void.

Becca skidded down the rock and ran towards him but she too tripped as the ground disappeared beneath her.

Liberty was quickly on the scene, clutching Doug's collar and hauling him out. She peered into the dark opening he'd crashed through.

"Looks like an old tunnel to me, Cousin Douglas." She yanked out a splintered plank. "Look. Timber-lined roof. They must've laid turf over the top."

Becca extracted her leg. "Where does it lead?"

"That way. Towards you. Has to be," reasoned Doug. "You can see the ground dipping."

"I see it, coz; you're right," said Liberty, squinting against the sun as she traced the course of the depression. "It leads back towards the pinnacle." She dropped feet first into the hole. "Let's take a look-see. Maybe we've found us a way off this island."

They edged down the tunnel at a stoop, adjusting to the darkness and the musty atmosphere; Liberty led the way with the faint beam of her pocket torch. It was dry and cooler than outside, but confined enough to make Doug feel a little claustrophobic.

"Look out for locals," Liberty warned. "Snakes 'n' spiders."

They went beyond the roof collapse made by Becca and found that the tunnel dropped steeply downwards. This section had been chipped out of the natural rock, complete with footholds and steps. At the bottom lay the remains of a rough wooden ladder.

The tunnel widened and progress became easier, but they had to crawl on all fours along certain sections. After a couple of minutes they reached a cave. Liberty's torch fixed on a decrepit table collapsed in the centre of the chamber.

"Look at this place. A regular hideout."

Liberty circled the cave with her light.

"It's some sort of a store," whispered Doug. "Look – shovels, axes, rope, lifting blocks, canvas…"

"Weapons too," said Liberty, fixing the beam on a row of dusty muskets; beside them five muzzle-loading cannon were arranged neatly against the wall, still on their carriages.

"They're identical to the ones we found outside."

"Yeah, but how did they get them in here?"

"This could've been an entrance," speculated Doug as he

Liberty and Sis explore the cave

From Doug's sketchbook. (DMS 3/56)

investigated a side passage blocked with rocks. "The tunnel we came down could have been an escape route."

In the spill of the light, Becca spotted a scrap of paper on the floor by the cannon, burnt around the edges. Somebody long ago had used it as an improvised taper. The page, brittle to the touch, was covered with a florid script in faded brown ink. Becca's voice echoed around the cave as she read it aloud:

"…20th day of Sept., 1723. From my Look Out on the hill beyond the Shore, I observ'd the Infernal Head Hunters paddle

away towards the Volcanoe; I have expend'd our last Supply of Gun-powder in this Attack – alas! it was not enough to Save the head of my dear Friend Adams, who was cut down by a poisoned Dart as he fish'd in the cove. I am afeared the Hunters will return for the Remainder of our Party at the next full Moon, as is their Wont, tho' they cou'd have Murder'd us all, had they so wished. Our Situation is very dismal indeed; we must labour hard to finish here. An Attack—"

The words ran out.

"Headhunters. Oh boy. I guess that explains those stiffs with the drastic haircuts." There was a chill in Liberty's voice.

"Of course," said Doug. "A surprise attack. Cut down by poisoned darts!"

"My head's stayin' right where it belongs," said Liberty, patting her blunderbuss, "planted firmly on my shoulders."

Becca examined the other side of the paper; smoke stains and age made the words difficult to discern. *"…yesterday eve. The work proceedeth: today Johns discover'd another Level on the 3rd Island, of the same configuration as the rest. We continue to Dyg at the Figure-head mine…"*

For several minutes they investigated the dusty contents of the cave, but they found little of value, and no further clues as to whom it all belonged.

"Whatever they were doin' here, they wanted to keep it secret," said Liberty. "Why didn't they just sail away?"

"Maybe they were shipwrecked like us," Doug replied. "We'd better get back to the *Expedient*. The captain should know about this place."

"Yeah, it's kinda givin' me the creeps."

HEADHUNTERS

Headhunters collected their enemies' heads as trophies; some tribes believed that this act transferred the victim's soul to the victor.

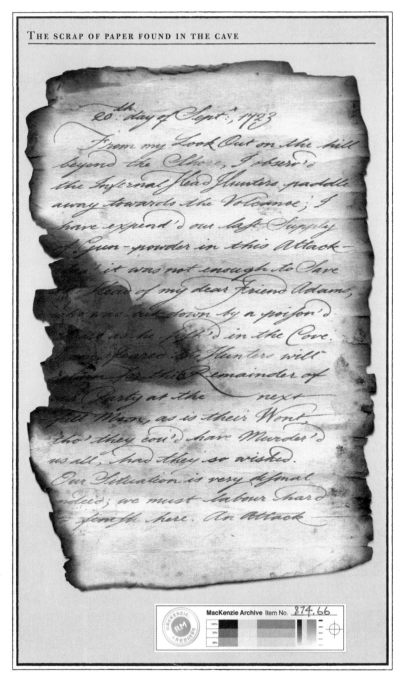

20th day of Sept:, 1723

From my Look Out on the hill beyond the Shore, I observ'd the Infernal Head Hunters paddle away towards the Volcanoe; I have expend'd our last Supply of Gun-powder in this Attack— but it was not enough to Save the Head of my dear Friend Adams, who was cut down by a poison'd Dart as he fish'd in the Cove. I feared the Hunters will return for this Remainder of our Party at the next full Moon, as is their Wont, tho' they cou'd have Murder'd us all, had they so wished. Our Situation is very dismal indeed; we must Labour hard to finish here. An Attack

Becca tucked the fragment of paper into her pocket. The voice of the long-dead writer chilled her. Despite the archaic handwriting the words seemed fresh and resonant – and terrifying. Was one of those skeletons the author of the journal?

The young MacKenzies had ten minutes left before dinner, yet neither was ready. Doug wiped his face with a grubby towel. In the cabin next door, Becca was reading the "Boat Work" section in *The Manual of Seamanship*. The steady *clomp-clomp-clomp* of rudder repairs reverberated through the bulkheads and pipework.

TACKING AND GYBING

Boats cannot sail closer than 45 degrees to the wind, as the sails cease to work; instead they tack and gybe to make progress. These manoeuvres change the direction in which the wind is blowing against the boat and sails.

TACKING *is cutting across a wind blowing towards the bow of the boat.*

45°

⬅WIND

45°

GYBING *is turning across a wind blowing across the stern of the boat.*

⬅WIND

Doug pushed open the connecting door. "You're going to take the dinghy, aren't you?"

"Well, I'm hardly going to swim across, am I?" Becca snapped.

"But you can't sail."

"You're hardly Joshua Slocum[6] yourself, Doug."

"At least I know how to tack and gybe. You'll be useless out there on your own. It's the open sea."

"I'll row the thing if I have to. I need those code books. Anyway, who said I was going alone?"

"Who would go with you?"

"None of your business."

"It *is* my business."

"Then come with me. Help me, Doug."

6 American mariner Joshua Slocum (1844–*c*.1910) was the first person to circumnavigate the world single-handed.

"I've sworn allegiance to the Guild. I can only go if the captain gives me the order."

"Push off then, and leave me alone," Becca seethed, kicking the door shut.

But Doug caught it and pushed it back open. "It's not Liberty, is it?"

Becca glanced up. "Good try. No."

"It won't be any of the crew. Though there's Charlie. He's been pretty disgruntled lately."

"Not Charlie."

"Have you thought about the tides and currents? You'll need to time it right."

Becca leant forward and chucked him a notebook. "Talked to Mr Ives. Checked the tides earlier. All taken care of."

"You told Ives?"

"No, I asked him about currents. I didn't tell him I was going to raid the submarine."

Doug was struck by an idea. "Oh no – not Xi? Tell me it's not Xi?" Becca's eyebrows twitched up. "I knew it! How did you persuade him?"

"Easy, actually. He wants to capture a Kalaxx ceremonial dagger. Says it'll prove him a true Sujing warrior."

"He's just mad enough to do it, as well," Doug said with a rising note of jealousy. "When are you going?"

"The captain plans to leave tomorrow night, so we'll have to go tonight. Come with us, Doug. I need your help."

"I can't, Becca. I really can't. Look – I've just made it into the Guild. I'll be able to find out lots more about what's going on from the inside; if I got caught I'd be sent straight back to Aunt Margaret's, and what use would that be? We don't know for sure if Borelli even has the code books. It's too big a gamble.

I have to start playing by Guild rules – or at least look like I am. I – *we* need to use my membership to our advantage, not throw it away."

Doug closed the door firmly as if to shut out temptation. For once in his life he was determined to act honourably.

But then Becca was off to raid a submarine.

CHAPTER SIX

Dinner dragged on until 9.30 p.m. Becca didn't eat much as she was so nervous about her plan. An hour later, she was finally on her way; she managed to slip out of her cabin and make it down the companionway ladder unnoticed in the darkness. Gently she lowered herself into the waist-high water of the bay, waded out until she couldn't touch the bottom and then swam towards the *Powder Monkey* anchored twenty yards off the beach. She found the transom and climbed in as quietly as she could.

"You can drive this thing?" hissed Xi, helping her aboard.

"Of course."

"Water. I hate water! We Sujing—"

"—only fight on land. I know. Thing is, Xi, we don't want to fight anyone tonight, understand? No one must know we've been to Sulphur Island. We'll row out. Once we're beyond the peninsula rocks we can set sail. Do you know how to row?"

"No," said Xi sheepishly. "We Sujing do not—"

"You steer with the rudder, then."

Becca began to row, dipping the blades in with gentle movements. The night was extremely dark, and she could only just make out *Expedient*'s shadowy form. Slowly the *Powder Monkey* made progress until the dinghy seemed to falter, and turn.

"We've hit a current," said Becca. "We'll never get there at this rate."

"Keep rowing!" ordered Xi.

"You'll never get there if you don't get the anchor up," came a voice out of the darkness. It was very close, and made Becca jump.

"Doug!"

"Told you you'd never make it. Help me aboard."

"Me too!" came another voice.

"Brother Xu!"

"I couldn't let you take on the entire Kalaxx army single-handed," said Xu.

Something woolly landed on the thwart beside Becca. "What's this?"

"My lucky socks," Doug whispered. "I'm trying to keep them dry. Had to swim with them clamped between my teeth."

"Get them away from me! They're disgusting! What changed your mind about coming?"

"Don't sound too enthusiastic. Code books or not, I fancied having a look at the sub."

"Well, it's good to have you on board."

"Right, let's get things shipshape," ordered Doug. "I'll get the anchor. Xu, Xi, keep watch. Becca, stay on the oars. I'll call out the channel."

"Who put you in charge?" she hissed.

The anchor tripped after a couple of pulls, and Doug carefully coiled the line down in the boat. "Anchor's aweigh."

Becca started to row, the oars slapping in time on the water. Within two minutes they were out of sight of the *Expedient*.

"Made it," Doug said as he hoisted the small jib. "We're safe now. Ship oars. Watch the jib sheets, Becca. I'm going to get the mainsail up."

"Is there enough wind?"

"A steady breeze. Ideal. We'll be there within the hour."

Doug untied the sprit and mainsail, which were lashed to the mast. He checked the snotter was properly attached and pulled hard to tension the rig. "Sails set, skip."

Becca sheeted in the mainsail, and the *Powder Monkey* immediately heeled and began to sail. Doug belayed the halyard and settled below the mast with a feeling of satisfaction.

"Plate down," whispered Becca. The *Powder Monkey*'s forefoot gurgled as it drove into the waves, the water slapping against the clinker hull. The power of the sails brought life to the tiller in Becca's hand. She felt for the direction of the wind as Charlie had taught her, turning her head left and right until her nose pointed directly at it. She adjusted her course and the small boat responded, putting on more speed.

Becca thought absent-mindedly that she ought to be terrified. If two months ago someone had told her she'd be sailing a boat in the middle of the night, she'd have laughed. Now her attitude was: *Why shouldn't I? How hard can it be?* Wenzi Island had changed Becca, and this was the moment she realized it. This new attitude seemed fleetingly dangerous, until she understood how powerful it was.

"Trim that jib, Doug," she ordered, "and then we're going to talk tactics."

Becca's plan was a simple one. Xu and Xi had forty-five minutes to capture their dagger, while she and Doug boarded the submarine to find the code books. They would all meet back at the boat.

Hunched down by the mast, Doug had been itching to take command. The fair wind carried them swiftly past the southern headland of the island, where the shallowness and conflicting currents made the sea choppy.

After Becca had talked through her plan, Doug took his turn on the tiller. He felt a surge of exhilaration as the small boat glided over the ink-black water. Above him the brilliant canvas of stars swayed against the gaff mast; he fixed on Polaris, the great north star, and for a few moments imagined himself some great sea captain commanding an ocean-going ship. Then he thought of the Kalaxx and the excitement drained from him as if a plug had been pulled; it was immediately replaced by a cold jangle of fear. Until now he hadn't thought much about his sister's crazy plan. *I mean, raiding a submarine? What are we thinking of? This message had better be worth it.*

They sat in silence for a while, then Becca's voice cut through the quiet. "The Kalaxx, your northern brothers, how did they end up here?"

"After the Ha-Mi Wars, the western chapter chased those dogs as far as the Russian steppe," said Xi.

Xu cut in. "In Russia they did a deal with Tsar Peter.[7] They fought alongside the Russian army for a hundred and forty years, and assumed Russian ways. But they were forced to leave when their leader insulted one of the Tsar's princes, so they joined the gold rushes of America, and opened diamond mines in Africa. They became rich, but their wealth was built on violence and ruthlessness."

Becca thought for a moment. "What happened to the southern chapter?"

"The stories say that they were lost before Alexander

7 Peter the Great (1672–1725), ruler of Russia from 1682.

himself was dead," Xu told her. "They disappeared with their gyrolabe and their quarter of *The 99 Elements*."

"You know the HGS is looking for these?" said Becca. "What will happen if they're found?"

"The gyrolabes are said to control a machine at Ur-Can—"

"Ur-Can?" she interrupted. Her mind raced back to the fireworks factory in Shanghai, and a conversation she and Doug had overheard between the captain and Master Aa. The Sujing leader had uttered those words then, but they'd meant nothing to her. "Is Ur-Can a place?"

Xi chuckled. "Ur-Can is a myth. It is supposed to be a lost city, said to contain a great machine that the four gyrolabes will initiate."

Xu continued. "According to *The 99 Elements*, all four gyrolabes are needed to start this machine. As you know, we gave ours to your forebear Kameroon MacKenzie to help his Guild in their research. It now resides in the Guild headquarters at Firenze. But our brothers the western chapter of the Sujing Quantou keep their gyrolabe at our temple in Khotan. If the great machine does exist, it cannot work without the Sujing—"

Xi could contain himself no longer. "They are all fools. No one has ever found Ur-Can. It is said to be in the Sinkiang; we, the Sujing Quantou, have travelled those deserts for twenty centuries, and still we have not found it."

"Perhaps Mother and Father were looking for Ur-Can," whispered Doug breathlessly.

"Ha!" said Xi. "They'll never find it."

By now they had reached the low headland of Pembleton-Crozier's volcanic island. Doug had spotted a small cove from the observation post and knew it would be ideal for hiding the dinghy: the submarine's bay would be a short walk over the headland of rock and scrub. Becca waited at the bow with the anchor as Doug sailed the dinghy as close into the shore as he dared.

"Let go!" he whispered.

It wasn't deep here; the flukes caught on the sandy bottom, stopping the dinghy with a jolt. Doug was already at work dropping the mainsail and jib.

"Right. Back here in forty-five minutes," said Becca, paying out more anchor cable.

"What's the code word?" asked Doug.

"Yes, what is it?" echoed Xi.

"Why do we need a code word?" asked Becca, irritated.

"It's a secret mission," pleaded Doug. "We've *got* to have a code word."

"All right, think of one," snapped Becca. "Quickly!"

"Er … lucky socks!" beamed Doug.

"Perfect. Now let's get going."

Doug hid his silver pocket compass, which had been proving unreliable since they'd reached the archipelago, under the stern sheets. One by one they slipped over the transom and into the neck-high water, and made for the small beach.

CHAPTER SEVEN

The mining compound opened up as they reached the top of the headland, the stark glare of its floodlights picking out a collection of craft anchored in the bay. The submarine lay three hundred yards away, moored to a wooden pier that jutted out from the beach, and guarded by a couple of Kalaxx.

From Doug's sketchbook: The submarine. (DMS 3/62)

"Forty-five minutes," repeated Becca to the Sujing twins. "And keep well away from the submarine."

"Sujing Cha!" whispered Xu and Xi, slipping away into the darkness.

"Can you hear that noise?" asked Doug. "The low hum? You can almost feel it."

"Probably the mining machinery. Let's get down to the shoreline."

They climbed down the headland path to the water's edge using the deep shadows of the rocks and boulders as cover. The night was so hot Doug found himself sweating, despite the dampness of his clothes from their short wade ashore. The submarine was less than fifty yards away now; its sinister outline looked like a malevolent mechanical shark surfaced to eye an easy offshore kill. It was massive in comparison to the nimble *Galacia*.

"We can't go clomping about on deck," warned Becca. "We'll hide our boots here. Remember this flat rock."

"I'm keeping my socks on."

"They'll come off when you're swimming, you idiot."

"Oh, right. Can't have that."

Barefoot, they waded into the water and started swimming for the stern. The tide was surging around the headland, tugging at their course. They both stretched out and swam hard, digging in to fight the current. Becca made it first, catching her breath in the shadows of the sub's hull.

"Go forward a little," whispered Doug, treading water. "We can climb up on the side buoyancy tanks."

As they moved off again, he could feel the steel hull flaring under his feet. They swam forward clutching the sub's casing until they could kneel. Getting onto the deck would be easy from here.

"There's no one about." The words tumbled from him, his breathing shallow as he began to shiver with nerves. His insides tensed and churned.

Becca pulled herself out of the water. "Right. Let's make for that open stern hatch."

Neither of the Kalaxx guards on the pier saw the MacKenzies as they sprinted along the deck as quietly as they could. Without hesitation, Becca climbed down the slender ladder inside the watertight hatchway. Doug waited, his gaze switching constantly between the guards and his sister; a strong smell of diesel fuel, sweat and rotting damp wafted up. Becca glanced fore and aft – it was all clear. She summoned her brother down.

They found themselves in the confined space of the engine room, dimly lit by bare bulbs. The claustrophobic compartment was packed with pipework and machinery, allowing only the narrowest of passages to squeeze along. The submarine was nothing like the *Expedient*: it was a cramped, tight, stinking space with none of the ship's elegant mahogany or bright brasswork; there was no refinement, not even the merest hint of comfort.

Doug looked about in wonder, lost in admiration that anyone could possibly know how to build such a vessel. "Lethal. Double lethal."

"Where's the wireless telegraphy office, do you suppose?"

"That way – forward," whispered Doug.

They were unsure if the submarine was manned; their time on watch at the observation post had suggested there was no one on board, but they couldn't be certain. The only noise was the whirr of fans circulating the stale air.

A watertight door led into the main body of the sub. More murky bulbs lit the way. The machinery and mechanical tangle of plumbing and valves didn't seem to decrease. The first compartment they reached was the galley, where unwashed pots sat in a basin of oily water. The next had tiers of bunks on either side, all of them unmade.

"Mrs Ives wouldn't put up with this," whispered Doug. Becca ignored him, her face set taut with determination.

The control room

From Doug's sketchbook. (DMS 3/64)

Another watertight door led them into the nerve centre of
the ship – the control room.

"We're getting closer," said Doug, looking around for radio
equipment. The cabin was arranged around the periscope: to
port was the chart table; to starboard, the trim controls and
helmsman's position. Doug could have stayed all night. Becca
grabbed his sleeve and pulled him away towards the next
compartment, where an oil-stained velvet curtain closed off
what she took to be the captain's quarters.

Doug spotted what he'd been looking for: a radio transmitter and receiver. "Becca! Here it is. The WT office."

The minuscule cabin was jammed with equipment. Doug

squeezed into the seat and started to inspect the locks of the desk drawers.

"Can you crack them?"

"You know me, sis." He pulled a pair of hairgrips from his trouser pocket and set to work. "There's the first." He grinned as he pulled the drawer open. "Haven't lost my touch."

"These are message duplicates." Becca wanted to read them all, but there wasn't time.

Doug had the second and third drawers open in quick succession. The paperwork was jumbled but there were no code books.

"No sign," he sighed. "That's it."

"Isn't there a safe?"

"Where? In here? There's barely room for a chair."

"Right, we'll have to look elsewhere then."

"Becca, there may not be any code books…"

But she was off. Doug set to work replacing and locking the drawers. He checked around to see if the code books might be jammed between the transmitters, but there was nothing.

His sister beckoned him on with a look of impatience. "What do you think of this?"

The small compartment was bare, but clearly much care had been taken over its construction. The heavy door was ajar, an open padlock hooked over the locking hasp. An arrangement of wires supported a gimballed steel container measuring a foot square, suspended in the very centre of the cabin; the wires were attached to the whitewashed wall with small dampener springs. Doug ducked through the door and opened the container. It was empty.

"Something delicate…" he said, nudging the container so

THE M5 SUBMARINE

The monstrous diesel-powered M-class submarines were developed by the British Royal Navy during the First World War. Their most notable feature was a single 12-inch gun with a range of 18 miles. The M5 was launched in October 1919, too late to serve in the Great War, and was fitted with only a 3-inch deck gun. Passed into private hands to be scrapped, she was instead sold to Borelli on the black market.

The M-class submarine had an unhappy history. M1 was sunk in a collision in 1925, with all hands lost; M2's gun was replaced with an aircraft hangar in 1927, and she foundered in 1932 with all hands lost; M3 was converted to a minelayer in 1927, and sold off to be scrapped in 1932; M4 was launched but never completed.

LENGTH:	303 ft
BEAM:	24.5 ft
DRAUGHT:	Forward 15 ft 9 in.; aft 17 ft 7.5 in.
DISPLACEMENT:	Full load: surfaced 1,691 tons; submerged 1,855 tons
SURFACE MACHINERY:	2 x 12-cylinder 1,200 hp diesel engines
SUBMERGED MACHINERY:	4 x 400 hp electric engines
SURFACED SPEED:	14 knots
SUBMERGED SPEED:	9 knots
FUEL:	105 tons of oil
RANGE:	6,000 miles at 11 knots
SUBMERGED RANGE:	86 miles at 2.5 knots
ARMAMENT:	3-inch deck gun; 4 torpedo tubes
DIVING TIMES:	To 16 ft: 1 min. 23 sec.
	To 30 ft: 2 min. 56 sec.

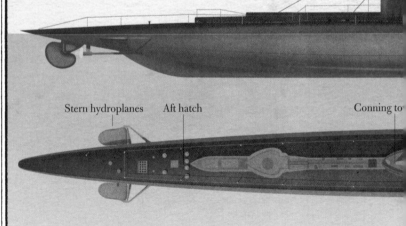

Stern hydroplanes   Aft hatch   Conning to

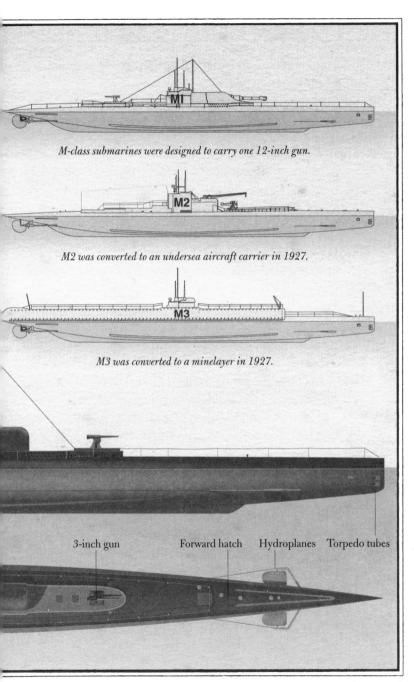

M-class submarines were designed to carry one 12-inch gun.

M2 was converted to an undersea aircraft carrier in 1927.

M3 was converted to a minelayer in 1927.

3-inch gun   Forward hatch   Hydroplanes   Torpedo tubes

that it swayed back and forth. "Something not to be dropped. Something to be handled very gently…"

"Zoridium!" they said in unison.

"Borelli's transporting zoridium. Has to be!" exclaimed Doug.

"Let's see what else he's got."

Becca stopped dead. Her voice dropped to a whisper. "Did you hear footsteps?"

Doug listened, but heard nothing. He looked aft and saw no one along the dim companionway. "Just your ears playing tricks on you."

Becca listened for a couple of seconds then pressed on, but slower and more stealthily. She was certain she'd heard something.

On tiptoe, they crept as fast as they dared to the last water-tight bulkhead. This was the torpedo room and crew's quarters, also deserted. A ladder led up to an open hatch, which made Becca feel more at ease. At least there was a way out.

An area measuring about fifteen feet by ten had been caged off; it was chock-full with hastily stacked packing cases, ancient books, scrolls and papers which had been carelessly thrown one on top of the other. An assortment of scientific instruments and antiquated devices lay jumbled within the hoard like some eccentric lucky dip. Bilge water had soaked into the lowest layer of the collection, and a smell of musty damp overpowered the stench of the submarine.

Becca read one of the aged files pressed against the mesh: "*Report on the recent expedition to Asia Minor… Honourable Guild of Specialists … 1810.* Where's all this come from?"

"No idea." Doug was struggling with the padlock on the cage door. "Firenze maybe?"

Suddenly they heard a voice on the deck above and the toe of a fine leather brogue appeared at the top of the ladder. This turn of events was bad enough, but what really struck an arctic chill into Becca and Doug's hearts was the crisp, clear-cut inflection of the words.

"...nonsense, Borelli! You'll be given the Nobel Prize, and fêted in New York, London and Paris. Don't worry about the Kalaxx, old boy."

It was a voice Becca and Doug knew all too well. Julius Pembleton-Crozier.

Doug's hastily improvised hiding place was not ideal. He was lying in the small space between the hull and one of Sheng-Fat's deadly torpedoes. The dragon's tooth motif painted on the side seemed to be taunting him. His nose was inches from the zoridium warhead, a device powerful enough to sink the submarine and several more like it in a single detonation. Becca was similarly positioned on the other side of the compartment.

But of more immediate concern were the two men smoking cigars. Both appeared to have just enjoyed a large meal. Borelli's cheeks were flushed with overindulgence and his moustache was indeed prodigious, just as their mother had described.

"What do you want done with all this rubbish?" asked Borelli, tossing the padlock key to Pembleton-Crozier.

"You could've tried to store it better." The Englishman's voice was suddenly cold and irritated. "It's damp. It'll rot, damn you."

"You try sailing through a typhoon with a useless engine and a crew of halfwits."

Pembleton-Crozier opened the door of the cage and clambered in, treading on the priceless files. "Is it here?"

"Yes, towards the back, I think. Somewhere … there… Julius, this cigar is magnificent. I left my Havanas in Firenze; the damp of the submarine ruins them."

Pembleton-Crozier began to rifle through the heap of papers.

"Your preoccupation with Ur-Can would be risible, Julius, if it wasn't so utterly pointless." Borelli smirked, wiping his fingers on a silk handkerchief. "It's a lost cause. The future lies with the new science and zoridium, not with long-lost Chinese cities. It's time to move on. The project here is a start. A fantastic beginning. By next year the Coterie will have the world at its feet."

Pembleton-Crozier paused. "You, Borelli" – his face broke into a smile as he pointed at his friend, the previous coldness forgotten – "you're a bloody genius. It's all down to you."

Borelli purred like a contented cat. "Mm, I know. Even I'm impressed with what I've achieved here. We just have one problem now – the Kalaxx."

"The Kalaxx will be taken care of, don't you worry. They've served their purpose. They'll not be getting their snouts in our trough."

"They're not going to like that. Not one little bit."

"They'll never know, if I have anything to do with it. Ah, here it is!"

Doug could just make out Pembleton-Crozier wrestling a large spherical object on a stand from under a pile of leather-bound books. It was a blue celestial globe, with constellations painted on its surface. Doug felt he'd seen the object before somewhere. Crozier spun it around with glee, then released a catch and opened the two hemispheres.

Inside was a gyrolabe, identical in size and design to the one the captain had aboard *Expedient*. Pembleton-Crozier picked it up as if it were a holy relic, his eyes wild with excitement.

"Happy now, Julius?"

"Happy doesn't describe this moment, Borelli. The genuine article! I have not seen this for fifteen years – the eastern gyrolabe."

"Don't show it to Master Kuibyshev. His Kalaxx troops would rip you apart for it."

From Doug's sketchbook: Pembleton-Crozier holds the eastern gyrolabe. (DMS 3/68)

Crozier continued to gaze at the elaborate workmanship of the artefact. "Did you get the northern gyrolabe too?"

"Ha! Fitzroy has it aboard the *Expedient*. He persuaded the board that he needed it for his Antarctic expedition. That's the one the Kalaxx really want. It's theirs, after all."

Pembleton-Crozier looked about him until he found an old canvas bag. Emptying out its dusty maps and notes, he placed the gyrolabe carefully inside.

"Now, old chap, how about a nightcap back at my villa? Lucretia has found a bottle of brandy I'd long ago given up for lost."

"An excellent suggestion. I should be delighted."

ALFONSO BORELLI

Board member and scientific director of the HGS, Borelli found the medieval structure of the Guild a great hindrance to his scientific ambition, although its research and papers, particularly regarding The 99 Elements, were in a large part responsible for his achievements.

Becca and Doug slipped out of their hiding places. They looked at each other in shock and confusion.

"Did you see it?" asked Doug.

"The gyrolabe? Yes, just about. The Guild must be breaking up. All this stuff's from Firenze! Borelli must have double-crossed the Guild. We haven't much time. We must find the code books. Where else would they be?"

Doug repeated his sister's question slowly, his mind working through the possibilities. "Where else would something important be hidden?" He had an idea. "What about the captain's cabin?"

They ran aft and pulled back the heavy curtain. There was a

small desk with a single drawer. Doug sat on the bunk and found his trusty hairgrips.

"Get a move on," Becca hissed.

"I'm going as fast as I can. It's not easy, you know."

The lock clicked and Doug yanked the drawer open to reveal a revolver, a box of cigars and some pens.

"Not here," said Becca.

"Wait a minute. Borelli said something about not keeping cigars on the sub, didn't he?"

Doug flicked the cigar box open, and there, in neat order, was a set of HGS code books.

Becca's face lit up. "I told you! I knew we'd find them!"

She took them out and wrapped them tightly in a waxed waterproof wallet. Doug relocked the drawer, and they hurried aft. As they reached the engine room, Doug stopped dead. "Wait. I've got an idea."

"We don't have time for ideas, Doug!"

"You go ahead. I need two more minutes." He turned and ran back to the control compartment, searching the bank of controls for the torpedo launch box.

"Come on, Doug!" called Becca. "Now!"

But Doug had found what he was looking for.

"What are you doing?" she fumed, looking at her watch.

"A little bit of insurance." He worked fast, undoing the connections on top of the panel. "When it's time for *Expedient* to make a run for home, I'd rather not be chased by one of Sheng-Fat's torpedoes."

He finished the job and tidied the cables, then winked at his sister.

Doug was glad to put his lucky socks back on. The sortie had gone well; the guards were still lounging at the end of the pier and there was plenty of time to make their rendezvous. Becca led the way back up to the headland, and in the starlight, Doug could see the dinghy riding at anchor.

"*Lucky socks!*" came a forced whisper. In the darkness, it was impossible to tell whether it was Xu or Xi. "Did you get the code books?"

"Of course," replied Becca haughtily.

"We saw Pembleton-Crozier and thought you'd been caught!"

"Caught? We MacKenzies do not get caught," mimicked Doug.

"Becca, Doug. We have found something. Something you should see," said Xu earnestly. "We … we cannot explain. We don't know what it is. This way."

They followed Xu and Xi along a rough track. The headland on their right rose and began to tower over them, but their path stayed level following the line of the cliffs. After ten minutes they found themselves on the far side of the *Powder Monkey*'s small cove overlooking a new stretch of land. This area had been hidden from the observation post by the hills and was not marked on Doug's map.

The low humming sound Doug had heard when they landed was much stronger here, and the air crackled with electrical activity. Xu and Xi dropped to a crawl and edged to the crest of the path. Below them was a circular building with a domed roof, perhaps four hundred yards in diameter, sunk into the ground. Blue light pulsed from vents in the side wall.

"Stay close to us," whispered Xu.

They scrambled down the bank to the wooden side wall.

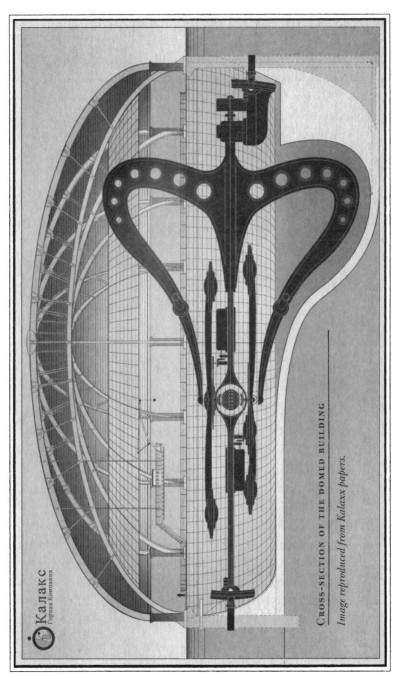

КАЛАКС
Горная Компания

CROSS-SECTION OF THE DOMED BUILDING

Image reproduced from Kalaxx papers.

Something swooshed past inside the building, then again and again – a continuous, regular sound.

Xu hurried them to a small round vent that offered a clear view of the space within.

Doug half expected to see the ancient ship Sheng-Fat had mentioned just before he died. But the building housed something quite different: a vast circular machine constructed within an excavation sixty feet deep. Two huge three-pronged wheels, lying on their sides, counterrotated around a central axis.

"The thing at the centre looks like…" started Doug hesitantly.

"What?" said Becca, jostling the others to get a better view.

"Well … like a massive gyrolabe."

Becca wasn't sure. "But we're not being dragged towards it. There's no gravitational pull."

The machine emanated portentous power and energy. Doug was fearful to be even this close to it: the low frequency hum that jarred his bones and the iridescent light gushing like mist from the spoke ends made him want to get a good, safe distance away from it. He looked again at the metallic sphere separating the upper and lower axis spindles. That was surely where the unbearable noise was produced – and the very core of the device.

Doug was mesmerized by the phenomenal scale of the engineering. Two huge steel arms reached out from the gloom of the side wall. The ground had been excavated deeper to accommodate this piece of machinery; its two extremities stretched out towards the upper and lower poles of the main machine, but didn't quite touch them. Brilliant blue light danced across the two polar gaps.

"What is it, Doug?" asked Xi, overwhelmed for once.

"I've no idea. But I think it must be the source of power for the digging machines."

"Let's get back to the ship," urged Xu. "The longer we stay the greater the risk."

"You're right. Let's hurry now," ordered Becca. "Doug, come on!"

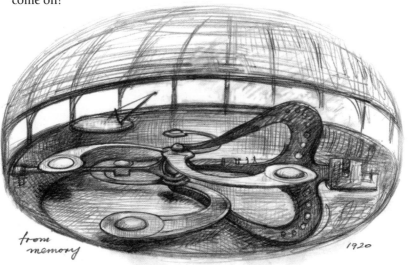

From Doug's sketchbook: The vast machine. (DMS 3/72)

Doug took a reluctant last look, then joined the others as they climbed back to the path. He had an uneasy feeling that this machine was somehow at the centre of Borelli's new scientific dawn. He walked back to the beach in a daze and climbed aboard the *Powder Monkey* without remembering swimming there.

"What an expedition – sorry you didn't get your prize," said Becca once they were safely under way.

"Who said we didn't?" said Xi, holding up a Kalaxx dagger.

Its ancient blade and gilt handle glinted in the glow from the mining complex. "Those dozy Kalaxx at the pier never even saw us!"

"But I told you not to—"

"Sujing Quantou!" chanted Xu, before Becca could get cross.

"Sujing Cha!" laughed Becca and Doug in reply.

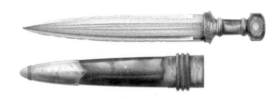

Kalaxx ceremonial dagger.

CHAPTER EIGHT

Caught. The captain and Master Aa were waiting for us back at the
Expedient. *They are both furious. We have to report to the captain's study at 8 a.m. Until then we are to rest and consider our
actions. At least we cannot be sent back to Aunt Margaret's for the
time being, no matter what Uncle threatens.*

*But I cannot rest. My head is reeling; I need to clear my
thoughts. I know the purpose of these gyrolabes, and we now know
where three of them are:*

NORTHERN GYROLABE: *in the captain's cabin.*

EASTERN GYROLABE: *stolen by Borelli from Firenze. Now in
Pembleton-Crozier's hands.*

WESTERN GYROLABE: *under the protection of the western chapter
of the Sujing Quantou in Khotan.*

SOUTHERN GYROLABE: *lost.*

POSSIBLE PURPOSES FOR MOTHER AND FATHER'S EXPEDITION:

1. *The hunt for Ur-Can.*
2. *The hunt for the southern gyrolabe.*

REASONS FOR P-C DESTROYING THESE ISLANDS? *Hunting for
the southern gyrolabe and the ancient ship? Or something more?
There's too much equipment here for just an archaeological dig. The
machine at Ur-Can must hold the key to Mother and Father's disappearance – yes, it* has *to be the machine.*

Now we must go and face our uncle's wrath. I've made Doug swear that he won't mention the submarine or that we've seen the eastern gyrolabe.

"Are you incapable of following orders? Insubordination is a disease. Much to my embarrassment it is a disease you seem to have infected these young Sujing with—"

"Xi couldn't wait to go," Doug interrupted.

"Silence, Douglas. I am not running a democracy here. This is a ship. I'm the captain; I'm in command. You will do as I damn well say, and my orders do not include running hare-brained missions into enemy territory. What if you'd been caught?"

"We weren't."

"Hardly the point. You put into jeopardy everything here. You have no regard whatsoever for your shipmates." Their uncle's face had reddened with anger, making veins bulge on his temples where his eyepatch cord crossed them. "What have you got to say for yourselves?"

Becca had decided to tell the captain everything they'd found out apart from their discoveries aboard the submarine, to divert attention from the real objective of the raid. She only hoped the others wouldn't give the game away. "We have information vital to the Guild and the Sujing Quantou," she began. "Doug wanted to have a closer look at the submarine, but it was too well guarded. Inland there was this huge machine – circular, with parts that spin around like … like a pair of bicycle wheels."

"Hell's teeth – are you sure?" asked the captain.

"It was huge," added Doug. "Three hundred yards across. A sort of electrically charged vapour came from its—"

"Master Aa, this changes everything. And you're certain you weren't seen?"

"Absolutely. We covered our footprints on the beach."

The captain nodded, then took a leather-bound book from his desk and leafed through the pages. "Did the machine look anything like this?"

The diagram was complex, but the notable features of central orb and spoked wheels could be picked out in section and plan.

Doug pointed at the core. "Yes, but there was a cupped arrangement above and below here on long steel arms."

"Could you sketch it?" asked the captain, finding him a pencil.

Becca's eye was drawn to the top of the page, across which was printed THE COTERIE OF ST. PETERSBURG.

"We heard Borelli and Pembleton-Crozier talking," Becca began. "They said that the Coterie would have the world at its feet."

"The Coterie?" gasped Captain MacKenzie. "The Coterie of St Petersburg? Tell me Crozier has not resurrected the Coterie as well as their diabolical generator!"

"So the machine *is* a generator," Doug muttered. "I knew I was right."

Becca looked puzzled. "Did this Coterie design the machine? Who are they?"

The captain took a great breath and began. "The so-called Coterie was set up by my father, your grandfather, forty years ago. It was made up of a faction of the Guild – several disgruntled board members. The original Coterie's aim was to exploit the practical applications of *The 99 Elements*, rather than merely study and protect them. They wished to bring about a new scientific dawn based on a partial understanding of these sciences and put what we thought we knew to practical use. So they built a machine similar to the one you have just described.

"The design was a crude enlargement of the gyrolabe – did you note that the central sphere and polar nodes were identical to those found on the gyrolabe I showed you?"

"Yes," said Doug. "But it had huge spoked wheels."

"Counterrotating?"

Doug nodded.

"So has the gyrolabe, if you remember – they rotate around its equator. These spokes are tweaks to the original design. The concept behind the first Coterie's machine was to run simple generators from the central spindle to create electrical power.

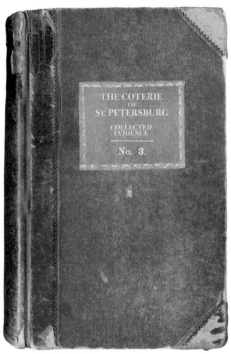

But that machine went wrong; it exploded, killing my father and most of the original Coterie members. Their drawings survived, and Borelli has obviously tried again. This machine you discovered is clearly a descendant of the generator constructed thirty years ago."

"It was working well enough last night," said Becca. "There wasn't any sign it was about to explode."

"That's as maybe, but it's a dangerous corruption. The gyrolabe is not meant

HGS publication from 1897.

(MA 46.15 HGS)

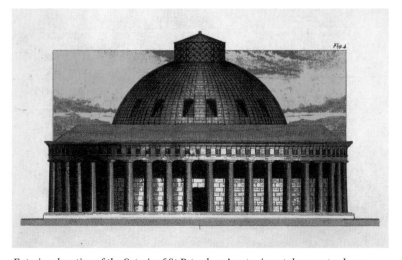

Exterior elevation of the Coterie of St Petersburg's experimental generator house constructed in Kazakhstan (illustration taken from The Coterie of St Petersburg, *Collected Evidence No. 3, 1897).* (MA 46.1528 HGS)

to be a power generator; it's an initiator, a starting device for the fabled machine at Ur-Can. These men are fools. They dabble; they copy; they misinterpret."

Doug finished the sketch and handed the book back to his uncle. The captain glanced at it.

"Ah, I'm beginning to see. All manner of things are falling into place. Some years ago Charlie retranslated a passage of *The 99 Elements* which related to my father's ill-fated generator. Soon afterwards his translation went missing; I suspect now that it was stolen, and the modification you've drawn here is based on Charlie's work."

The captain began to pace the cabin. "This refinement explains why Borelli's machine is operational while the Coterie's prototype ripped itself apart. It should have occurred to me that Pembleton-Crozier would be mad enough to try again with this infernal generator. But he didn't have the scientific knowledge. Now I know Borelli's involved, it's all making sense."

"At least now we know how they're getting electricity to run their drilling machines," said Doug.

"Is the generator zoridium powered like the gyrolabe?" asked Becca. "Is that how it works?"

"Of course it is. But where's Borelli getting his zoridium?"

"We saw, um, we think that Borelli has been transporting zoridium in a special container..." Doug glanced at Becca.

Xi suddenly stepped forward and addressed Master Aa. "The Kalaxx are refining Daughter of the Sun. Their star-shaped building is identical to your descriptions of the refining chamber at Khotan."

"What?" roared Master Aa. "Damn this Kalaxx treachery! Is there no part of our heritage they will not sell? Are you sure of this?"

"We saw inside," said Xi.

"We are certain," agreed Xu.

"This is most alarming." Master Aa's knuckles whitened as he gripped the arms of his chair. "We must act, Captain. We must stop the production of refined Daughter of the Sun, whatever the cost."

THE TEMBLA

Constructors of the gyrolabes, authors of The 99 Elements, *and the first manufacturers of refined Daughter of the Sun. The secrets of the ancient Tembla civilization were at the very heart of all the HGS and Sujing Quantou sought to protect.*

"But that would bring you into conflict with the Kalaxx. You said you did not wish to fight them."

"I have sworn oaths, Captain. We came here expecting to find Crozier excavating a ship. The plan was a simple arrest. Instead we discover the Kalaxx destroying islands, refining Daughter of the Sun and constructing machines based on Tembla technology. I would suggest there is a simple fact here – one we must face with all its terrible implications."

"The Tembla mines?"

"Yes, Captain. Pembleton-Crozier and the Kalaxx are extracting Daughter of the Sun from these islands. They have found the lost Tembla mines. They are not hunting for a ship with those machines; they are mining raw Daughter of the Sun. These matters far exceed in importance the survival of my chapter of the Sujing Quantou. It would be months before I could assemble my brothers from Khotan into an alliance against the Kalaxx. By then it will be too late. We must act now, for the greater good."

"Then we are united in our resolve, Master Aa. I too am sworn under oath to stop any practical applications of *99 Elements* science. However, we are outnumbered, and my ship is still unfit to sail."

"If these children can infiltrate the island, so can we," said Master Aa. "Two carefully placed bombs, one at the refining house and one at the generator, will put a stop to both activities. If timed with our retreat from this island, we need never fight the Kalaxx."

"Can you build such bombs?"

"It can be done. The refining house will require a special charge, which will take some time to prepare."

"My laboratory is at your disposal, Master Aa. But I should like to place these charges myself. Your talents will be better employed in the defence of the *Expedient*. We must leave this island tomorrow night. Herr Schmidt assures me all will be shipshape by then."

Master Aa stood. "Very well. Our plan is set." He shook hands with the captain. "The alliance lives on, Captain."

"It is an honour, Master Aa."

The captain turned to the crew of the *Powder Monkey*. "A most valuable piece of reconnaissance work. However, you must still be punished for taking my dinghy without permission."

Doug's heart sank. They'd been within a hair's breadth of getting away with it.

"Coconuts. I'm sick to death of coconuts. What sort of punishment is that?" Doug booted the wicker basket like a football, sending it high into the air. He and Becca were alone on the flat ground where the skeletons had been discovered. Six neat mounds marked their fresh graves.

"Here's Mrs Ives's book if you fancy trying to find something different."

Doug read the title without enthusiasm: *"God's Garden: A Missionary's Guide to Edibles Found in Tropical Climes."*

Becca settled next to one of the cannon barrels that pointed forlornly towards the beach. She pulled the code books and her mother's message from her pocket and spread them out on the ground.

"Do you know how to decipher this stuff?"

"No. I think you need a number key or something." Doug looked across to the redoubt. Xu and Xi were being put through martial arts exercises by Master Aa as part of their punishment. It looked a lot more fun than coconut gathering.

They puzzled at the various codes and the cipher, trying to make sense of it. Nothing emerged except more jumbled letters.

"This is so frustrating," said Becca. "We have the cipher, we have the books, and *still* we can't crack it."

"We could ask Sparkie."

"He'd tell the captain. They're all very touchy about the secret stuff."

They struggled on for several minutes until Doug's mind drifted off on a wave of defeated boredom. Becca plugged away writing out trial sentences, determined to get at least one word right.

A glint of metal in the disturbed earth where one of the skeletons had been prompted Doug to stroll over and unearth the hand guard to a sword. The lump of misshapen rust that had once been the blade snapped immediately, leaving him with a jagged stump. He swished it about, imagining its owner fighting the headhunters in that last desperate battle.

"D'you think he had a chance to use this cutlass before he lost his head?"

Becca glanced up from the cipher to examine Doug's find. "It's not a cutlass," she said, scribbling down another number sequence.

"How do you know?"

"It just isn't."

Doug poked about in the soil and found the bone handle of a dagger, its blade intact but deformed. The handle was edged with strips of braided silver.

The bone-handled dagger. (MA 00.23910 MAC)

"What's that?" mumbled Becca, pencil between her teeth.

"A dagger – or are you going to say it isn't?"

Becca spat out her pencil. "Let me see, Doug."

He held it up.

"It isn't a dagger."

"It *is*!" he insisted. "Look at it! How could it be anything else? Just like that used to be a cutlass. Look at the thickness of the blade!"

"Give it here."

After some hesitation, Doug handed her the dagger, which she inspected with a trained eye.

"What are you thinking?"

Becca started to grin. "Of course! I'm beginning to see!"

Doug looked confused. "See what?"

"I think we should go and have another look at that cave, Douglas."

CHAPTER NINE

Master Aa and the Sujing had already unblocked the cave and removed the cannon for use at their own defences. The broken foliage and wheel marks made the entrance easy to find. Mosquitoes flitted in the sunlight that filtered into the gloom through the low arch of rock. After a few moments, their eyes adjusted and they could see quite well. Doug was still puzzled by what Becca had seen in the old dagger and sword, but he knew from the glint in her eyes that she was working on something.

The Sujing hadn't touched the various barrels, boxes and stores, which lay as Becca and Doug remembered.

"What are we looking for?" asked Doug.

"Anything."

"Right. Anything in, er, particular?"

"Let's see what's here. Check everything."

They started tentatively, but after a few minutes they got into the swing of things, each holding their discoveries aloft, calling out what they'd found to one another like auctioneers. There were barrels containing salted meat and ship's biscuits; a coat; three pairs of boots; a bundle of surgical instruments, including an extremely nasty-looking amputation saw that Doug thought might still be quite useful; a collection of books; quill pens and an ink pot; carpenter's tools in a chest; a kitbag stuffed with what might once have been a shirt. The list grew.

Doug was enjoying himself, although he couldn't really

Artefacts from the cave

From the MacKenzie Archive: early eighteenth-century artefacts "rescued" from the cave by Doug: (1) stub of a clay tobacco pipe; (2) pewter gambling token engraved with the image of a ship; (3) horseshoe found in kitbag; (4) carpenter's nail inaccurately labelled 4-inch surgical pin! in Doug's handwriting; (5) gaming marbles, a popular sailor's pastime.

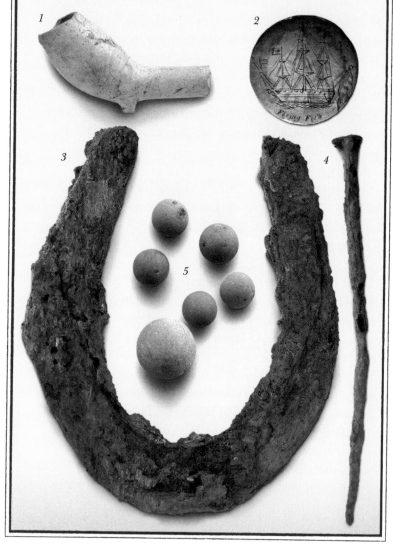

see the point of the exercise. Becca seemed determined to examine absolutely everything.

There were five large barrels marked SALT HORSE, which were going to be harder to move. Doug wondered briefly why anyone would choose to eat horse, and sneezed from the dust. "After these last barrels there's nothing else left, sis."

"Move them into the light. I want to see it all."

Doug sighed. The barrels came up to his shoulder. He tried to push the first but couldn't shift its great bulk even an inch. He decided the best way was to try to topple it over and then roll it. He managed to get the barrel to wobble, but nothing more. He put his back to it and braced both feet against an outcrop of rock. He gave it a good hard shove and the barrel teetered; then, with an alarming crack, the rock gave way beneath his feet.

"Doug! What are you doing?"

He stumbled, fighting to stay upright. "Becca, look at this! This rock just gave away. I think it's plaster."

Becca moved across to inspect it. It was about two feet in diameter, blended into the geology of the wall; in the gloom there were some very faint lines and she ran her finger over them, tracing what looked like a numeral or letter.

"This whole section is plaster," she said, rapping it with her knuckles. "It's been painted to look like rock."

"What does it say?"

"I–s–e–e," said Becca.

"Isee? What does that mean?"

"The last two letters are difficult to read." Becca took a sharp intake of breath. "I've got it. It's not Isee – it's 1533!"

"The year of the founding of the Guild?"

"Exactly."

"But what was the Guild doing here?" Doug peered closer and tapped the plaster.

"Hunting for the same ancient ship as Pembleton-Crozier?" Becca guessed. "Pass me that musket, the one with the bayonet."

She knocked the wall with the butt of the gun then turned the musket around and aimed the tip of the bayonet at the centre of the numerals – it pierced through easily. Doug grabbed another musket and started to help. Great chunks of plaster crumbled and dropped to the floor. Soon they began to pull at it with their hands.

"There's something inside."

"Treasure?"

"Grow up, Doug."

"Come on. There might be."

There was. A neat pile of gold coins was stacked in a niche beside a simple square slate on which words had been carefully etched. They looked as fresh as the day they were written.

If the Year fifteen thirty-three and the words that follow hereafter mean nothing to thee, dear Traveller, then I do beseech thee to Despatch this humble missive to the Palazzo de Selve, Firenze. Say that an Honourable Gentleman directed thee; there shalt thou be rewarded handsomely for thy great kindnesse.

Firstly:—The shadow of the Sun on the sun-dial mark'd with a Compass giveth the number of Feet.

Secondly:—This must be multiplyed by its many Faces to yield a distance.

Thirdly:—To this figure must the angle of the crane be join'd to establish a course.

Begyn at the mark'd Key stone outside; and with these measurements, thou shalt find what is Lost.

"Firenze! I knew it. Those skeletons were guildsmen!"

"How?"

"The cutlass, as you called it, was a claymore. The dagger's a dirk. We've seen those weapons a thousand times in the painting above the fireplace at home. They belonged to Duncan MacKenzie. No wonder he disappeared – he was killed on this island!"

"Lethal! But what was he doing here?"

"These islands are the key to something, Doug. Pembleton-Crozier, the ancient ship, the Daughter of the Sun mines, the Kalaxx, this Guild message written by a MacKenzie – they're all connected to this archipelago. We have to work out what this message means. We might not be able to crack Mother's cipher, but we have a fighting chance with this one."

"Do we?" said Doug, looking over the words again. They were just as mysterious as the encoded message.

"It's in a language we can read. That has to be a start."

Doug slid down the last few steps of the boiler-room ladder by hooking his feet onto the hand-rails and landed with a

From Doug's sketchbook: The slate and the coins. (DMS 3/81)

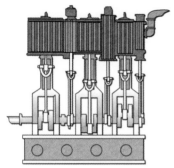

TRIPLE EXPANSION STEAM ENGINES

A type of engine which used high-pressure steam three times before expelling it. The steam entered the first high-pressure cylinder, then the intermediate cylinder, followed by the low-pressure cylinder. Each cylinder drove a piston which was connected to the crankshaft. The crankshaft then drove the propeller shaft turning the screw (propeller), pushing the ship forward.

clatter on the steel grating. With the ship beached and the boilers cold, the engine room seemed as lifeless as a fairground shut up for winter. The two massive triple expansion engines which had brought them so bravely through the typhoon lay dormant on either side of him. The smell here was unlike anywhere else on the ship: a rich miasma of engine lubricant and steam boilers. He gazed up at the skylights above, marvelling again at the complexity of piping and ducts that blew air into the furnaces to heat the steam and propel the ship.

The captain saw his nephew and gave him the briefest of nods. He was engaged in conversation with the Chief, Herr Schmidt, who looked tense and agitated. The engine-room crew were hard at work on the thrust block bearing. Further down the starboard propeller shaft, the next bearing had been removed entirely. To Doug's eye, it looked as if the work was far from completion.

"Very good, Chief. Report to me in an hour. Douglas, good man!" The captain's demeanour was unexpectedly friendly, given last night's sortie. "Follow me, if you will. We'll talk as we go. I must inspect the rudder repairs next." The captain swung up and scaled the ladder with surprising speed. "Now, I want to know if you are continuing your academic studies."

"Well, there's not been much chance…" mumbled Doug, nervously fingering the pewter gambling token in his pocket.

"That's no excuse. Despite our situation here, we must not neglect your education." The captain strode along the walkway beside the idle boiler. "I see you with a sketchbook and pencil in hand rather more often than a Latin primer."

As they climbed the steep ladder to the deck there was a loud explosion from the laboratory.

"No cause for alarm, nephew – it is only the Sujing Quantou at work."

The Duchess, who was stretched out in the shade of the alleyway, craned her neck as a drift of blue smoke wafted out. She dragged herself sleepily to her feet and leapt deftly onto the roof of the submarine deckhousing, where she settled, yawned, and started to clean her paws.

In the distance they could see Charlie out fishing in the cove. Since their arrival on the island he'd gradually withdrawn from the life of the ship, barely speaking to anyone and taking his meals apart.

"Charlie's a bit off colour, isn't he?" Doug asked.

"I'm afraid so," replied the captain. "He came to my study this morning full of a lot of rot about building himself a canoe and making for Mindanao."

Doug fell into step beside his uncle. "Is he a coward, do you suppose?"

"How do you mean?" They passed the empty submarine hangar and crane. "Mind this cable here, nephew."

"Well, he doesn't seem to want to fight – that means you're a coward, doesn't it?"

"Some of the bravest people refuse to fight."

"But Charlie said he wanted to talk rather than fight. Seems he's gone soft or something."

"Charlie has won medals in battle. He's no coward."

"Then why's he so upset?"

The captain sighed. "This section of *The 99 Elements* he retranslated has clearly enabled Pembleton-Crozier and Borelli to overcome the problems the first Coterie encountered when they built their generator. These machines create a gravity vortex at each pole of their axis." He held open the door to the stern cabins. "This is what the original Coterie did not understand. It was this defect that caused their machine to explode; it cracked the earth's crust. Charlie's reinterpretation of the translation uncovered a way to contain the vortex to prevent this happening."

"What do you mean – a gravity vortex?"

"The vortex is still little understood by the Guild. But imagine a tornado. The destructive energy is concentrated as it spins. The gyrolabe exhibits this on a small scale – you saw how it burnt through the desk when I demonstrated it to you. If you look up" – the captain pointed to the ceiling – "you will see similar scorch marks. *The 99 Elements* reveals a way to dissipate such energy. That is what Borelli has mastered with Charlie's unwitting help, and Charlie feels responsible."

Doug nodded. But Charlie had been acting strangely before they'd discovered what the Coterie was up to on the island. There had to be something else, a deeper reason for his misery, but Doug couldn't fathom it.

The atmosphere in the steering gear compartment was as tense as in the engine room. Ives wrapped an oily rag around a spanner and tightened a bolt as hard as he could. Slippery Sam, Leaky and Grease were all pulling on a rope to support the turning arc's weight.

"Captain, the rudder's still outta true. We've tried everything," said Ives.

"So the Chief says. But it'll work as a temporary repair."

"The pintles need remachining. We ain't got time for that. We'll just buckle the steering arc the second we put steam through it."

"At least she's set amidships now."

"That's fine if we only wanna steer in a straight line, Captain."

"Then, Mr Ives, we must be satisfied with our progress. We arrived steering by propellers and that is how we shall leave."

"Look, Captain, I love this ship as much as you do, but if she was a dog, you'd put her down."

From the faces of the other crewmen, it was clear that they felt the same.

"She'll get us away from here, mark my words."

ERASMUS IVES

As a young deckhand, Ives had saved the captain from drowning when their ship went down in an Atlantic storm off Nantucket Island. They had remained firm friends ever since.

Half an hour later, Becca grabbed Doug's arm and pulled him into the captain's day cabin.

"Hey! What are you up to?"

"Fifteen thirty-three!" whispered Becca excitedly. "The number in the plaster's a clue. Has to be. This message must be decipherable by any guildsman. What's the common denominator? What do both the captain and Mother and Father have hanging on their wall?"

"A reproduction of *The Ambassadors* painted in 1533?"

"Exactly. Duncan MacKenzie was surrounded by head-hunters, and he had to hide whatever he'd found here."

The Ambassadors by Hans Holbein the Younger, oil on oak, 207 x 209.5 cm, National Gallery, London © National Gallery Company Ltd

HANS HOLBEIN'S
THE AMBASSADORS

Many details in this painting hint at a secret meaning – one which has eluded centuries of scholars.

However, documents from the MacKenzie Archive insist that the painting celebrates the founding of the Honourable Guild of Specialists in 1533.

"The ancient ship?"

"Perhaps."

White dust sheets had been draped over the furniture by Mrs Ives, but Becca soon found the captain's reproduction of *The Ambassadors*. She pulled her diary from her pocket and Doug read the clues aloud as she scanned the painting.

"Firstly:—*The shadow of the Sun on the sun-dial mark'd with a Compass giveth the number of Feet.*

"Secondly:—*This must be multiplyed by its many Faces to yield a distance.*

"Thirdly:—*To this figure must the angle of the crane be join'd to establish a course.*

"*Begyn at the mark'd Key stone outside; and with these measurements, thou shalt find what is Lost.*"

"There's no crane in this picture."

"There are several things that look like sundials."

The two subjects of the painting, Jean de Dinteville and Georges de Selve, leant against a table cluttered with scientific instruments and gazed out of the canvas with a mesmerizing stare. Slashed across the lower foreground was the mysterious distorted skull motif, with a neat hole where a parrying dagger had once landed.[8]

Doug recognized an object that had been niggling him since the submarine raid. He moved in closer to inspect it.

8 A dagger thrown by an enraged Becca, much to the horror of her uncle. (See Book I, Chapter 2.)

"Becca, the globe in the painting – it's the same as the one we saw on the submarine!"

Behind de Dinteville's left arm was a blue and gold celestial globe identical to the one housing the gyrolabe which Borelli had handed over to Pembleton-Crozier.

Doug read the name of the nearest visible constellation. "Galacia! The name of the captain's submarine."

Becca had seen something else that confirmed this was indeed the gyrolabe case. "Look, the ram's head. The downturned horns. The sign of the Sujing Quantou."

"Where?"

"Supporting the band running around the equator of the globe. You can only see two of them, but they're positioned at the quadrants, so there must be four in all. The four chapters of the Sujing; the upholders and protectors of the gyrolabes."

"Could that be the sundial?" Doug's attention had fixed on an object lying on the table. "It looks like it has a small compass built into it."

"How many faces does it have?"

"I see four."

The object was very finely painted; delicate triangular veins projected from each face to create a measurable shadow. Each side was marked out as a clock face.

"What does the shadow read?"

"A little after ten o'clock on the top, a little before ten on the side one, a little after ten on the other – he wants to wind the thing up."

"Shut up, Doug. Shall we average it out at ten?"

"Ten times four … forty feet. Has to be."

"But there's no crane in the painting. Could he mean a bird?"

"I suppose that quadrant thing looks a bit like a dockyard crane if you squint. It's at an angle."

Neither of them thought much of the idea.

"It *has* to be here. It really does."

They could hear someone approaching. Becca and Doug ducked under the dust sheet and nipped through the door onto the deck.

Becca lay awake searching for an answer to the clue. All that day it had consumed her. *Crane*. What could it mean?

Outside her cabin she heard a clatter of feet on the ladder, and then running. Someone was hammering on the Iveses' cabin door.

"Coxswain! Charlie's running away," shouted Laughing Boy Messop. "He's climbing aboard the *Powder Monkey*."

Ives burst out of his cabin and bounded up the ladder three steps at a time.

Becca sat up and put her head out of the scuttle. She could see Charlie rowing away into the gloom. On deck above her, the captain's voice boomed out. "Charlie! Ship those oars."

"I must ... I must..." came a faint reply.

"Come back to shore immediately!"

Ten Dinners and Slippery Sam swam out after the dinghy, but Charlie had an excellent lead. He'd already got the sail up and, catching the wind, was gone.

CHAPTER TEN

At dawn Doug wandered along the shore to recover the anchor and line. He didn't understand why Charlie had deserted, and wished he'd tried harder to find out what had been troubling his friend. The captain gazed out into the cove.

"I wonder what made him do it?" started Doug as he coiled the rope down and lashed it to the anchor stock.

He was interrupted by a shrill voice. "Captain … Captain MacKenzie," called Mrs Cuthbert, the leader of the ladies' choir, striding purposefully towards them.

"Good day to you, Mrs Cuthbert. I'm glad to see you on your feet."

"I'm glad that row boat has gone. I thought you might suggest we all squeeze aboard it and paddle for freedom."

The captain swung his walking stick up under his arm so he could light his pipe with both hands.

"The dinghy was integral to my plans. I am forced to consider other alternatives. No matter. How can I help you, madam?"

"Why, I'm here to help *you*, Captain. All of us in the fo'c'sle hospital are sick to death of sitting around doing nothing with that Mrs Ives of yours fussing about us like a Fifth Avenue sales assistant. We want to help."

MRS CUTHBERT

A formidable widow from Virginia who sang in the face of adversity, she startled even the ferocious warlord Sheng-Fat by belting out Wagner for the entire time it took him to cut off her little finger.

"That's a fine sentiment, but everything is in hand."

"Everything is not in hand. We can all see that."

"Tonight, madam, we shall set sail from this island. You have my word."

Mrs Cuthbert was not to be put off. "We know Pembleton-Crozier, that ... that crony of Sheng-Fat's, is all but an island away. We're ready to man the redoubt and fight."

The captain gave a stunted laugh. "If I recall, you are the leader of a choral society, are you not? Can you still sing?"

"Trah-lah-lah-lah-laaahhh!" she trilled in reply.

The captain flinched. "I see. I may ... yes, there may be a moment when I should very much like to hear a requiem. Which do you consider the best?"

"Mozart's always a good bet. But don't expect it to sound too spectacular. Sheng-Fat cut our numbers some. And that's not all he cut," she said, holding up her bandaged hand.

"Then Mozart it is. You can leave any fighting to Master Aa and my crew and we shall look to you for support of a more spiritual nature."

"Very well, Captain – you, me and Mozart, we have a deal."

The captain was discussing the loss of the dinghy and its implications for their plan with Master Aa.

"Could a simple gunpowder rocket really hit the dynamite store from this distance?"

"There is nothing simple about Sujing gunpowder, Captain. Once the rocket is fired, we'll be committed to the retreat. We must get away before the Kalaxx have time to retaliate."

"It seems to be our best chance. I can see no other option."

SUJING QUANTOU ORB BOMB

Many times more powerful than the Sujing battle discus (see Book I, Chapter 14), this palm-sized demolition charge was ideal for the sabotage of buildings and machinery; the timing was controlled by an adjustable fuse. The explosive was a formulation of unstable chemicals which required very careful handling.

"The two orb bombs to destroy the generator and the refining house are complete. They are delicate and uncommonly powerful; they will require careful handling. I will set to work on the rocket immediately."

Liberty bounded down the companionway and waded towards them. "Hey, Skip!" she shouted. "Did I just hear right? That gibberin' Limey's run off with the row boat?"

"Yes, Charlie had something of an anxious moment."

"*An anxious moment?* I'm havin' an anxious moment right now, darn it! I want off this island. Where's he gone?"

"We are unsure. He's not been spotted by our lookouts," admitted the captain. "Tell me, how *badly* do you want to get off this island?"

"What?" Liberty could smell trouble, and reined in her attack. "I don't trust you, Cap'n. Somethin's comin' and it's gonna slap me right in the face."

"Would you be prepared to help?"

"Whaddya mean, help?"

"It is imperative that I destroy the generator on the other island."

"Why, I'd be delighted, Skip," mocked Liberty. "Shall we signal ahead so they can send us over a boat?"

"This is no joke, Miss da Vine. You have something I need. Something that none of my crew have."

Liberty's eyes narrowed. "What, exactly? Wit, charm and a passion for haute couture?"

"No. The ability to fly. I want you to pilot my plane."

"What plane?" she scoffed. "Y'all gonna build one outta bamboo?"

"An FE2. A pusher plane. I have one aboard ship."

Liberty searched the captain's face to see if he was joking.

"You're tellin' me you had a plane on board all this time, and you didn't think to mention it?"

"My aeroplane is not for hire, madam."

"And what exactly makes you think this pilot is?"

"Once you land, I'm sure you'll be able to recapture *Lola*, and then you may make for civilization in any way you see fit."

"Why, you sly ol' galoot. What about the Kalaxx?"

"It isn't my intention to tackle them. I intend to plant the Sujing bombs and leave. *Expedient* will launch at the same moment that a diversionary rocket hits."

"And then I just fly off, is that it?"

"I would be most obliged if you could deliver me back to the *Expedient* first."

"Oh, so now I'm a taxi service? Anyhow, they'll see us comin'. Sure to hear us too, once the engine's fired up."

"We'll float out on the current. When we're clear of this island we'll take off, circle around, climb as high as we can, cut the engine and glide in from several miles out. I plan to undertake this mission in the dark, naturally."

"Mm, how romantic. I'll wear somethin' special. Now let me think: a night flight, landin' on water with the engine cut. Almost impossible."

"But, Miss da Vine, I heard you were a great pilot! Perhaps I have overestimated your skills? If such a request is beyond your capabilities then we'll forget I asked, of course."

"Whoa, easy now, partner. I can get you in, you bet I can. When d'y'all plan to put this crazy scheme into action?"

"Tonight."

"*Tonight?*" Liberty's face contorted into a scowl. "But if it means gettin' *Lola* back ... shoot, why not?"

"Then we have a deal?"

"Shake on it, Skip."

"One more thing," he said. "The *Ladybird* needs a little work before she'll fly."

"What?"

"Reassembly and some light repairs, that's all."

"No, not that. What did you say she was called?"

"The *Ladybird*."

"The *Ladybird*?" spat Liberty. "We're changin' the name, and that's a fact."

"Do you know of any cranes in Sujing mythology?" Doug asked Xu as he poured a mug of water for his friend. The young Sujing were on watch at the redoubt, peering over the sharpened bamboo barricade. There was some movement in the jungle ahead.

"Cranes? The birds?"

"Or lifting gear, I suppose," added Doug.

"No. The crane is used in oriental and ancient European mythology. It can represent many contrary things. You will need to tell us more."

"Does an angled crane mean anything?"

Xu looked blankly at his brother and shrugged his shoulders.

They were interrupted by the sound of gruff voices.

"Here they come!" whispered Xi.

Four Sujing broke cover, hurrying two captured Kalaxx in front of them. They were surveyors, the tools of their trade carried on their backs.

"There. The vile dog-faced Kalaxx," spat Xi. "They were captured in our hidden traps near the observation post."

Hat with ram's head badge.

Detail of ram's head badge.

KALAXX (NORTHERN SUJING): FULL BATTLEDRESS

The costume of the Kalaxx order was heavily influenced by their exile to Russia (1720–1861). Equipment included gunpowder charges worn across the chest in the Cossack style; a fighting sword with ram's head motif; a Caucasian flintlock pistol; and a Kalaxx ceremonial dagger tucked into the Sujing Quantou red sash.

From Doug's sketchbook: The Kalaxx captives. (DMS 3/86)

"What are we going to do with them? Won't they be missed?" Doug asked.

"The Kalaxx are closing in on us. Very close now. But we're ready. We'll fight," vowed Xu.

Despite these words, Doug noticed that Xu and Xi drew away slightly as the Kalaxx approached. Their blood enemies were as huge in stature as the Sujing themselves, with the same sunken eyes. Their clothing was not so elaborate, influenced more by Russian tastes than Chinese or Japanese. They both had long, unkempt beards and wore a red sash tied around the waist of their smock tops, with baggy trousers tucked into knee-high leather boots in the Cossack style.

"That's two down," enthused the ever optimistic Xi.

"Just about four hundred and ninety-eight to go," added Doug.

Becca, standing on the fo'c'sle, watched with fascination as the curious aeroplane emerged in sections from the *Expedient*. She'd seen it once before, below deck, but it had been dark, and had only left an impression. In the daylight it didn't look at all as she'd expected. The wings and fuselage were already on the beach, where Lucky and Leaky were arguing about the order in which the plane should be reassembled. Liberty was lost in thought, clearly trying to make sense of the bizarre-looking vehicle and how the pieces should fit together. Becca had never seen her quite so absorbed in something; her eyes were bright with excitement as she stalked back and forth issuing impatient commands.

"Careful with that tail section," she shouted, as the last piece rocked and jerked into the air on the end of the purchase. "We're not lassoin' a steer here; we're liftin' a darned plane!"

The damage was clear to see: the airscrew was splintered, and the tailplane in tatters. "Light repairs, my..." Liberty's words were lost. "Betcha the crankshaft's outta true."

Becca looked around for Doug, but luckily he wasn't in earshot.

Liberty guided the tail section onto the sand and undid the lifting line. She jumped up into the nacelle and yelled out, "What happened to the last pilot?"

Captain MacKenzie, watching proceedings from the beach, replied, "He died. Dangerous business, flying."

"His darn blood's all over the controls. Hey, you got a spare airscrew?"

"I believe we do."

Becca climbed down and waded over to see the plane close up. "What do you think? Can you make it work?" she asked.

LUCKY AND LEAKY

Lucky, the ship's carpenter, and Leaky, the Galacia's *mechanician, bickered constantly, and could easily be goaded into an argument whenever entertainment was required by the crew. They were utterly charming to everyone but each other.*

"Gimme a pair of wings and I can make a brick house fly. A good pilot's a good ground engineer, that's the first thing I was taught. Jump up and sit in the cockpit to steady her, coz. I wanna swing the airscrew – what's left of it – see if she's seized."

Becca clambered up with butterflies in her stomach. She hesitated.

"Come on, coz, you're hardly gonna fly anywhere without fuel or wings."

"Just … just felt a bit funny. All right if I stand on the seat to climb in?"

"Get in, for pity's sake!"

As Liberty tinkered with the engine, Becca settled into the wicker seat; there was indeed dried blood on the instruments, but it didn't put her off. The dials and switches indicated a variety of measurements of which she had no knowledge: turn indicator, tachometer, aneroid, velocimeter, magneto switch. Two of the instruments she did understand: the compass (after lessons from her father while crossing the Hindu Kush) and the clock, which she adjusted to read the correct time and wound up, feeling satisfied that she'd achieved something. Then she found the rudder bar and control column, and, in a sudden electrifying instant, knew what she wanted to do for the rest of her life – fly.

In her enthusiasm she waved at her uncle. He waved back with a quizzical smile that warmed into a nod of agreement. "It suits you, niece!"

Becca called down to Liberty. "What exactly is a crankshaft, and how do you fix one?"

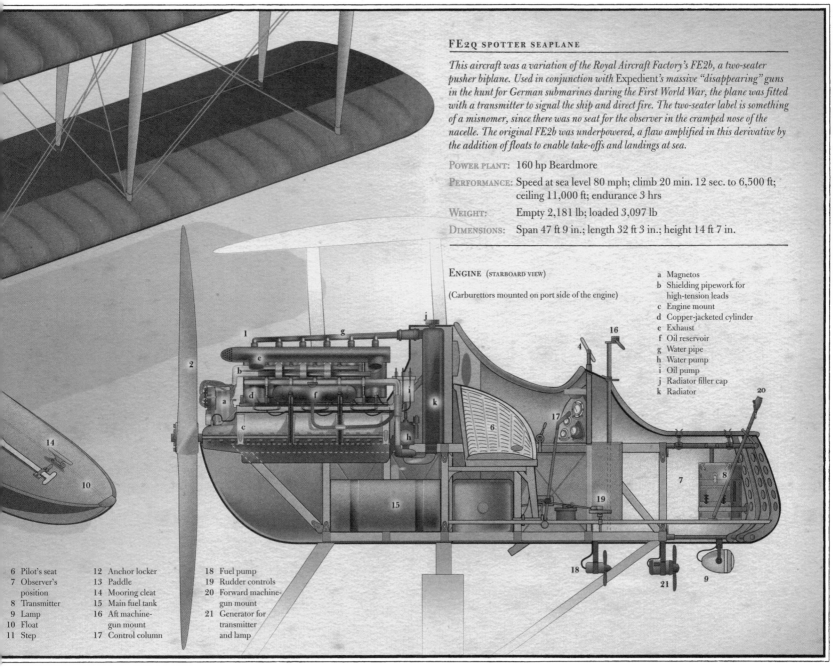

FE2Q SPOTTER SEAPLANE

This aircraft was a variation of the Royal Aircraft Factory's FE2b, a two-seater pusher biplane. Used in conjunction with Expedient's massive "disappearing" guns in the hunt for German submarines during the First World War, the plane was fitted with a transmitter to signal the ship and direct fire. The two-seater label is something of a misnomer, since there was no seat for the observer in the cramped nose of the nacelle. The original FE2b was underpowered, a flaw amplified in this derivative by the addition of floats to enable take-offs and landings at sea.

POWER PLANT: 160 hp Beardmore

PERFORMANCE: Speed at sea level 80 mph; climb 20 min. 12 sec. to 6,500 ft; ceiling 11,000 ft; endurance 3 hrs

WEIGHT: Empty 2,181 lb; loaded 3,097 lb

DIMENSIONS: Span 47 ft 9 in.; length 32 ft 3 in.; height 14 ft 7 in.

ENGINE (STARBOARD VIEW)

(Carburettors mounted on port side of the engine)

a Magnetos
b Shielding pipework for high-tension leads
c Engine mount
d Copper-jacketed cylinder
e Exhaust
f Oil reservoir
g Water pipe
h Water pump
i Oil pump
j Radiator filler cap
k Radiator

6 Pilot's seat
7 Observer's position
8 Transmitter
9 Lamp
10 Float
11 Step
12 Anchor locker
13 Paddle
14 Mooring cleat
15 Main fuel tank
16 Aft machine-gun mount
17 Control column
18 Fuel pump
19 Rudder controls
20 Forward machine-gun mount
21 Generator for transmitter and lamp

TOP VIEW

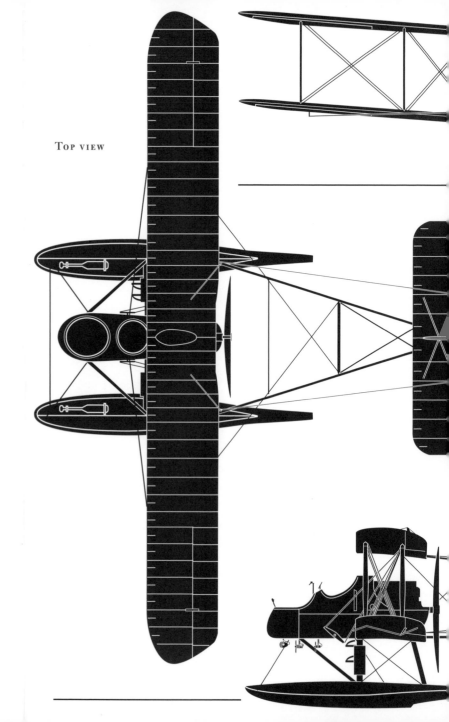

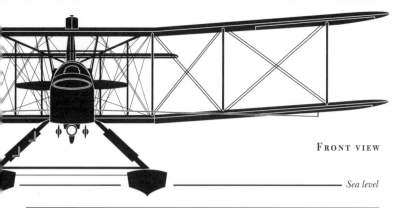

——— *Sea level*

OPTIONAL ARMAMENT

The FE2q was armed with two .303 Lewis machine guns. Both were operated by the observer. Neither safety harness nor parachute was supplied.

Provision was made for a bomb rack carrying four 25-pound bombs which were dropped via a cable release system operated by the pilot. Their extra weight made these weapons extremely unpopular; the underpowered aircraft was already *overburdened with the heavy floats and radio transmitter vital to its role as a spotter plane for* Expedient, *and for this reason these additions were rarely carried. It took a pilot of rare bravery to take off on a choppy sea carrying live bombs slung only inches above sea level.*

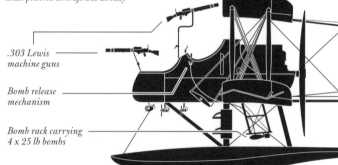

*.303 Lewis
machine guns*

*Bomb release
mechanism*

*Bomb rack carrying
4 x 25 lb bombs*

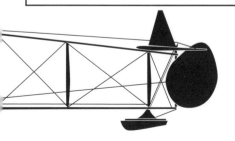

PORT SIDE VIEW

FEET

0   5   10

——— *Sea level*

INSTRUMENT PANEL

I   Bank and turn indicator
II   Tachometer
III   Clock
IV   Water temperature
V   Air pressure

VI   Compass
VII   Velocimeter
VIII   Aneroid
IX   Magneto switch

1 160 hp Beardmore engine
2 Four-blade fixed-pitch airscrew
3 Auxiliary fuel tank
4 Pilot's windshield
5 Air intake

Becca's diary: 11th May a.m. 1920

We are both outraged. Doug and I have been sent back here to the peninsula with a set of books and an essay title to work on. Neither of us can believe that the captain can think of essays at a time like this! Two hours of academic work, he says. "You must not let your education slip."

Just as we set out we received some astonishing news from the observation post. A huge airship has landed over on the other island. What on earth is it doing there? We saw nothing of it, of course, as the Expedient *is so hidden from view. Even so, we were lucky not to be spotted. Doug is jumping about wanting to go up to the OP and have a look, but the captain has expressly forbidden it. Slippery Sam has reported that ten passengers disembarked, but their identities are unknown.*

As to my own flying news, I think that sitting in the cockpit of the plane has been the highlight of this awful year. I want to know all about how it works and how to fly it. How I wish I were there helping Liberty fix it up!

Since the raid on the submarine, Doug seems much less keen on his new status as a guildsman. He didn't want to tell the captain about Duncan's message. I think he's wising up to the fact that the Guild is in trouble. Mother and Father must have suspected it. Now we do too.

Time is running out here. It cannot be long before the Kalaxx discover they are missing one of their survey teams and send out search parties. The anticipation of discovery tingles in the air. How can we possibly concentrate on schoolwork?

Chapter Eleven

On Becca and Doug's return to the ship for lunch, the captain was inspecting the engine repairs again. The young MacKenzies dumped their books on the galley table, grabbed a biscuit and rushed out to check on Liberty's progress.

A canvas tent-like structure had been hastily constructed around the aircraft in case of discovery. Inside, the plane was looking more like it might fly. The wings and floats were attached, the broken airscrew replaced and the fuel tank filled. Liberty was working feverishly, every so often urging herself on with: "I'm gettin' off this island. Nothin's gonna stop me. No sir. *Pass that goddam wrench!*"

The *Ladybird* – rather optimistically renamed the *Fighting Dragon* by Liberty – was an odd-looking machine; its big, rounded two-seater nacelle jutted out like a prominent chin in front of the wings, giving it the appearance of a friendly face. Liberty immediately set the two MacKenzies to work, instructing them to paint everything black – "To make this flyin' bathtub look a little more mean."

Doug had an idea for painting a celestial dragon along the side of the plane with a pot of red paint he'd found. "You betcha!" sang Liberty. "Just like *Lola's*." Becca quite liked the idea too, and after an hour's work the little pusher plane was transformed into an aerial dragon, a great fanged beast, that looked surprisingly effective on their limited resources.

The final touch was a Texan lone star on the tailplane. As Doug filled in the outline he quizzed Liberty. "How did

Pembleton-Crozier swindle you out of your aeroplane, Liberty? You must have known him pretty well in Foochow."

"What, that low-down rustler? Yeah, but don't you make it sound like I was his friend nor nothin'. He's the worst kinda double-dealer. Things turned ugly when he found out who my father was."

"But why were you there, in Foochow?"

"I was there doin' business. Meetin' a contact of my father's, name of Capulus. Ha. That guy and Pembleton-Crozier … what a duo. Capulus was Russian, I think – said he was a cinnabar ore trader from Samarkand, wherever the heck that is. We all met in a bar one night. P-C started up tryin' to extract information from this here Capulus about some place called Hurricane … Sugar Cane … Tin Can" – Doug glanced at Becca – "somethin' like that."

"Could it have been Ur-Can?" Becca asked.

"Yeah, that's the joint. *Ur-Can*. Sure sounds like a one-horse town, don't it just? Capulus didn't seem to know anythin' about it and Pembleton-Crozier just went crazy. He pulls a gun on the guy, startin' up a brawl, then Capulus gives Crozier the slip by jumpin' out the bar window and scuttlin' off across the rooftops. Next thing, P-C's jabbin' the gun in *my* side and handin' me over to Sheng-Fat on that finger-choppin' ransom racket. Then, to add salt to my wounds, I hear that Crozier's made off with *Lola*. Boy, I can't believe how dumb I was!" A wry smile cracked her face. "I still got one over on the both of them, though."

CINNABAR ORE

(Mercury sulphide – HgS.) Cinnabar is the main ore from which mercury is extracted. Bright red in colour, it is also known as vermilion; small droplets of mercury metal are sometimes found within the ore itself. The main centres of cinnabar mining are Italy and Spain.

DOUG'S ORIGINAL DESIGN FOR THE LIVERY OF THE FIGHTING DRAGON

Before Becca or Doug could ask what she meant, the captain cut in, surprising everyone as he swung aside the canvas door. "Douglas, perhaps you could help Mr Ives shift some pipes and ducting for Monsieur Chambois. My, what a transformation, Miss da Vine," he remarked as he saw their progress. "And painted black for night camouflage too – what a clever touch!"

Gesturing rudely at the captain as he left the hangar with Doug, Liberty said, "Swing up into the cockpit, coz, and give her all the starboard pedal she's got. I'm gonna adjust the control cables."

Becca was filled with a surge of anticipation as she clambered back into the cockpit of the *Fighting Dragon*. For the next half-hour she did as Liberty asked, pressing the pedals and pushing the control column back and forth until they were all adjusted and fully functional. With each movement of the controls, Liberty explained how it would affect the aeroplane. Finally, she climbed the ladder and laughed. "Well, look at you, Cousin Becca. I've never seen a smile like that on your face. I'd say it's time for your first lesson."

"But we can't take off."

"Don't jump the gun now. Plenty to learn on the ground." Liberty spoke slowly and seriously, as if she was telling a secret she didn't want everyone to know. "You gotta watch for downdraught. When you're flyin' in mountain country, remember that. It's no good just pilin' on the juice. Next, icing…"

And so the lesson continued. All the switches and dials were explained, some of which Becca understood, a lot of which she didn't. But she loved it all. The plane was so exciting just to sit in; she could only imagine what it would be like to actually fly her.

"Here's a cloth. Get that darn blood off the dials. That guy must've cracked his cranium good 'n' proper to make that God-awful mess."

Outside, Becca could hear Chambois cursing in French as he wrestled to complete his flooding channel.

"Cranium," echoed Becca pensively. "*Cran*ium, but in French – of course!" She leapt out of her seat.

Crane – not a bird or a lifting derrick, but *le crâne*, the French word for skull, derived from the Latin word *cranium*. The combination of hearing Chambois's accent and Liberty talking about the pilot cracking his head had jogged Becca's mind into the answer to the third clue.

Liberty raised an eyebrow and handed the cloth to Becca. "Feelin' all right, coz?"

"When I explode the cordite charges dug in around the perimeter of the *Expedient*, sea water will flood in," explained Chambois, wiping sweat from his face.

Doug liked the sound of this. "Cordite charges? Lethal."

Chambois rolled his trousers up and waded deeper into the water. "We must artificially lower the beach if we are to set sail. I have placed twelve of these charges. The pipework I've installed will break the suction between the sand and the hull."

"I … I don't understand."

"As an additional measure, I intend to pump air under the ship. Imagine your boot stuck in mud. If you could distribute air around your boot – *voilà*. It would pop out of the mud with ease."

"So your flooding channel will bring the water closer in. The air will break the surface tension, and we'll sail away. Won't the explosives just blow the hull open?" asked Doug doubtfully.

"No. I have angled the charges outwards, away from the hull. As extra protection I have attached the molecule invigorator to the stern of the ship to strengthen it."

"But that much steelwork will soak up the power, surely?"

"You always try to think of problems, Douglas! *Expedient* will glide away from the shore like a newly launched ship."

The battered superstructure of the ship looked about as far from newly launched as you could get.

"Let's be honest, Monsieur Chambois, she's one step away from the scrapyard."

"Nonsense! Just a coat of paint, a little repair here and there. You should be more loyal to your ship."

"I saw Slippery Sam ten minutes ago, and he says the starboard propeller bearing is nowhere near fixed. He says there's another day's work on it – that's if they can fix it at all. With no rudder and only one propeller, we won't be gliding any further than the far side of the cove."

"Gossip and rumour! I have spoken to the captain and he insists we shall leave the island tonight."

Doug helped Chambois route the mass of hoses under the ship, but he couldn't

SLIPPERY SAM

Sam's curious nickname may have come from his reputation as one of the best salvage divers and swimmers in the business. However, a second possibility is proffered in Becca's diaries: a rumour circulated the ship that he was closely connected to a family of cockney safe-crackers renowned for accessing bank vaults via London sewers.

CHAMBOIS'S
FLOODING CHANNEL

The storm surge caused by the typhoon had left the Expedient stranded high on the beach. With neap tides during their stay at the island, the captain would have had to wait for higher spring tides to float the ship off. Chambois's idea was to lower the beach beneath Expedient's stern to ease their departure from shore. He created this effect using cordite charges sealed in watertight tubes, linked to an electric firing mechanism. Steel plating dug into the sand angled the explosion outwards and away from the ship. The molecule invigorator was attached to the stern to strengthen and protect the hull.

From Doug's sketchbook: Chambois at work on the flooding channel. (DMS 4/09)

help feeling that their situation was slipping. Perhaps Liberty had been right all along about their escape from the island.

Becca came running from the aeroplane tent bursting with excitement. "Doug, Doug – I've got it!"

"Got what?"

"The clue," she breathed. "The last clue! I know what the crane is. Come on, I need your help."

Doug looked at Chambois, who nodded his consent.

With so much activity about the ship, Doug was able to sneak into the day cabin while Becca kept lookout. He slipped in under the dust covers and found the painting of *The Ambassadors*.

Taking out his protractor, he measured the angle of the distorted skull in the foreground, wrote it down, and made a hasty exit.

SPARKIE WATTS

Sparkie was the ship's electronics and radio expert. He was also an exceptionally gifted mathematician and cryptographer who once played and won five chess games simultaneously while wearing a blindfold.

A series of explosions boomed out high on the ridge. Everyone on the beach stopped what they were doing and gazed up. A cloud of smoke blew away on the breeze. Sparkie ran out onto the boat deck and called to the captain, who was inspecting Chambois's work.

"It's the observation post on the telephone." He held the receiver up. "They're under attack."

A further exchange of distant shots confirmed this.

"So it would appear," answered the captain. "How many Kalaxx?"

"Four. Two have escaped and are making for their encampment below the OP."

"Tell them to pull out and get back to the redoubt as fast as they can. Send word to the engine room to fire the boilers."

Sparkie ducked back inside the wheelhouse.

"Oh no. We'll never get back to the peninsula now," sighed Becca.

Doug shrugged. "Why not? This ship isn't going anywhere yet. The boilers take hours to heat up."

Liberty burst out of the tent and intercepted the captain. "Where does this put your little plan now, hey, Skip? We'll never get over there."

"There's still a chance. They may not have seen the ship. There's only an hour until nightfall."

"So what?"

"We may still have the advantage."

"Advantage? This isn't a game of lawn tennis."

"Is the plane fit to fly?"

"As best as I can guess without a proper riggin' diagram or engine test."

"I'm willing to risk it if you are, madam."

"I'll paddle that plane back to Manila if I have to. I'm not stayin' on this island and puttin' my faith in that floatin' junk-yard," she said, pointing at the *Expedient*. "I'm goin' after *Lola*."

"Shall we say departure in an hour and a half?"

"Sweet music to my ears, Cap'n."

It was music to Becca's ears too. "Let's get some kit together," she whispered to Doug.

"Shouldn't we tell the captain?"

"No. This is up to us, Doug. We've got to find out anything we can before it's too late."

CHAPTER TWELVE

Two more things have happened that make me feel we really are on borrowed time now. First Lola suddenly roared overhead, curving around in a swooping arc. Pembleton-Crozier was flying so low that both Doug and I fell to the deck. The screech of the engine was extraordinary – as were the expletives from Liberty as she bawled at the plane, shaking her fist. "Give her back, you dirty rustlin' rat! You're cruisin' around in my bird while I'm stuck on the ground with this piece of stinkin'—"

D.M. 1920

From Doug's sketchbook: Pembleton-Crozier flies over in Lola. (DMS 4/13)

Lola made another circuit, much slower this time, as P-C observed our position. He gave us a casual wave, and was gone. How I dislike that man!

Doug thinks P-C might not send in an attack until daylight tomorrow as the Expedient *still looks as if she's going nowhere.*

Then there's been a further skirmish, this time at the redoubt. I can't see much from my scuttle, as it's almost dark. There were some bangs and flashes, and a lot of shouting. All's quiet now, but it feels extremely creepy. Doug thought it was probably the Kalaxx testing our defences.

Doug and I are going to see Liberty and the captain off. If Liberty recaptures Lola, *this will be the last time we see her. I'll miss our new Texan cousin, and my flying lessons.*

There is so much activity that we've been able to assemble our equipment for tonight's sortie quite easily. We have a rope, a lantern and candles, a protractor and some cordage which Doug is now measuring and marking to forty feet.

Doug managed to use the trapdoor in the bathroom to climb down and check on progress in the engine room. They're still working on the propeller shaft. He doesn't think it'll be ready. Nearly all the crew are down there, which will make our absence less conspicuous.

"Now listen here, cousins," said Liberty, her face indistinct in the darkness. "Y'all watch out for yourselves; and Doug, for the love of God, ditch those socks. No girls'll wanna kiss you with that stink waftin' around."

"Can we write to you?" asked Becca.

"Yeah, well, I'm kinda always on the move."

"You must have an address."

"Address? The sky's my neighbourhood, coz." She pulled her flying goggles up and settled them on her forehead. "Becca, Doug – it's been an absolute blast."

The last canvas panel covering the *Fighting Dragon* was taken down. The crew began to push the plane into the water.

"We shall paddle out to the point where the tide will carry us around the headland," said Captain MacKenzie, stepping aboard the float. "It's going to be hard work against the current."

"Hey, let's get one thing straight here. I'm the skipper on this trip," called out Liberty as she threw an oar to the captain. "And you're rowin'."

"Mr Ives, the diversionary rocket will be fired at 0100 hours. Coordinate Monsieur Chambois's charges to detonate in the flooding channel simultaneously. You are to launch the ship and make for the open sea with as much haste as Herr Schmidt will allow, whether I return or not. Is that understood?"

"Aye aye, Captain."

"Master Aa, can you infiltrate back up to the ridge to launch your rocket?"

"One of my best men has been given the task, Captain. He will not fail us."

"Ives? Make with all speed for Manila once the ship's afloat. Douglas, Rebecca, you are to follow Mr Ives's orders to the letter. Now, Miss da Vine, are we all set?"

"Ready for action, Skip."

"Take care, Liberty," said Chambois, holding the plane's wing. "I've added some acetone to your fuel to give you more power, but be careful – this engine is not built to race with. And if you're ever in Paris, remember to … look me up."

Liberty climbed onto the plane's float and waved her bandaged hand. "See y'around, Chambois."

As the crew stood and watched the plane being paddled into the darkness, Becca and Doug pulled up the collars of their sea coats and slipped away towards the peninsula.

They were about to enter the cave when Doug was tackled to the ground.

"What the … Xu?"

"Xi actually. What are you doing here?"

"None of your business. What are *you* doing here?"

"We are on guard," answered Xu. "All our Sujing brothers and sisters are at the redoubt. We are keeping watch for Kalaxx; Master Aa thinks they may land near here and storm the beach."

"What happens if they do?"

"If the ship will not float, Master Aa has a plan to mount a final defence here on the peninsula, at the pinnacle above us. It is much easier to defend, but it will mean—"

"—abandoning the *Expedient*. We know," sighed Doug. He was beginning to think that no one believed the *Expedient* would sail again.

He started to hunt about with the lantern until he found a skull carved into the top of a square stone just beyond the cave entrance. It was cut as a compass, with north, east, south and west marked. Three hundred and sixty notches were carved in a neat circle around the edge.

"This has to be the marker," he said. "They must have aligned it to Polaris, the north star. Compasses are useless around here – all the zoridium, I suppose."

"What are you doing?" asked Xi, intrigued by the MacKenzies' actions.

Becca took out the measured cordage. "We found some clues left by … by a guildsman in the cave. We want to find out where they lead. Will you help?"

Xi was defensive. "Why didn't you tell us before?"

"We only cracked them this afternoon."

"I'll help," said Xu. "It beats guard duty. Xi, you stay here in case Master Aa checks on us."

"Why me?" he snapped.

"You are the Sujing Quantou prodigy," replied Xu. "You will have the honour of guarding the peninsula, and I will help Becca and Doug."

Xi's voice wavered. "I will stay with you."

"Frightened of the dark, brother?" taunted Xu.

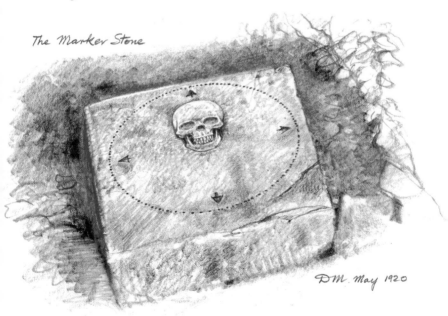

The Marker Stone

DM. May 1920

From Doug's sketchbook. (DMS 4/17)

"At least I'm not scared of heights, like you—"

Becca sighed. "Are you two going to stop bickering?" She lit a small candle and handed it to Doug. "All the clues are taken from the painting *The Ambassadors*, by Holbein. Do you know it?"

The young Sujing nodded. "The founding of the Guild painting," said Xu. "We know it, but have never studied it."

She shielded the flame and checked through the clues. *"Firstly:—The shadow of the Sun on the sun-dial mark'd with a Compass giveth the number of Feet.* We know that's ten. *Secondly:—This must be multiplyed by its many Faces to yield a distance.* That's forty. *Thirdly:—To this figure must the angle of the crane be join'd to establish a course.* That's sixty-three degrees. *Begyn at the mark'd Key stone outside; and with these measurements, thou shalt find what is Lost.*

"We need some sticks for the keystone, Xu. A thick one for the centre, and one thin enough to fit in the edge notches."

Doug set to work counting sixty-three notches round from the north. Becca counted with him to check he'd got it right.

"Will these do?" asked Xu.

"Ideal." Doug took the thickest stick and stuck it in the centre hole which had been carved in the skull's nose. Becca put the thinner stick in the sixty-third notch.

Doug squatted down and lined them up. "This is just like taking a bearing at sea. It's that way, whatever it is."

Becca tied one end of the measured cord around the centre stick and the other to her brother's belt loop with a bowline. "Hold the lantern and I'll keep you on course," she said. "I'll give one tug on the line for you to walk to starboard, two to go to port."

"Right. The distance is forty feet on an angle of sixty-three degrees true."

Doug started to walk down a bank in the direction of the sea, Xu and Xi moving branches and foliage from his path, until the cordage tugged him to a stop. Becca pulled at the line to correct his course to the left, then ran down and joined them.

"Here! Right on course."

They hunted around but there was nothing unusual about the flat piece of ground. They started to dig with their hands, but the soil was thin and immediately they hit bedrock.

"There must be something." Doug's voice was choked with disappointment.

Xu shook his head. "Solid rock. There's nothing here."

"Search out a bit," said Xi. "The angle might not be right."

"The angle *was* right," Becca said indignantly.

For five minutes they scrambled around trying to find something that might be construed as strange or out of the ordinary. There was nothing.

Becca's voice was tinged with exasperation. "Think. Where have we gone wrong?"

"The distance *has* to be right. The sundial had four faces," said Doug. "Four times ten is forty. Forty feet."

"Which sundial?" asked Xu.

"The one in the painting!"

"A sundial with four faces? I've never seen such a thing. The geometry could not work. Describe it."

Doug tried to explain. "It's an odd shape, like two cubes stuck together, but the two end faces are smaller. Here, I'll draw it." He scratched out a drawing on the loose soil.

Xi chortled. "That would have ten sides, not four."

"Of course," deduced Becca. "A decahedron! If the sundial was three-dimensional it would have ten sides, not just the four we can see in the painting. Ten times ten would be a hundred feet – we're sixty feet off."

"And you only have a forty-foot rope," said Xi.

"Stand there, Doug. You'll have to walk another forty feet, then we'll halve the rope to make up the last twenty. If Xu stays here holding the candle, and I put the lantern on the marker stone, you can align the two lights and get the bearing. I'll fetch the other end of the rope."

The new plan was put into action. Xu sat on the ground and held the candle above his head as a beacon at the forty-foot position. Becca gave him the end of the rope to hold, then sent Doug off. All Doug had to do to stay on course was walk backwards, keeping Xu's flickering candle in line with the distant glow of the lantern. When he reached the eighty-foot point he gave a couple of tugs on the rope to signal he'd arrived.

Becca ran forward. "Halve the rope, and we're there."

Xi held the rope at the eighty-foot mark, and Doug set off again, all the time keeping his bearing. He was a few paces from the hundred-foot mark when his progress was halted by a thicket of scrub on a low mound. It was covered with creeping plants, but looked somehow unnatural.

"A hundred feet's in the middle of that," said Doug, untying himself.

Becca pulled back a branch and clambered onto the mound. "Well, whatever's hidden must be under here."

The glow of the lantern and candle signalled Xu and Xi's arrival. They began digging with gusto and found the earth fine and easy to move.

Duncan's riddle is solved by studying *The Ambassadors*.

1) The first and second clues refer to the sundial with inlaid compass seen lying on the table (fig. a). The shadows falling from the vanes onto the four clock faces all mark time either a little before or after ten o'clock. Becca and Doug average this out to ten, giving them the solution to the first clue.

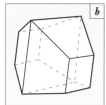

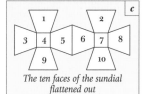

The ten faces of the sundial flattened out

2) Their mistake is to assume the second clue refers to the number of faces of the sundial that are visible in the picture, which is four. The real sundial painted by Holbein would have been a polyhedral object (fig. b); as Xu observes, there could not have been just four faces – Becca and Doug had neglected to count the other six faces (not visible in the painting) which would be required to make the object three-dimensional (fig. c). These six "invisible" faces, plus the four visible faces, give the solution to the second clue, which is ten. By multiplying the results of the first two clues together, the answer is 100 (10 x 10).

3) The third clue refers to the angle of the distorted skull seen in the foreground of the painting. When measured along its jawline (fig. d) this gives an angle of 63 degrees from the perpendicular (due north) axis, and the solution to the final clue.

"There must be something here," Becca insisted, slicing at a thick tangle of roots.

For several minutes they worked away, clearing back the vegetation. Suddenly Becca touched something smooth and metallic, stuck solidly into the ground.

"Pass me the lantern."

She held it close, and gasped as the light glinted off a piece of bronze carving.

"It can't be!" whispered Xi.

"Can't be what?" asked Doug.

They all began to dig furiously. Within minutes the sculpture resolved itself into an exquisite animal's head.

Xi turned to his brother, then Becca and Doug, playing the candlelight across their discovery. "A ram's head with downturned horns."

"The mark of the Sujing!" exclaimed Becca.

Doug and Xi ran back to the cave and found some of Duncan's old tools, which accelerated their progress considerably. They worked away with renewed energy, clearing the earth around the sculpture.

The ram's head had a fierce beauty, with menacing eyes. Becca expected to see the creature's body appear, but the deeper they dug, the more it became apparent that the head was cast on an elongated neck.

"Did your clue say what it was?" asked Xi, struggling with Duncan's old wooden shovel. "Why it is buried here?"

"No, nothing."

The deeper they went, the more inexplicable it became. They reached bedrock at about three feet, but the neck continued on into the ground. It seemed to be set solidly into the rock.

"This rock must be millions of years old," said Doug. "It doesn't make any sense."

"I've found something," said Becca, working on the opposite side of the ram's neck. "There's wood here, a plank or something…"

They all moved to her side and worked fast to uncover a small trapdoor, carved with the numerals 1533. With help from Xu and Xi, she lifted it to reveal a narrow tunnel that descended into the rock.

"Tie the rope around the statue." Doug took hold of the lantern and waved the beam back and forth into the opening. Deep footholds had been cut into the rock shaft's walls.

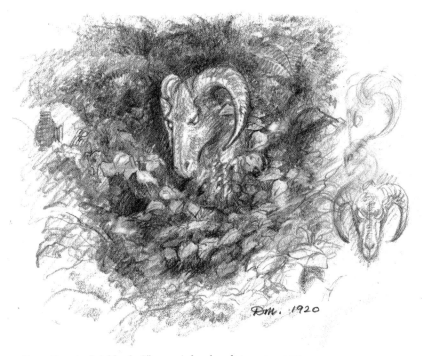

From Doug's sketchbook: The ram's head sculpture. (DMS 4/20)

Becca handed him the coil of rope. "Here! Be careful."

Doug made sure of his feet and began to descend. "It's an easy climb, sis," he said, promptly slipping.

Becca clambered down after him, her heart racing. "I'm coming with you."

"We must return to our watch," said Xi. "We cannot leave our post any longer."

"Then come after us if we're not back in fifteen minutes."

CHAPTER THIRTEEN

The narrow tunnel shaft dropped down for ten feet, then turned abruptly and levelled to a steady slope on which Doug found he could walk. At this point they lost sight of the bronze neck, which presumably continued its course down through the rock. The lantern light guided the way as they forged ahead into the blackness, the damp, musty air cool after the heat of the night outside. The tunnel had been built on a downward curve, and after twenty feet the hard rock surface suddenly gave way to a much softer mud.

Doug slipped a few feet. "Watch it here." He turned a corner, inadvertently plunging Becca into darkness. The gradient levelled and Doug saw that he'd entered a huge chamber which had been dug out by hand – the cut marks could still be seen in the soft mud of the walls beside him. The lantern cast its yellow beam into the gloom: they were at the mouth of a long cavern. Shapes and forms dissipated into the murky darkness.

Becca took two steps forward. "What is it?"

"It looks like some sort of underground fortress."

"D'you think people lived down here?"

Doug could see before him what appeared to be a substantial wooden wall, holed and revealing a further framework beyond. He waved the lantern high above his head, and saw that it had been painted.

"Wait a minute… No, Becca, look! It's a ship. I think we've found the ancient ship!"

"Are you sure?"

"It's... It is! It's a trireme."

"Oh. I was expecting to see something, more ... well, ship-like." Becca looked again at the tangled and broken construction and realized they were standing at the bow, which towered above them.

"It was rowed by hundreds of oarsmen. Look! It even has a battering ram built into the bow for sinking other ships. Lethal!"

Doug moved the lantern aft and the shape of the ship became more apparent. The trireme lay decaying in the muddy cave surrounded by hundreds of broken oars which crisscrossed the floor at crazy angles; it looked like the flattened ribcage of some fossilized dinosaur. With a start, Becca saw that the oarsmen still crewed their vessel: their bones lay all about where they'd died at their stations. Some still clutched oars, their moment of death frozen in time. She backed away, uncertain if they should disturb the stillness of this cavernous ossuary.

"Never mind them," said Doug, shifting the lantern's cast. "Their fighting days are over. This way." He whistled through his teeth. "This ship is huge." Despite being broken in half towards the stern, the hull was still remarkably intact.

"But how did it get here?" wondered Becca. "That's rock above us. It makes no sense."

"Igneous rock. This archipelago is volcanic. The ship must've been trapped by a sudden mud slide first, then the lava from an eruption covered the mud. Look, you can see how the oars are burnt where they've touched the rock. The ram's head sculpture is the figurehead; it's mounted on a great stalk of bronze and must've been left poking out above the lava. When he discovered it, Duncan just cut a tunnel and followed it down. Once they got through the rock, it would've been a fairly easy excavation."

They followed a small pathway to the hull, where a hole gouged in the side allowed them to climb aboard. A huge eye painted on the bow stared at them. Doug tentatively kicked one of the ship's timbers.

"The wood's still firm. This ladder leads up to the deck. Just think, Becca, we're the first people to see this for two hundred years!"

They proceeded with great care, testing every tread before standing on it.

"You know, Doug, these islands aren't very lucky for ships. This trireme was buried here. Something must have happened to Duncan's ship, and the *Expedient* was almost wrecked by a typhoon."

"Why was this ship here in the first place, though?" mused Doug.

Xu's voice cut through the darkness making them both jump. "It belonged to our lost brothers, the southern chapter."

"Xu? The lost chapter of the Sujing Quantou? Lethal!"

"The warriors who crewed this ship were Greeks who had fought side by side with Iskander the Great himself. Our brothers, yes, but they were never known as Sujing Quantou. You have found the original southern prodromoi.[9] As you say, Doug, *lethal!*"

Xu scaled the timbers and joined the MacKenzies on the deck. His voice filled with awe and reverence. "This ship sailed down the Indus. Just think – a vessel from the navy of Alexander the Great!"

"Where were they headed? Why did they sail so far into Asia?"

9 The southern division of Alexander's elite fighting force, guardians of the southern gyrolabe.

"Our Sujing lore tells that their quarter of *The 99 Elements* detailed Tembla mines of Daughter of the Sun; that they set off to hunt for them after they split from Alexander's army at Hyphasis. Pembleton-Crozier must have found out about these mines somehow."

"D'you think he's after this ship?"

"Only as an additional prize. Daughter of the Sun is infinitely more valuable." Xu was deep in thought. "But how did he find out this location? The clues that led you here were Guild clues?"

"Yes. But they were hidden in the cave. We think Duncan MacKenzie left them."

"Dooncarn? They were *his* clues?" asked Xu, scratching his head. "No wonder he disappeared. He must have discovered the location of the mines when he was in the Sinkiang, come here to find them and found this ship as well. The southern prodromoi and he were looking for the same thing – the Tembla mines – but two thousand years apart. The clues he left were for guildsmen – and guildsmen only search for very specific things."

"You mean the southern gyrolabe and the missing quarter of *The 99 Elements*?" Becca speculated.

Xu's eyes were bright. "Have you found them?"

Doug gestured astern. "They must be over there."

"Why?"

"Doesn't matter how old it is, a ship's a ship. The important stuff's always kept in the captain's cabin, and the captain's cabin is always at the stern."

The lantern picked out a red wooden box, four feet square, mounted between the thick beams of the trireme's hull. They looked at one another, eyes wide with anticipation.

"Who's going to open it?" Becca asked.

Xu's words were fast and edged with nervousness. "You do it, Doug. You should have the honour."

Doug nodded and handed the lantern to Becca. With all the deference he could muster he slid the heavy bronze bolt back and lifted the lid.

They all moved in closer. The spill of light fell across a collection of objects that were at first hard to discern. The largest artefact was a second square box, inlaid with intricate gold and silver in complex geometric patterns, with sturdy bronze handles on the sides. This box too had a bolted lid, and Doug bent down and opened it. As the lid was raised, they could see a dark spherical dome crossed with golden meridian lines. Xu carefully edged his hands in and lifted it out. It was a celestial globe, identical to the one they'd seen in *The Ambassadors* painting and on Borelli's submarine.

"I must open it as we have been taught," breathed Xu. He touched a button on the equator line, and hinged the globe open.

It was there.

Resting on an exquisite metal stand was the missing southern gyrolabe. The gravity device glittered in the light as brightly as the day it was made. Xu tentatively reached in and handed it to Doug; it was heavy, and he wondered if it was loaded with Daughter of the Sun. Doug could scarcely believe his eyes. This was an object of almost unimaginable antiquity, sought across the continents for centuries – and they'd found it.

"It's so beautiful…" whispered Becca, mesmerized by the object.

"Look, there are more things in here," said Xu excitedly.

Becca's attention turned to the other objects in the cargo box. She could see two books at the bottom. The first was an old, leather-bound volume; she took it out, opened the first page and read the copperplate script. "This is the ship's log from the *Flying Fish*, dated 1721. That must have been Duncan's ship."

"And he put it in here for safe keeping?" suggested Doug.

Xu lifted out the second book of parchments, which was bound in a completely different way. "This one's Chinese. Hold the lantern closer." He flicked through the pages. "It's Mandarin … written by a Ha-Mi scribe." Xu read from the first verses, then stopped in surprise. "It … it is a translation of hieroglyphics taken from the walls of Ur-Can. So it really does exist! It describes the location of the Tembla mines on these islands. These must be the pages that guided Dooncarn here from the Sinkiang."

Handing the book to Becca, Xu carefully lowered the lantern into the very bottom of the cargo box – and gasped. "Becca, Doug! The missing chapters of *The 99 Elements*… They … they are no longer missing. Look!"

He lifted out a small, humble wooden chest, warped with age. Its lid was carved with two circles forming the ancient Indus symbol for south.

"The last quarter of *The 99 Elements*," he whispered reverently. "The missing Tembla chapters. This box is identical to ours in Shanghai. It is sacred."

"Go on," urged Doug, eager to see what all the fuss was about. "Open it."

Xu hesitated for a long, tense moment; then he gingerly opened the lid. Inside was a stack of thin wooden strips covered with columns of minute hieroglyphs. Their simplicity was not what Doug and Becca had expected of such a powerful text.

Xu suddenly panicked and pushed the lid shut. "We must not look! It is only for Master Aa to see—"

As he spoke, the ground began to shake.

A whistling, metallic hum vibrated the ancient ship's timbers. The noise crescendoed into a deafening industrial row, metal rasping against rock, until the red-hot teeth of cutting blades smashed into the cavern. Doug could just make out the front of a tunnel-boring machine as it roared to a halt beside the ram's head tunnel, virtually blocking them off.

"We're trapped," he yelled.

A storm of rocks and grit hurtled around the cave as the cutting head decelerated. The machine's surface was so hot that melted rock flowed out beneath it, and steam from the boiling mud belched up to fill the chamber. Murky amber light glowed from portholes in the machine's filth-encrusted sides.

Xu grabbed the wooden chest containing *The 99 Elements* in one hand and the Ha-Mi translation in the other, his eyes fixed on the slender gap between the cutting head and the exit tunnel. "I must get back to the surface. I must warn Master Aa!"

"But you'll never get past the machine—"

"Sujing Cha!" he shouted, already running.

Struggling to keep hold of the wooden box, Xu jumped down through the ship and reached the painted eye at the bow. On the ground, he dodged the last of the flying rocks, slipping and sliding on the mud as he ran. There was barely a slither of space between the slowly rotating cutting head and the cavern floor. He careered to a stop, dropped down onto his back and slid under the terrifying machine, the searing hot cutting teeth inches from his face. He made it through, sprang up and sprinted for the shaft to the surface.

Doug stuffed the gyrolabe into his pocket while Becca attempted to hide the *Flying Fish*'s logbook beneath her sea coat. They jumped down from the ship, looked at each other, and then at the tiny gap Xu had escaped through.

"We can make it!" Doug shouted, just as floodlights clicked on from the dreadful machine, blinding them both. A door in its side clunked open, framing a figure in a ghastly metal mask and breathing apparatus. It kicked out a ladder, flicked on an industrial torch and removed its headgear.

It was Julius Pembleton-Crozier.

He fixed the brilliant white beam on the Greek trireme … and then Becca and Doug.

"You two!" he said with a false smile. "You're as persistent as your wretched parents." He looked back at the ship. "Perhaps as useful as them too."

Six Kalaxx miners climbed out of the tunnelling machine behind him. Pembleton-Crozier strode forward and grabbed Doug by the collar, the smile mutating into a hard sneer.

"You had a lucky escape on Wenzi Island. Well, I've news for you, MacKenzies. Your luck's just run out."

Doug felt himself choking. Pembleton-Crozier pushed him back into the mud, sending the gyrolabe flying from his pocket. It thudded into the sludge and lay glinting in the glare of the lights like an ancient jewel.

Pembleton-Crozier picked up the device and held it for a

From Doug's sketchbook: The tunnelling machine breaks through. (DMS 4/29)

moment, turning the mechanism until he found the Indus symbol on the top. He cleaned it delicately with the tip of his finger.

"Well, well, well. Here it is at last – the lost southern gyrolabe. After four hundred years of bad sport and miserable disappointment, gyrolabe collecting now seems to be no bother … no bother at all."

He turned, his eyes fixed in an inimical stare. "You, Rebecca. That book – give."

He snatched the ship's log from her and flicked through it, immediately disappointed.

"Looking for something?"

"The lost chapters. Come on, where are they? They must have been with the gyrolabe."

"The captain will have them by now." Becca smiled. "You're too late."

He slammed the logbook shut. "Oh, really? Fitzroy's going

nowhere. The *Expedient*'s a wreck; we have him surrounded. But it is indeed too late – too late for the Honourable Guild."

Xu climbed out of the tunnel and found Xi beside the ram's head statue.

"Where are the others?"

"A tunnelling machine cut us off. I escaped, but Becca and Doug did not follow, so I went back to find them and heard the voice of Pembleton-Crozier. He has captured them, I am sure. We found the ancient ship, Xi. But there are many Kalaxx too."

"Those Kalaxx dogs are everywhere," spat Xi. "Seventy of them have landed on the peninsula in three motor boats. I counted every one as they stepped ashore. They are down there hiding beside the path. We must warn the *Expedient* and the redoubt."

"What about Becca and Doug?"

"It's too late. If we wait here we will be caught as well. What use would that be?"

They set off silently in the direction of *Expedient*. Xu was the first to spot two Kalaxx scouts blocking the path ahead. They climbed back towards the pinnacle, hoping to find another way down to the hourglass beach.

"Cha!" came a whisper from close by. It was Master Aa and Ba'd Ak. "Why aren't you at your post? We've been looking for you. You are to return to the *Expedient*. Ba'd Ak will keep watch here."

"But, Master Aa, the Kalaxx are already here. The path is blocked. And we have found something."

THE SOUTHERN QUARTER OF THE 99 ELEMENTS

These photographs show the humble chest that housed the southern quarter of the ancient 99 Elements. The picture below details the engraving on the lid: the Indus symbol for south.

Xu handed the wooden chest to Master Aa.

"What is this?"

"Master, I believe it is the lost chapters of *The 99 Elements*. Becca and Doug have found the ancient ship."

Master Aa took the chest and examined it closely in the darkness. "Can it be?" he murmured, tracing the circular symbol with his finger. "At last?"

"Pembleton-Crozier has captured Becca and Doug and the missing southern gyrolabe," added Xu. "We also found this Ha-Mi translation of—"

Ba'd Ak signalled silence; there was movement in the jungle close by. The Sujing dropped to the ground and watched twenty Kalaxx steal past.

Once they were a safe distance away, Master Aa whispered, "We cannot risk the capture of *The 99 Elements* by the Kalaxx. We will never make it through the enemy lines. To the pinnacle – we will conceal ourselves among the rocks and boulders there."

"But what about the *Expedient*?" protested Xi.

"Have I taught you nothing?" hissed Master Aa. "Ownership of *The 99 Elements* surpasses all other missions. These writings have been lost for over two thousand years. The importance of the secrets they contain is beyond measure, as is the honour their recovery will bring to our chapter. The protection of this ancient box eclipses the Treaty of Khotan and my covenant with Captain MacKenzie."

"But that means leaving our friends to die at the hands of the Kalaxx," argued Xu.

"It does not," replied Master Aa. "Captain MacKenzie is a resourceful man. He will find a way to defeat the Kalaxx horde without us."

After crawling for a few minutes, they found shelter on the

north side of the pinnacle in a gap between two boulders which commanded a clear view of the hourglass beach and the *Expedient* below. Occasional rifle fire cracked out from the redoubt into the still of the night as they settled in to keep their vigil. For Xu and Xi, it was a troubling dilemma that they should have to sit and guard an ancient artefact while a battle of bloody proportions prepared to unfold on the beach below them.

CHAPTER FOURTEEN

The tunnelling machine, thought Doug as he was dragged into its control room, warranted further examination, and had it not been for the fact that Pembleton-Crozier had him by the scruff of the neck, he might have been able to dawdle and make some sense of the thing. It was a complex piece of machinery, and he could see immediately that Chambois's molecule invigorator was at the core of its workings. He did some quick calculations, recalling that Chambois's invention was capable of strengthening steel by a factor of twenty-five. No wonder the machine could cut through rock so easily.

They squeezed back along a narrow, sweltering corridor lined with pipes and wires. They reached a squat steel door with a watertight seal, which Pembleton-Crozier opened and forced them to climb out of, into the tunnel behind. It was scorching hot; the tunnel walls had been cut with such heat and speed that the rock had melted.

"Glass," said Becca, peering at the compressed rock.

"The centrifugal forces generated by the machine compress the excavated rock so hard and fast that it seals the tunnel," Pembleton-Crozier informed her with a smug smile. "We add silica to form a glass lining when we hit soft ground like mud. This thing can bore ten miles of tunnel in an hour."

Becca could feel the scorch of the smooth tunnel surface through her sea boots. The air was so foul it made her gag.

Crozier hit a button and uncovered a motorbike and trailer

in a compartment at the back of the tunelling machine. He lowered it to the tunnel floor.

"Hold this position and await orders," he shouted at the machine's driver. He kick-started the motorbike. "You two MacKenzies, get on."

Becca and Doug were barely seated before Pembleton-Crozier let the clutch out, spun the metal-studded wheels on the glass surface and accelerated away. The bike picked up speed, banking steeply on the corners, faster and faster until Doug could see by the speedometer that they were going at fifty miles an hour. After a couple of terrifying minutes, Crozier slammed the brakes on hard as they reached a junction where several tunnels met, widening into another chamber. He gunned the engine then screeched to a stop outside a sentry post.

He grabbed a field telephone and wound its handle. "Master Kuibyshev, it's Julius. Get the attack under way... Tell your troops that the bounty is half a million dollars for whoever captures the *Expedient* and her captain. Get word to the other tunnelling machines, and send everything over there... Tell them to drill through his damn hull if they have to... Start the surface attack immediately. You've got machine guns and dynamite. Use them."

He slammed the receiver down and jumped back onto the motorbike. "You two might prove useful yet."

After another dizzying ride through endless black tunnels under the sea, the bike began to ascend then broke out into the mining compound on Sulphur Island.

Pembleton-Crozier frogmarched Becca and Doug into his villa, which seemed bizarrely out of place in the industrial wasteland that the island had become.

"Turn out your pockets." He jabbed a finger at the table. "Come on. I don't have all night."

There were three sharp knocks on the door. Posh Charlie was pushed in, his hands tied, followed by Borelli and three Kalaxx miners.

"Good Lord. Charles!" said Pembleton-Crozier. "I thought I caught a glimpse of you at Wenzi Island, but I wasn't sure in all the thrill."

"J-J-Julius. Heavens – Becca and Doug too?"

"Yes, do join our little party." Pembleton-Crozier scraped back a chair and shoved Charlie towards it. "Where did you find him?"

"Wandering around on the north side of the island," said one of the Kalaxx in a heavy Russian accent. "He says he sailed here from Mindanao."

"Well, that's not quite true, is it now, Charles?"

"I b-beg you to stop this, Julius," pleaded Charlie. "I came here to try and t-t-talk to you, to p-p-persuade you to give yourself up to the Guild."

Pembleton-Crozier laughed. "Give myself up to the Guild? What an amusing notion."

Borelli smirked. "It's rather too late for that."

Crozier started to inspect the items turned out by the two MacKenzies. His attention fixed on the coded message. Becca froze as he picked it up.

"Well, well."

"Leave my things alone," she demanded, but he was already walking over to his writing bureau.

"I've seen what you're doing here, J-Julius. You have to s-s-stop all this. My retranslation of the gravity vortex references was not made with the assumption that anyone would try and couple it to a zoridium g-g-generator. Thirty years ago the device cracked the earth's surface, for g-g-goodness' sake; the p-p-potential for catastrophe is—"

"Oh, do shut up, you stuttering fool," barked Pembleton-Crozier as he took out a set of HGS code books and settled down to decipher Becca's mother's message.

"B-B-Borelli, you are a director of the b-b-board," said Charlie, "sworn to defend these secrets. You have gone against hundreds of years of tradition—"

"Tradition! A tradition that suppresses a science of this magnitude? We could change the planet with these machines. We could all be rich instead of grovelling around running secret missions for any government that'll pay. The Guild's become a gang of mercenaries, just so it can balance the books and persist with this laughable devotion to an archaic secret."

"But this technology could destroy the planet – that's what *The 99 Elements* warns! Our civilization is not sufficiently advanced to use this knowledge wisely!" Charlie's stutter vanished as he reddened with anger.

"Nonsense. The time is right. Civilization's at its peak. We have steam trains that can achieve almost a hundred miles an hour. We have electric trams, aeroplanes and automobiles. What better time?"

"You forget our history, Borelli."

"History? What history?"

"Four years ago I was in France, lying in a stinking trench near the Somme, ready to launch myself towards all the ingenuity

THE GREAT WAR AND THE BATTLE OF THE SOMME

Better known today as the First World War (1914–18), the Great War was a conflict on a scale previously unknown and fought mainly in Europe. The Battle of the Somme (1916) has become synonymous with futile slaughter: it lasted for almost five months and 420,000 British, 200,000 French and over 600,000 German troops were killed or wounded.

of mankind – machine guns, poisonous gas, bombs, tanks…
Mankind is still barbaric, Borelli; prone to cruelty, rarely to be
trusted with its discoveries and careless of the planet."

"Such pessimism," interrupted Pembleton-Crozier. "You
can't stop progress, Charles old boy. Can't uninvent it. The
future is already here. It's powering this damned light
bulb."

Julius lit a cigar and read over the message again. He
seemed to have finished decoding it. "So your parents were
on the hunt for Ur-Can," he said, puffing out a cloud of
smoke. "What have you heard of Ur-Can then, Rebecca?"

"Nothing."

"I don't believe you. Been sworn into the Guild, have you?
Honour, duty or death?"

"I'm not in the Guild," she stated bluntly. "I shan't join the
Guild until I've seen my parents."

"Certain you *are* going to see them? Sure they're not …
dead?"

"Look, we don't know anything about Ur-Can," said
Doug.

"If you tell me, young MacKenzies, you can have this message. Otherwise…" Pembleton-Crozier held his cigar to the
sheet of paper until it started to curl and singe.

Becca couldn't stop herself. "All right, we've heard Ur-Can
mentioned, nothing more. But if you're trying to find out
what our parents were doing in the Sinkiang, you'd better join
the queue, sir!"

Pembleton-Crozier gave a hollow laugh. "My my, how
you sound like your mother when you're cross, Rebecca.
What about the machine that the gyrolabes initiate? Has
Fitzroy told you about that too?" He held the cigar closer.

The message was beginning to smoulder and flicker into flame.

"No ... no ... we know nothing."

Pembleton-Crozier dragged on his cigar until the tip glowed a bright orange.

"What about the Tembla? It says here: *We're going to locate the site of the ancient machine at Ur-Can created by the Tembla civilization.*"

Becca could barely contain her rage. "I've never heard of the Tembla or an ancient machine, all right?"

"It goes on... Oh dear ... it's so difficult to read through the smoke..."

Becca turned to Doug for help. He could offer none.

"Let me tell you about the Tembla, shall I? See if I can ring any bells. The Tembla were a great southern ice civilization, who sent emissaries to the Indus Valley in the time of epic India. Heard the captain mention Antarctica, have you? Ah, I can see you have. Your eyes betray you."

A small flame licked up the edge of the paper.

"I insist you stop!" shouted Charlie. "The Tembla are not to be spoken about in this way. These children know nothing of interest to you."

"I'll gag you if you don't shut up, Charles." Pembleton-Crozier took a revolver from his belt and placed it on the table.

Doug thought about making a lunge for the gun, but didn't rate his chances. He recognized the look of fury in Becca's eyes; Crozier had pushed her too far. With a move so fast he almost missed it, she reached for a glass of water and hurled the contents at the burning message, extinguishing the flame and dousing Pembleton-Crozier's cigar with a hiss. He

From Doug's sketchbook: Becca confronts Pembleton-Crozier. (DMS 4/33)

sprang up, dropping the message, and grabbed the revolver. He wiped his eyes with his sleeve, blinking rapidly.

At that moment, Lucretia Pembleton-Crozier swept into the room. The atmosphere changed immediately, the balance of power shifting from Julius to his wife. His moustache twitched nervously as he greeted her. "Ah, good evening, my dear."

Lucretia acknowledged her husband with raised eyebrows, then turned her attention to Charlie.

"Charles. How nice to see you."

"G-g-good evening, Lucretia."

"I wondered if you'd turn up. And these must be the young MacKenzies. Charmed, I'm sure. Julius – the Coterie is assembled."

"The Coterie of St Petersburg?" gasped Charlie. "Here?"

LUCRETIA PEMBLETON-CROZIER

Daughter of a Portuguese jade dealer, she was renowned for her icy intellect and fabulously expensive lifestyle. She was reputed to have scandalized polite London society at the age of eighteen by winning a gentlemen's pistol-shooting contest dressed in the disguise of a tweed suit and wig.

Lucretia's scarlet lips curled into an icy smile.

Pembleton-Crozier lifted his revolver. "On your feet, all three of you. Now."

"How the heck did I get into this? I should be flyin' planes, not paddlin' them like some trapper's canoe. Where did it all go wrong?"

The *Fighting Dragon* bobbed up and down in the swell. Liberty and Captain MacKenzie had made steady progress along the narrow channel and had followed the coast to the island's last headland, which loomed over the *Fighting Dragon*'s starboard wing.

"Probably when you met Pembleton-Crozier in Foochow."

Liberty stopped paddling and glanced over at the captain. "Don't get smart with me, Skip. I just want *Lola* back. Remember that."

"Tell me, madam, what do you know of this fellow Capulus?"

"Why d'you ask?"

"It's possible he is connected with Rebecca and Douglas's parents somehow."

"Capulus, Pembleton-Crozier ... you. That's the trick here, isn't it? Knowin' who to trust. From my perspective, you're all just different shades of the same grey. I'm caught, you see. Bit like those kids. Smack in the middle of all this. I seem to have landed up on your side, for what little thanks I get. But is it the right side?"

"I am most grateful to you for saving my ship at Wenzi Island. Perhaps I've not made that clear enough. You also took care of Douglas and Rebecca, for which I am again deeply grateful."

"Yeah, well, force of circumstance, nothin' more."

"I find they are a most headstrong duo. I can command a ship, but I seem unable to control a pair of children."

"How d'y'all get lumbered with those two anyhow? You're not exactly father material, scootin' around the globe in that gunboat of yours, tryin' to keep ahold of all those dusty secrets. Did you ever have kids of your own?"

The captain didn't answer.

"You sly old dawg. Gal in every port, I bet."

"If you insist on persisting with this line of questioning, then I must tell you that my wife died during childbirth, many years ago. She and our child are buried in … well, it's immaterial where they are buried. The matter is closed."

For some moments the only sound was the drip of water running off the paddles into the sea.

"I sure am sorry to hear that, Captain. I had no idea."

Liberty dug the paddle blade deep into the water and pulled; up ahead the surf was breaking as they approached the headland.

"If it's any use to you – to Becca and Doug's hunt for their parents, I mean – Capulus approached Mallagerty offerin' him a sample of this Daughter of the Sun stuff."

"Mallagerty?"

"The boss of my father's Shanghai office. Dad has oil

exploration teams all over the world, especially here in Asia. Capulus sent a letter claimin' this new mineral had the potential to kill the oil and petroleum industry dead. Mallagerty said the guy was a nut, which he was, but not in the way we thought back then. I had a week to spare before I was due to ship out for the States, so I thought I'd take a look at the guy's proposition. Dad told me not to go, which was an added incentive, of course. What did I have to lose? A plane and a little finger as it turned out, but I wasn't to know that then. I never heard Capulus mention the name MacKenzie, though."

"Well, it was a long shot."

"Hey, Skip – I'll let you in on another secret."

"Don't tell me you're planning to join a convent after this?"

"Those kids, Becca and Doug, they like you."

"Sentimentality doesn't suit you, Miss da Vine. I fear I'm more comfortable with your famous Texan wit."

"Yeah, well I'm more comfortable in the air. Are we through with paddlin' yet?"

"Almost … we are clear of the island. The current will carry us to the south-east at about three knots by my reckoning." The captain checked his pocket watch. "By 0030 hours we'll be a good six miles away from any Kalaxx. It will be safe to start the engine then."

Liberty clambered up into the pilot's seat and patted the little plane's side. "Let's see if there's any fire in this dragon's belly."

Chapter Fifteen

Even before Julius Pembleton-Crozier had slammed the door and locked it, Doug was looking for a way to escape from the cellar beneath the villa. Crozier's lantern had revealed a candle and matches on the table. Now, in the pitch-dark, Doug found them and quickly had the candle lit. In the orange glow he saw Charlie had slumped in the corner, a defeated man.

"What made you run, Charlie? What made you sail here? The captain will be furious."

"Untie my hands, will you? You assume m-m-many things, Doug old chap. First, that we will s-see the captain again; and second, that he'll ignore the f-f-fact that you're here too."

"Did you really think Pembleton-Crozier would listen to you?" asked Becca, untying Charlie's hands.

"I thought I could p-p-persuade him to stop ... turn himself in. I s-see now that he has lost his head."

"We could've told you that." Doug sighed. "We need to get out of here as quickly as possible." The cellar contained nothing helpful to effecting an escape. As far as Doug knew, a collection of wines and spirits was not much use for removing a door. He took a bottle from the rack and read the label. "Château Latour, 1893."

"N-n-nice drop that."

Doug rolled it across the floor towards Charlie. "There's crates of the stuff." He yanked at a metal rack, making the bottles shake and clink. He kicked one of the bars at the corner, dislodging the rusty bolt with a crack. Three hundred bottles lurched and threatened to fall.

"Help me out, sis!"

They worked fast, unracking the wine and placing it on the floor.

"Righto, stand back." Doug twisted the bar back and forth until the metal fatigued and broke. "One iron bar."

"What are you going to do with it?"

"Remove one of the floorboards from the room above us. Plenty of leverage on this. What we need is a bit of a gap and we're in business."

The iron bar was surprisingly heavy. They wormed one end into a small gap between a floorboard and joist, and worked the bar up and down until they gained a purchase. With a crack and a groan the board began to lift.

© Science Museum/Science and Society Picture Library

ARCHIMEDES

Greek mathematician (c.287–212 BC) known for his work in physics, geometry and mechanics, including the properties of levers and pulleys. Famed for discovering Archimedes' principle of fluid displacement in his bath and running naked through the streets of Syracuse shouting "Eureka!" ("I have found it!")

"Stop there," ordered Doug as the tips of nails emerged. He pulled the table closer so he could stand beneath the joist and pushed the floorboard up. "Right, lever up the other end while I keep the pressure on here."

Charlie and Becca repositioned the bar at the opposite end of the board and started work. After a few moments, it was free.

"Law of the lever," sniffed Doug. "Give me a place to stand and I'll move the earth."

"I doubt Archimedes had a rack of vintage p-p-plonk in mind when he thought that one up, Douglas."

They had the second board up within a minute, and their escape route lay tantalizingly open.

"Give me a leg up. Let's see what we've got."

Becca helped her brother haul himself up through the gap until he was seated on the edge of the opening.

"All clear?"

"Yes," he whispered, "but keep your voice down and watch for the nails. I'll pull you up."

Becca grabbed the joist and clambered up without Doug's help. Charlie came next.

"G-g-good work, Doug."

Doug put his fingers to his lips in warning. Voices could be heard in the next room.

"The Coterie," whispered Charlie, eyes wide.

They tiptoed to the door. Through a crack Doug could just see Lucretia standing at the head of a long polished table, the rest of the Coterie arranged around it. Her voice was measured and steady.

"Borelli, are you satisfied that the research on the prototype generator is now complete?"

"Absolutely." Borelli's smug grin cut through the curls of blue cigar smoke. "The data the machine has supplied means we can proceed with Project Avalon. I'm confident that next time we can contain a more powerful gravity vortex."

"Should we decommission and dismantle the prototype?"

"Decommissioning is unnecessary and expensive. It has served its purpose. My recommendation is to destroy it *in situ*."

"Harry? Extraction and refinement – do we have enough zoridium?"

"Our yield from the tunnelling machines has been falling

BARON VANVORT

The archaic structure of the Guild meant his position as treasurer and loyal member of the HGS had gone unaudited for nearly a decade. Vanvort had set about destroying the Guild from within by burdening it with crippling debts. By 1920 he had syphoned off virtually all the Guild's assets into the bank accounts of the resurrected Coterie of St Petersburg, which fed on the Guild like a parasite in matters both scientific and financial.

consistently for the last six months. However, our stockpile of refined zoridium now stands at three tons."

"Is that enough to sustain our development programme?"

"Three tons is enough to last the next two hundred years."

Lucretia nodded. "Julius, what about the weapons programme?"

"Our development of zoridium weaponry has proved a success," he stated, "despite the destruction of the production facility at Wenzi Island."

Lucretia folded her arms. "An unfortunate loss, but our research institutions in Zurich and San Francisco can bridge the gap. Baron Vanvort, please outline our financial position."

The cold distance in this man's eyes sent a chill through Doug. Baron Vanvort's jet-black hair was lacquered so tight against his skull it looked as if it was stretching the skin on his face. When he spoke his voice was as precise and remote as his stare. "There is sufficient finance to proceed with Project Avalon."

"Excellent," said Lucretia. "Then I move that we initiate Project Avalon immediately. Are we all in agreement?"

The Coterie nodded their assent.

"This is a spectacular moment for the Coterie, gentlemen. Spectacular."

"One moment, Lucretia," said Baron Vanvort with slow

THE COTERIE OF ST PETERSBURG

The Coterie of St Petersburg was founded in the winter of 1880 by a faction of disgruntled HGS board members striving to break free from the medieval constraints of the Guild. Their express aim was to realize modern, practical applications of the science of The 99 Elements. *To demonstrate their ambition they created an electrical power generator based on the gyrolabe. The machine was constructed outside the city of Alma-Ata, Kazakhstan.*

The first test ended in the catastrophic destruction of the generator, vindicating the Guild's long-held belief that The 99 Elements *should be studied and protected until properly understood. The few Coterie members who survived the test were captured and put on trial at the HGS headquarters in Firenze. (Illustration taken from* The Coterie of St Petersburg, Collected Evidence No. 3, 1897: *shows the original Coterie of St Petersburg's headquarters in Russia.)*

deliberation. "With so much renewed investment we can also continue our exploration for more of the Tembla secrets. A sustained search for Ur-Can may deliver us a far more powerful machine."

"We must not be swayed from our current purpose," retorted Lucretia. "You speak like a guildsman."

"We still do not know what the Ur-Can machine is, or what it is capable of," persisted the baron. "I mean no offence, Borelli, but if the warnings in *The 99 Elements* are to be heeded, your generator is a mere toy by comparison."

"This is an old Guild argument, an academic exercise of little value," snapped Borelli. "The future lies with our successful harnessing of zoridium in a working electrical generator. Let us enjoy that success and forget the gyrolabes and Ur-Can."

"Nevertheless, it is still possible that Ur-Can holds the ultimate secret," Pembleton-Crozier argued. "Your generator is a work of brilliance, Borelli, but don't let this blind you to further, greater possibilities. While we have achieved something extraordinary here, we have within our grasp the summit of our ambitions."

Borelli banged his fist on the table. "This is pointless! If nothing else, you'd need all four gyrolabes to work this mythical machine!"

"We have two of them, and I know exactly where the other two are. We're halfway there, my friend."

Borelli sat back in exasperation. "You still have to find Ur-Can! The Guild has wasted centuries on that fruitless search. Why rehearse old mistakes?"

Lucretia resumed control. "Let us leave this debate for now; we have more pressing matters. I suggest we close down our operation here. The world must never know the source of our zoridium. The question of our connection to the Kalaxx must also be resolved."

Crozier laughed. "After tonight, there will be no connection, I assure you."

"And you are confident the *Expedient* won't cause us any trouble?"

"She's trapped on a sandbar with drilling machines tunnelling towards her rusty hull. The *Expedient*'s arrival is to our advantage. Nearly all the Kalaxx have been lured there with the promise of battling the Sujing Quantou to the death. Let them have their internecine war." Crozier grinned. "And they can kill Fitzroy while they're at it. In the confusion, I'll slip over and collect the northern gyrolabe."

Lucretia paced towards the window. "Then we all leave tonight. Borelli, the last consignment of zoridium will be loaded onto your submarine immediately. The rest of you will leave aboard the airship. We will reconvene in Alexandria in two months' time."

As the chairs scraped back, Becca, Doug and Charlie made a dash for the door at the rear of the villa. The compound's perimeter wire was an easy sprint away but the ground offered little cover.

"Do you know those people, Charlie?" asked Doug.

"One or t-t-two of them, yes," he admitted. "Now, we really should find a way b-back to the *'Pedie* and inform the captain of all this."

"No need. He's coming here with Liberty. They're planning to land at the cove where we beached the *Powder Monkey*," said Doug. "Start running and don't stop till you've reached the wire."

The Captain's diversion

From Doug's sketchbook. (DMS 4/38)

They sprinted off together, their pace quickening as adrenalin surged into their muscles. They had not gone more than twenty yards before a shout went up from one of the Kalaxx guards and searchlights raked across the churned-up surface, hunting them out.

"Stick with me, sis!" yelled Doug, swerving from the track of the beam. Becca ignored her brother and jinked left. The burning white light locked onto Doug momentarily, until he ducked out of it. Almost immediately a second beam found him. A machine gun fired a line of warning shots into the ground ahead of them, bringing them all up short.

"Ah, I think on reflection I s-s-should have s-s-stayed in that cellar and had a drop of Latour," said Charlie, raising his hands.

As the Kalaxx guards ran towards them, Doug's eye was drawn to a rocket arcing through the sky from South Island. It landed with a deafening explosion on a large wooden

building at the far end of the compound, and flames ballooned into the sky.

The captain's diversion had begun.

The ground suddenly shook and reverberated, and the four
cramped Sujing could only watch from their hiding place as
the red-hot cutting head of a tunnelling machine smashed up
through the hourglass beach, spraying out a whirlwind of
sand. A searchlight on *Expedient's* bridge snapped on with
blinding brilliance. The aft twelve-pounder opened fire, hit-
ting the machine head-on and setting it ablaze.

In the flare of light, Kalaxx miners could be seen moving
down the ridge path from the observation post. Xu could just
make out the Sujing fighters deploying along the redoubt.
The Kalaxx threw a volley of dynamite sticks towards the
defensive line, which exploded with a deafening report.

As if in answer, the *Expedient's* horn sounded – the signal
to warn of the imminent detonation of Chambois's flooding
channel charges.

"They're going to launch the ship," whispered Master Aa.

"Take cover! Take cover!" came a shout clear through the
night air. Seconds later a series of charges blasted beneath
the *Expedient*, allowing the sea to surge up and surround the
ship like a moat. The advancing Kalaxx slowed, staring in
awe and confusion as tons of sea water and sand hailed
down onto the beach. To anyone who didn't know
Chambois's plan, it looked as if the ship had just been
mined.

"Is she floating?" whispered Xi.

The ship settled, and the sea spray was carried away on the breeze. *Expedient* was certainly much lower in the water now. Her engines kicked into life, the partially covered propellers thrashing the shallow water into a foam. But the ship didn't move an inch.

The *Expedient* was stuck hard.

The *Fighting Dragon*'s engine ticked and pinged as it cooled on the beach. The captain's plan had worked so far – after drifting away from the archipelago for two hours, they had taken off, gained height and looped back towards Sulphur Island. As they approached, they saw the explosion as the Sujing rocket hit the dynamite store in the compound at precisely 1 a.m. Liberty used the flames as a beacon and glided down until they landed on the water, then paddled the last few hundred yards into the bay.

"Tie her off, Skip. I'm gettin' my insurance policy."

"Insurance policy?"

Liberty climbed up to the cockpit and took out her twin-barrelled blunderbuss.

"I'm surprised the barrels are still in proof after that last shot into Sheng-Fat's powder magazine."

"Plenty of life in the old girl yet. Master Aa gave me some more trick gunpowder."

"Did he, indeed? Well, just warn me before you pull the trigger this time.

"The compound is this way," said Captain MacKenzie. "We shall start with the refining house."

"We? *We?* Shoot – are you expectin' me to help you?"

"We're bound to get more done as a team, don't you think?"

"Why, of all the—" began Liberty as the captain threw her a rope and started to scale the perimeter wire.

In the distance, an airship engine fired into life, and moments later the vast machine was released from the lattice mast and soared into the sky above them. Light glimmered in the windows of the gondola hanging beneath it.

"Pretty," said Liberty, "but you'd never catch me in one. Like a flyin' bomb with all that hydrogen aboard."

The engine note deepened and the silver airship slipped away into the night.

Captain MacKenzie and Liberty set off moving fast and low. They reached a truck parked beside the villa and stopped to catch their breath. Liberty could see the aircraft hangar less than two hundred yards away, and it was all she could do to stop herself from making a run for *Lola*.

"Look – there's Borelli," hissed the captain.

The Italian appeared, framed in a doorway at the back of the villa. He glanced around anxiously, descended the steps and walked hastily to an outbuilding.

"Let's take him hostage," whispered Liberty, cocking the blunderbuss and starting for the outhouse. "Might help our cause some."

"Miss da Vine, I insist that this is done my way—"

Secondary explosions erupted from the dynamite store. Many of the buildings surrounding it were now ablaze. A line of narrow-gauge railway trucks was blown into the air as its cargo caught fire and exploded. Smoke swallowed the night sky.

They reached a window opaque with dust and peered in.

"Borelli's laboratory. My God…" breathed the captain. "I must see what has been going on in here."

"Don't start with all that spooky Guild stuff, Skip. We're here to plant a couple of bombs and liberate a plane. Time's a-wastin'.'"

"Just a few moments, Miss da Vine," whispered the captain, nudging the door open. "This could be vital."

At the centre of the laboratory stood a huge silver globe lit from above by a single powerful bulb. From the chiaroscuro gloom the soft glow of dials and gauges described racks of complex measuring apparatus angled towards the sphere. The machinery was powered by a lattice of thick electrical cables which snaked across the floor in great curves and loops. Borelli was there, hard at work filling a suitcase with manuscripts and papers.

"Going somewhere, Borelli?"

"MacKenzie. Ill met by moonlight."

Borelli continued to pack, seeming unconcerned by their presence. His movements were fast and precise. "Julius and I have a very good set-up here, don't you think? With my scientific brilliance and Pembleton-Crozier's knack for skulduggery – why, we're unstoppable."

The captain withdrew the blade from his sword stick. Its razor-sharp edge glinted as he stepped closer. Liberty followed behind, blunderbuss at the ready.

"All I see here are the dreadful workings of a madman."

"In your eyes, perhaps. In other eyes I am considered a genius."

"Oh, *you* are a genius, Borelli, I know that. But Pembleton-Crozier is nothing more than a manipulator, a gentleman reduced to the company of mercenaries and criminals. He has turned you into everything you once despised."

"So we've built a zoridium-powered generator – what's

the great crime, Fitzroy? This is the launch of a new industrial age! Which scientist wouldn't crave such an
accomplishment?"

"You. Or rather the man I knew five years ago wouldn't.
You've sold out."

"Sold out? As a guildsman I've lived in poverty and obscu-
rity, hiding this great secret, waiting ... always waiting. Well,
I can wait no longer, Fitzroy. I have a year to live. I'm dying.
And I choose to die as the most famous scientist since
Newton."

"Fame – is that it? I'd always thought better of you, sir."

"...And fortune, naturally. Think of the profit! Cheap, easily produced power. Even a one per cent stake in such an
enterprise would make the Coterie rich beyond our wildest
dreams!"

"I found Pembleton-Crozier in league with the most notorious pirate in the South China Sea. Is this the company you
wish to keep in your dying days?"

"That? Sheng-Fat was just a fund-raiser. The Coterie were
short of money, and the Kalaxx were getting awkward."

The captain sighed heavily. "So what now? Are you going
after Ur-Can? You believed in it once."

"Ur-Can? Nobody has ever found Ur-Can. Nobody even
knows what it is, so what's its value? No, the value is in these"
– Borelli flicked through his papers – "the blueprints for my
generator."

"How did you find these mines?"

"Elena's translation of the Capulus hieroglyphs. Most
obliging of her."

"Surely she's not a member of the Coterie too?"

Borelli laughed. "No, and she never knew I was. Her

research led Julius here in 1916; for four years we've been extracting and refining Daughter of the Sun."

"How low you've sunk," said the captain, raising the tip of his sword and resting it against Borelli's chest.

Suddenly the door behind them was kicked open. They turned to see the muzzle of a pistol aimed directly at Liberty as Lucretia stalked in, wearing a smart flying suit.

"Drop your weapons."

"Lucretia! You're in on this too?" said the captain.

"I said *drop your weapons*. You, put that … *thing* on the floor and kick it over here," she ordered, gesturing at Liberty's blunderbuss.

Liberty scowled, but had no choice.

"It's been a long time, Fitzroy," Lucretia said coolly as she stooped to pick up the ancient gun. "And just for the record, using Sheng-Fat was my idea. Never underestimate the influence of a good wife." She turned to Borelli. "It's time you left. Are you ready?"

"Almost. What shall we do with Fitzroy and the woman?"

"Take them to Julius; he can deal with them. Then we can get off this godforsaken island as well. I want to be bathing in vintage champagne by tomorrow afternoon at the very latest."

Chapter Sixteen

Borelli pushed the captain and Liberty into the generator house with a smart shove.

"Visitors for you, Julius," he called, nudging his two captives onto the high walkway with the muzzle of his pistol. Their shoes clinked on the ironwork. Below them the huge arms of the generator swung by with a low electrical hum.

"Dear God, what have you done?" the captain murmured, incensed at the sight of the vast machine.

"Fitzroy! How's the leg? Miss da Vine too. You've met my other two guests, of course."

"Becca? Doug? How on earth did you get here?"

"And Charlie's here to make up the numbers," Pembleton-Crozier shouted with mock joviality.

"Push the machine up to a thousand kilowatts, Julius. That'll see an end to this island, and anyone on it." Borelli wiped the sweat from his forehead with a silk handkerchief and made for the door.

"This machine is monstrous," gasped Captain MacKenzie. "Monstrous!"

"I prefer to call it … marvellous, old boy," replied Pembleton-Crozier.

"It's lunacy! We still don't know enough about the gravity vortex. This goes against everything the Guild stands for!"

"We're only carrying on the work started by your father, Fitzroy. He and the original Coterie had vision. Why, if they'd been allowed to continue we could all have been rich decades ago. We could have advanced mankind's scientific development by fifty years in a single step."

"Advances like these cannot be risked without understanding the science!" the captain fumed. "You ignore the warnings of the true inventors of this technology!"

"You really are such a bore, Fitzroy." Pembleton-Crozier suddenly booted the captain's bad leg, bringing him to his knees. He aimed his gun at his head. "Your father died in his generator. Well, Fitzroy … like father, like son."

A second kick sent the captain sprawling backwards over the gangway into the blue glow of the gravity vortex. He was immediately carried away, as if trapped in a whirlpool; held in the vortex's grip, he orbited the machine at the same speed as the huge rotating arms.

"How does it feel, Captain?"

The captain was surrounded by the blue electrical glow, his arms and legs outstretched. He was clearly in terrible pain.

Pembleton-Crozier stepped up to the central control platform. "Now, with a little adjustment, I can finish the Kalaxx as well. It'll be no bother … no bother at all."

Doug could see that as Crozier wound the metal handle the zoridium nodes moved closer to the central sphere, and the huge arms began to spin faster. Crackling electricity flashed between the two poles, and a ring of blue light grew between the rotating arms.

Pembleton-Crozier pointed the gun at his captives. "Move to the edge of the walkway – all of you."

From Doug's sketchbook: The captain trapped in the gravity vortex. (DMS 4/41)

"Julius, s-s-stop this," pleaded Charlie, stepping forward. Crozier fired a shot, but the bullet was pulled off course by the gravity field, and clipped Charlie above his right elbow.

"It's time to join your captain," he sneered, driving Becca, Doug, Liberty and Charlie back to the edge of the gallery, until they too fell one by one into the gravity vortex.

Doug felt as if he were being stabbed by a thousand needles. Rippling pulses of current flowed around him. His back burned and ached as he swung round, the machine gathering speed all the time. He tried to crane his neck to see Becca just beyond the arc of the spoked wheel, but could only make out her arm.

Pembleton-Crozier tucked the gun into his belt and returned to the controls. He cranked the generator up even faster, causing the vortex to glow more intensely. Pain surged through Doug's body.

"It'll take ten minutes to reach one thousand kilowatts." Crozier wound another of the controls to tilt the machine. "Let's see, that should be the correct angle."

With that he took a spanner and unscrewed the control wheel, then threw it into the vortex. His captives were spinning faster and faster, the machine humming as the energy danced and surged around the central sphere.

"That's the end of you, Fitzroy. The Guild is finished. You lose." He waved as the captain spun by him, threw the spanner in for good measure, then left.

"Douglas, Rebecca, don't try to move," shouted the captain. "You are safe in the vortex's centre line. If you move, the centrifugal forces may suck you towards the axis of the machine."

"Is there any way out of this?" Becca called.

"Not as far as I know."

"I … I may b-be able to reach the centre, Captain. Dislodge the p-p-polar node enough to break the vortex temporarily. I can reach one of the arms."

"You would never survive. Don't try it, Charlie."

"This is my fault, Captain. My own work made this monstrosity p-p-possible…"

Charlie stretched behind him and grasped the steel arm, dragging himself backwards. He twisted around, screaming with pain, until his upper body broke through the luminescent barrier, his legs propelled up, his hair flying back. Clutching the edge of the arm, he began to work his way towards the centre of the generator like a man clinging to the edge of a building.

"Charles, stop! Come back!" ordered Captain MacKenzie.

But Charlie, bathed in violet light, was now halfway down the spoke, where the curious effects of the machine allowed him to drop to his knees and move more easily. A little further in he was able to run, but Doug saw his body oddly blurred and displaced from his legs like a distorted reflection in a circus hall of mirrors. Then he was struggling again, his silhouette fading as the colossal machine pulsated with a blue and orange glow. As the hum became a low mournful scream, Charlie appeared at the centre, as if in the eye of a storm, his face bleached white by the brightness of the sparks.

Lightning shot out of the top axis in a mesmerizing flash. Charlie climbed up one of the fine meridians towards the polar node, every muscle straining against the current.

"Captain, the shield is moving," he yelled over the drone. "I'll try and dislodge the polar node. A small movement may be enough to distort the gravity field and allow you to escape."

"Be prepared for anything," roared the captain. "Brace yourselves!"

"Now!" called Charlie.

As he pushed the heel of his boot onto the node, the generator wobbled. Doug felt the pull of the vortex weaken then strengthen again.

Charlie began rocking and kicking the node, sending waves of imbalance rippling through the machine. All the time, the shield was edging away. Charlie tried it again, and the vortex shifted slightly, seeming to escape the shielding band; suddenly the captain broke free and landed with a crack on the walkway.

"That's it, Charlie! Do it again, when I say!"

Doug and the others circled around again.

At the point where he had escaped, the captain yelled out, "Now!" Doug and Becca were released at the same time, spinning out and landing heavily. They scrambled away, fighting the machine's pull as the vortex snapped back into its orbit.

"Where's Liberty?" cried Becca.

"I'm here, coz! I made it out too," shouted Liberty, running for the ladder.

"What about Charlie, Captain? The shield is still moving. We must try to stop it," implored Becca.

Doug and the captain ran up the steps to the central control platform which hung suspended from the ceiling above the generator.

"Pembleton-Crozier's sabotaged the machine. There is nothing we can do. Once the gravity vortex shield is removed, it will crack the earth's surface. I came here to destroy this infernal device, but Pembleton-Crozier seems to be doing it for me."

Doug looked at the controls. "But how?"

"The vortex will spin at such a speed that it will act like a drill and burrow into the bedrock – like a gyrolabe, but vastly more powerful."

"Well, the earth's pretty thick."

"Not here. We are on a volcanic island, nephew. He has angled the machine so that it will pierce the magma chamber beneath the volcano, causing it to erupt in the direction of the *Expedient*."

"And he's sent the Kalaxx over to attack," said Doug. "We heard him say they wouldn't be a problem after tonight. He means to bury us all in pumice and lava—"

"Get out!" bellowed Charlie from the vortex. His voice was distorted, amplified and deepened as the machine gathered speed. The roof was beginning to break up; beams and planks were being sucked towards the generator.

"Charlie," yelled Captain MacKenzie. "Get to the top of the shield – it's your best chance of safety!"

Doug was still staring at the controls. "Perhaps we can change the angle of the machine, even if we can't stop the shield from moving. This handle alters the machine's pitch; I saw Pembleton-Crozier use it. Which way do you want the magma chamber to erupt?"

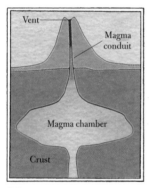

MAGMA CHAMBER

The chamber beneath a volcano where the magma (molten rock) is held before an eruption. The eruption is caused by the build-up of pressure in this chamber and its sudden release by fracturing.

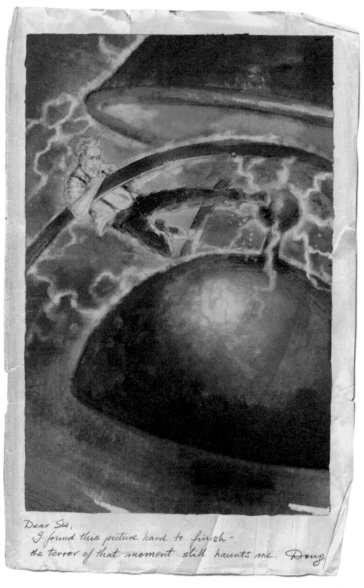

Dear Sis,
I found this picture hard to finish —
the terror of that moment still haunts me. Doug

CHARLIE IN THE GENERATOR

"Straight up. It will strain the earth's mantle the least."

Doug wound the handle until the angle on the dial read ninety degrees. The generator began to straighten.

"Hang on, Charlie," Doug whispered, turning to see his old shipmate climb through the arcing flashes and perch at the top of the shield, a vivid blue aura encircling him as he screamed out in agony.

Chapter Seventeen

"Captain, that star-shaped building you were so keen on blowin' up is already alight. We need to get the hell outta here," yelled Liberty as they sprinted out of the generator house.

"I concur, Miss da Vine. Events are outpacing my sabotage plans. We must get away immediately."

"We can't leave yet," said Becca.

Liberty looked shocked. "I can't think of a single good reason to stay."

"We found the trireme, Uncle, the missing Greek ship. Pembleton-Crozier has the southern gyrolabe, a secret message from our mother, the ship's log for the *Flying Fish*—"

"Duncan MacKenzie's ship," added Doug.

"—and my diary. He took them from us at the villa. We *must* get them back. Please? I know where they are."

"You two found the ancient ship and the gyrolabe? What about the missing section of *The 99 Elements*?"

"Xu has *The 99 Elements* and the Ha-Mi texts that guided Duncan here."

The captain let out a loud belly laugh.

"What's so funny?" asked Doug with annoyance.

"After four hundred years of searching, it was you two?"

Becca and Doug looked at each other. "Well … yes."

The captain looked at a truck parked in the shadow of the generator house. "Do you still want to try for *Lola*?"

"Stupid question, Skip," replied Liberty. "She's our best bet of gettin' off this island in a hurry."

"Can you get this truck to work?"

She grinned. "Do skunks stink?"

"All aboard. We must work fast."

Liberty had the engine fired within seconds. With a wheel spin, they set off through the compound, which was now well ablaze. Dynamite from the store targeted by Master Aa's rocket continued to detonate in thudding explosions. Liberty drove fast, swerving to miss machinery and buildings alike, but never using the brake until she screeched up beside the villa.

"You've got three minutes," she warned, "then I'm off to get *Lola*, with or without you."

Becca and Doug ran up the steps and burst into the villa, the captain close behind them. Becca made straight for the parlour, where they'd been interrogated by Pembleton-Crozier. The bureau was locked, but with the help of a letter knife she forced it open. The message from their mother was still there, along with Crozier's singed translation and the code books tucked into her diary.

"The gyrolabe's gone, but the *Flying Fish*'s logbook is here," said Doug, pulling the volume from a drawer.

"He will have kept the gyrolabe close to him," said the captain.

Outside, Liberty was already pounding the truck's horn.

The captain turned to leave, but something caught his eye. He picked up Liberty's ridiculous blunderbuss and slung it under his arm like a gamekeeper. "Obviously not Lucretia's style. We'll have it back, I think. Now, as Liberty would say, *time to get the hell outta here.*"

As they reached the back door, a huge section of panelling twisted off the generator house and flew into the air. It orbited once then slammed down into the villa. The blue glow inside the dome pulsed brighter; Doug felt the structure of the villa creak and moan. The air was now thick with choking smoke that billowed across the compound, and flames licked upwards from buildings all around them.

Outside in the truck, Liberty waved frantically for them to hurry; the young MacKenzies leapt onto the flatbed. Becca took the blunderbuss from the captain and scrambled over boxes to the passenger seat. Doug helped his uncle onto the open tailgate. Liberty crunched into first gear and floored the accelerator, steering for *Lola*'s hangar.

"Can Charlie survive, Captain?" shouted Doug.

"The mechanic working on my father's generator did. He was trying to shut down the machine by prising the polar node away when it exploded. Whether the generators are comparable, only Borelli knows."

Liberty swerved and snaked the truck. Ahead were twenty or so armed Kalaxx making for a boat beached beside *Lola*'s hangar. They saw Liberty at the wheel of the careering truck and began to fire, forcing her down a side track into the protection of a line of buildings.

"We'll never get to *Lola*!" she yelled, gunning more speed out of the engine. "We'll have to make for the *Fightin' Dragon* instead."

At that moment, there was an almighty explosion, and a blinding flash of blue-white light.

"It's gone! The shield is off!"

The truck seemed to slow as it was sucked into the generator's unleashed gravitational force.

The villa started to crumple and bow towards the generator house. Seconds later it moved sideways, the roof hinging open like a doll's house. Equipment, storehouses and miners were all impelled towards the unshielded vortex. A vast cyclone of whirling blue light burst upwards into the sky like an inverted tornado.

Liberty found second gear and tried to accelerate. An astonishing gale howled past them as air was sucked towards the generator.

"More throttle, Liberty!" the captain called.

"Gee, you mean if I press this pedal down the truck'll go faster? It's a crazy notion, Skip, but I'll give it a try."

The truck crawled along, the canvas tilt ripped from the rear body. Doug and the captain clung desperately to the roof frame.

"We're gonna make it, guys—"

As Liberty spoke, three boxes flew up and crashed into the captain, knocking him off the tailgate. Doug grabbed his arm as his feet scraped against the gravel.

"Hold on, Uncle! Stop, Liberty, stop!"

"No," shouted the captain. "Keep going. Let go of me, Douglas, I order you!"

"I won't," Doug bellowed. "You'll be sucked into the vortex!" But his grip on the roof was weakening.

A second later, the hoop was torn from its mounting, and they both flew from the back of the truck, tumbling towards the appalling machine. For fifty yards they bounced and slid, unable to resist the pull. Ahead was the entrance to one of the tunnels; they were being dragged directly into it. There was nothing Doug could do to stop his progress as he spun and somersaulted. The captain hit the tunnel first, crying out with pain as his damaged leg was battered and scraped. Inside, the glass lining offered nothing to clutch at. Now they slid even faster, the gravitational effect no less strong underground than it had been on the surface.

The tunnel curved, then dropped down steeply. Doug pawed at the smooth glass wall, twisting and writhing to slow himself down. The curve tightened where the tunnelling machine had altered course, and by the apex of the bend he managed to come to a stop. It was then that Doug felt the full impact of the gravitational force, which seemed to compress his very skeleton.

The captain struggled in vain to stand up. "What a remarkable effect," he commented, before the growing pressure on his injured leg made him crumple.

Doug tried to move, but he was completely immobilized. Some years before, he'd been on a funfair ride in Chicago called the Spinner of Death – he'd climbed into a large drum that rotated so fast he'd been pinned to the wall by way of centrifugal force. This was the same, only there was no fun involved, and far more chance of death.

"We are powerless against this machine," shouted the captain. "We did the best we could. Thank you for trying to save me, nephew."

Doug watched, horrified, as the skin on his uncle's face rippled with the pull of the vortex. With a shock he realized he could feel his own face doing the same. Doug's vision began to grey, then the edges darkened, until he finally blacked out as the blood was drained from his brain.

G-FORCE BLACKOUTS

Unconsciousness can occur if a person is subjected to extreme gravitational forces. Blood is forced towards lower areas of the body, depriving the brain of its normal supply and starving it of oxygen.

Becca pleaded with Liberty to stop.

"If I stop we both die!" Liberty yelled, the wheels of the truck skidding and scuffing to keep a grip on the ground. Becca felt numb, unsure if she should try to go after her brother. Her hand moved towards the door handle.

"No! Stay here, Becca. There's nothin' you can do. We'll probably be joinin' them in a few seconds anyhow.

"Come *on*!" Liberty bawled at the truck, dropping to first gear.

Suddenly Becca was dragged from her seat and flipped over into the back. She gripped the seat, kicking to find a foothold. The last of the cargo slewed across and was yanked out. The vortex was pulling her towards the tailgate; she realized with panic that her life depended on a bent and rusted seat back.

The truck seemed to dip down as it crested a ridge, and accelerated slightly. Liberty pulled out her blunderbuss, aiming at a gate to her left. She fired, sending a flash of blue flame towards the lock and blasting the gate open. The truck laboured on, dropping down the incline on the other side. She spun the wheel and headed towards the undergrowth, and slowly the pull of the vortex began to diminish. Liberty found second gear as Becca managed to scramble back into her seat.

"We must go back!"

"The only place we're goin' is that aeroplane down there. I'm sorry, coz."

Becca's eyes welled with tears.

THE GRAVITY VORTEX

These diagrams show the gravitational field of the zoridium-powered generator. Fig. A shows the first Coterie's machine, built in Kazakhstan, with poor shielding above and below the centre nodes. This created a gravity vortex, seen spiralling dangerously up and down from the top and bottom nodes. Fig. B shows the machine on Sulphur Island, with shielding based on Charlie's retranslation of text from The 99 Elements. This generated what Borelli described as a "farfalla" (butterfly) shaped field, contained and under control. Note the weakening of the field along the radius arms, compared with the intense field at the centre axis.   (See Appendix 3.)

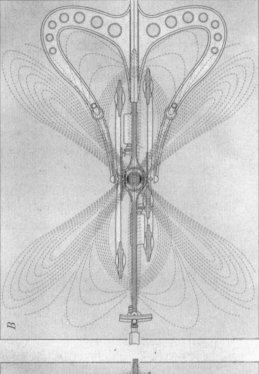

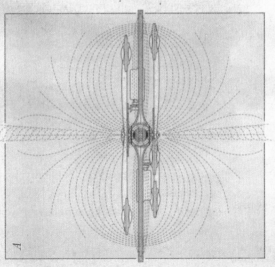

"Hey, no time for that!"

Liberty pushed on, smashing through the jungle, until the truck bounced and crunched into a tree. "End of the line; all change. The beach is just down there. Run!"

Becca ran, but it was like running in a dream. She could still feel the influence of the vortex, which slowed the movement of her arms. It was as if she was struggling up a hill, although she was now sprinting down the beach towards the *Fighting Dragon*.

Liberty slung the blunderbuss into the cockpit and started to push the plane. Becca helped her turn the nose out to sea, all the time fighting the force of the generator.

"Get in the pilot's seat and set her up to take off. I'm gonna swing the prop."

Becca climbed into the pilot's seat, wiped her eyes and tried to concentrate. Liberty's lesson flooded back. She found the throttle. "Switch on! Ignition. Contact!"

"Good," shouted Liberty, swinging the airscrew. The engine sparked into life. Liberty climbed along the floats and jumped up into the navigator's position. "What are you waitin' for? Get us out to sea and away from that wacky carousel."

"You want me to take off?"

"You wanna stay here?"

Quickly they left the shore, and picked up speed, the pull of the vortex weakening as they headed further out to sea. The velocimeter registered forty miles an hour. Becca tried to remember how fast the plane had to be going before it lifted off. Liberty was busy reloading her blunderbuss, pouring in the Sujing gunpowder and ramming it home with a wad. She looked up at Becca, giving the thumbs up.

"You're goin' great. We're safe now. Cut the revs."

The *Fighting Dragon* slowed half a mile from the shore. As the engine idled, Becca stood up and looked back through the blur of the airscrew at the island. The sight of the vortex climbing into the blue-black dawn sky, edged with the red glow of a tropical sunrise, was breathtaking.

"I can see a plane, Liberty. Just taken off."

"Where?"

"Just there. Is it—"

"—*Lola*. It's that darned rustler Crozier!" spat Liberty.

She clambered into the pilot's seat as Becca struggled forward. "He won't see us comin', not out of the dark west horizon." She jammed the throttle forward and turned the plane, pulling down her flying goggles. The *Fighting Dragon* skipped across the waves before lifting out of the water and banking around. They climbed towards *Lola*, now much clearer against the dawn light to the east. Becca felt a tap on her shoulder; Liberty passed her a pair of goggles.

"He's trapped, can you see?"

Becca suddenly understood that *Lola* was caught within the vortex, flying at full power but unable to break free of the gravitational force.

"He's just makin' headway. He set off too late – ha!"

As they climbed to five hundred feet, Becca could make out an almost perfect outline of rippling water around the island. Liberty was studying it too. "The limit of the generator's influence," she shouted. "We're all right if we stay outside it. Hell of a crosswind, but we're flyin' just fine."

The plane climbed higher. But instead of steering towards the relative safety of the *Expedient*, Liberty was going after Pembleton-Crozier. "We've got him now!"

"But the generator's boring into the earth's crust," reasoned

Becca. "The whole thing will explode!"

"We might get to squeeze off a couple of shots first. I'm gonna give him a broadside."

Becca just wanted to get as far away as possible. "Can't we just leave him? We're all going to die!"

"Scores to settle, coz. Nobody steals my wings."

"But look at the generator!" The rotating arms could hardly be seen in the detritus and flashing forks of lightning. The cone-shaped vortex glowed with a clear bright light.

Liberty steered as close in to *Lola* as she dared, then pulled out the blunderbuss. Becca could see Lucretia in the front seat aiming a pistol. She didn't hear the shot, but she saw the flash; the bullet struck Liberty's right forearm, ripping into her flying jacket and causing the plane to swerve away.

"Would you look at that. I've been shot, darn it!" Liberty pulled back her sleeve and inspected the wound, which trailed blood back to her elbow.

Becca hung on as the plane dived, losing altitude.

"You know that flyin' lesson you wanted, coz? It's about to start."

"What do you mean?"

It became quite clear what Liberty meant as she gained height, levelled off, then began to stand up.

"This is a little seat-swappin' trick I used to do in the flyin' circus. But you gotta be quick, d'you hear?"

Becca looked dubiously at the pilot's seat. Doing this when stationary was one thing, airborne was quite another.

"Oh, come on, coz!"

Becca stepped up and clambered in. It was quite a squeeze.

"There's the control column. Find the rudder bar."

Liberty put down the blunderbuss and scrambled forward.

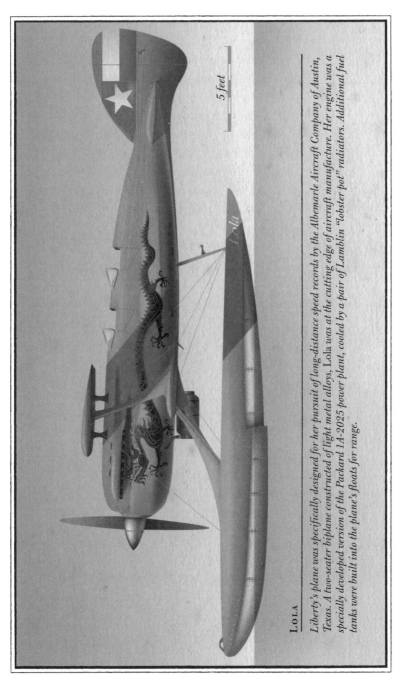

5 feet

LOLA

Liberty's plane was specifically designed for her pursuit of long-distance speed records by the Albemarle Aircraft Company of Austin, Texas. A two-seater biplane constructed of light metal alloys, Lola was at the cutting edge of aircraft manufacture. Her engine was a specially developed version of the Packard 1A-2025 power plant, cooled by a pair of Lamblin "lobster-pot" radiators. Additional fuel tanks were built into the plane's floats for range.

"Now, nice and steady. Bring us around for a shot."

"If I'm flying, we're going straight back to the ship."

Even over the roar of the engine, the low rumble of the generator could be heard as it cracked through to the dormant magma chamber of the volcano. The sea close to the beach seemed to kick up, then a hot red jet of lava shot up into the air, heralding the most extraordinary volcanic eruption.

The vortex had drilled down. The earth's crust was pierced.

CHAPTER EIGHTEEN

Once the generator had been destroyed, the gravitational pull which held him fell away, and Doug now lay slumped on the tunnel floor. He came to with a start and found himself staring at the Duchess. Fresh blood was on her muzzle, teeth and paws. The tiger was growling and pushing his shoulder with her enormous paw, trying to rouse him.

"Duchess," he gasped, sitting up.

The big cat picked up the captain's stick and walked over and nudged her owner, growling at him too until he stirred.

The tunnel was shaking alarmingly and the glass walls were beginning to crack under the stress of the volcano's eruption.

From Doug's sketchbook: The Duchess wakes the captain. (DMS 4/51)

"Are you alive and in one piece, nephew?"

"I think so. The Duchess must have come through the tunnels."

"Not so lazy, hey," said the captain, stroking her massive head. She roared and began to pace away, her tail flicking from side to side. "We must get off the island. Immediately."

At that moment, lava burst through a crack about sixty feet away down the tunnel, glowing red in the dark.

"Run!"

Doug scrabbled to his feet, his mind numbed by the after-effects of the gravity. His legs felt heavy and slow, but he forced himself to find hidden reserves of energy. The Duchess set the pace. They slipped and struggled up the smooth glassy incline to the surface, spluttering as they emerged into the foul air of the compound – or what was left of it.

A burning red lava jet rose four hundred feet in the air in front of them. Huge lumps of lava rained down all about and a thick sulphurous dust hung in the air. It was so hot they both backed away, lifting their coats over their heads to protect themselves.

"To the sea, Douglas! We need to find a ship."

But Doug could see that his uncle's leg was causing him great pain. "Lean on me. I can take some of your weight."

They dodged between the lava bombs, finding the path to the bay. The few surviving buildings were all askew, ripped from their foundations and leaning towards the ruined generator. All were ablaze, adding to the scorching heat.

In the confusion, Kalaxx miners were swarming out of the tunnels into the ash-clogged air and running for the beach.

"We must find a boat, anything that'll float."

They sheltered in the lee of a half-collapsed building.

From Doug's sketchbook: Escape! (DMS 4/52)

The Duchess's ears twitched. She stood stock-still then gave one of the lowest growls Doug had ever heard her make. It was the sound of an animal about to make a kill.

"Easy, Duchess," soothed the captain. "What have you seen?" He spotted her prey – an unfit man running as fast as he could towards the wooden pier. "Borelli! Where's he going?"

"To his submarine, must be."

"Then so are we, nephew. It's time we reminded him of his oath to the Guild."

The *Fighting Dragon* rocked all over the sky as Becca fought to follow Liberty's shouted instructions.

"Right rudder – too much! Left … straighten up. Too much –

use gentle, small movements. Left pedal, coz… Straight and level, that's the way."

"You'll have to take over," insisted Becca.

"You're doin' just fine. Now the rustler's right on your tail, so give her more revs, and I'll try and get a shot in."

Becca edged the throttle forward as *Lola*, finally released from the vortex, roared overhead. Lucretia, leaning out of the cockpit, was aiming her pistol at Liberty, and instinctively Becca pulled the stick left and they cut under *Lola*'s tail. Liberty had a clear shot, but her injured arm had no strength to lift the blunderbuss.

"Bring her round. I'll be ready for them this time. Right pedal. Right stick … straighten her up."

As they circled, the volcano erupted for a second time, propelling a rush of rock and lava skywards. Their plane bucked violently, forcing Becca to battle with the controls. The searing heat scorched her face.

Liberty turned and pointed. "Forget the volcano, coz. Look behind you!"

Lola was onto them again, weaving and looping back for another attack. Liberty gritted her teeth and wrapped her arm around the barrels, readying her shot. "Straight and level, coz … straight and level." Just as she was about to fire, another shock wave rocked the *Fighting Dragon*, and Liberty's shot caught only the floats and tail. She slumped back, cradling her arm.

Lumps of falling pumice began to strike the plane. Becca watched one piece drop straight through their thin fabric wing, leaving a neat smouldering hole.

Liberty grimaced. "Ah, yeah – we may be at some disadvantage here."

Becca weaved to avoid more falling boulders. "How d'you mean?"

"*Lola* has metal wings. Ours are just plain flammable. Follow Crozier. Give her everythin' she's got. I still have one barrel left."

"Can't we just *go*?"

"Follow him. We both have debts to collect on."

Becca wasn't sure the debt was worth dying for, but she put the nose down and tried to catch *Lola*. Liberty raised the blunderbuss and loosed off a shot, but they were outclassed in both plane and pilot. Pembleton-Crozier waved his hand in victory as he gunned the engine, pulled a roll and climbed away for clear air.

Liberty chucked the blunderbuss down in disgust, sat down and put her feet up on the edge of the nacelle, muttering, "Darn that dirty rustler..." Her expression turned to horror. "Becca! The wing. It's alight! Land her. Land her fast."

"*Land her?*"

"Just do what I say and we'll get her down easy. Cut the power right back – that's it. Turn into the wind. Nose down a touch – *not that much!* – let the speed drop off ... that's right... Now, don't worry about the sea; it looks like it's comin' up to hit you but it ain't. Keep her steady ... little bit of right rudder – no! Too much. Straighten her up ... stick back, and..."

The *Fighting Dragon* touched down, water spraying up from the floats to douse the flames. Becca cut the power to idle and the little plane coasted to a halt.

"Why, you're a natural! My, that was just about perfect. Put the fire out too. Just look at that."

Becca pushed her flying goggles up onto her forehead and let out a long breath. Her mouth was dry, and she suddenly felt sick. She looked back at Sulphur Island: the volcano was pumping out clouds of ash in a dark, menacing column.

The awful shock of what had happened to Doug hit home. She shut her eyes and saw him tumbling from the truck. He couldn't have survived such a catastrophic event. It was just not possible.

"I've been on that submarine, Uncle."

They were running after Borelli as best they could. The Italian had not seen them in the smoky confusion of the eruption. He leapt aboard with uncharacteristic grace and ran towards the conning tower, yelling instructions to his crew to get under way.

"Really. You surprise me, Douglas." The captain grimaced. "Your sister too? When you took the *Powder Monkey*, I suppose?"

Doug nodded. "There's an engine-room hatch, a conning-tower hatch and a fore hatch that leads into the torpedo room."

"Let's get aboard. They've already slipped their mooring lines."

Doug and the captain ran along the pier and managed to board the stern as the engines accelerated and the sub pulled away. The captain collapsed on deck and caught his breath as the Duchess padded down beside them.

"What if they dive?"

"They're running the diesels. The boat is much quicker on the surface. Stay close, Douglas. I shall need your help." He whispered something to the Duchess and she prowled forward towards the bow. The captain took out the two Sujing bombs from his coat pocket, smiling grimly. "I think we can say with some degree of certainty that these contrivances are not as delicate as Master Aa suspected. Follow me."

They made for the open engine-room hatch and the captain stole silently down the ladder.

Two engine-room stokers had their backs to the MacKenzies and didn't hear their approach over the fierce clatter of the diesels. The captain advanced slowly, sword stick in his right hand and a bomb in his left. He tapped the edge of the blade on the first stoker's shoulder.

"I have a bomb. Forward please, gentlemen."

The cramped space was so confined that it was impossible for them to attack him. They raised their hands above their heads and did as they were ordered.

Beyond the next watertight door, they found the cook, who was nursing a nasty lava burn to his shoulder. He immediately grabbed a meat cleaver, but froze when he saw the bomb.

"That's it, nice and steady. Keep moving forward."

The control room beneath the conning tower was crewed by four men. The

SUBMARINE ENGINES

Submarines of this era generally had two sets of engines. The main engines were powerful diesels (a type of internal combustion engine invented by the German engineer Rudolf Diesel in 1892). These could only be used when running on the surface because they required a constant supply of air to enable the fuel to combust inside the cylinders, and also expelled noxious fumes. The diesels charged the batteries that powered the secondary electric engines. These were used when the boat dived beneath the surface, as electric engines did not require oxygen to function and produced no toxic exhaust fumes – ideal for use in the sealed environment of a submerged submarine. However, their range was limited by the batteries, and they propelled the submerged boat at much lower speeds than the diesels.

captain pushed his captives in, but hung back by the door. "Gentlemen," he said coolly, "I am taking command of this submarine."

The men jumped up towards him.

"He has a bomb!" yelped the cook.

"Yes, and what's more, it's set to explode when I drop it. Where's Borelli?"

"On the bridge," said a squat man with a Spanish accent, who appeared to be the skipper. He scrutinized the Sujing device. "That isn't like any bomb I've ever seen." He took two more steps forward.

"Borelli!" shouted Captain MacKenzie up the conning-tower ladder. "Borelli, damn you!"

Borelli's voice echoed down from the hatchway above. "MacKenzie?"

"Yes, Borelli. I have a Sujing Quantou bomb, and will have no hesitation in sinking this submarine if you don't get yourself down this ladder."

The captain turned to the submarine skipper. "What's the complement? Come on, how many are aboard?"

The man laughed and crossed his arms. The rest of the crew joined in, and started to crowd closer.

Borelli climbed tentatively into the control room.

"Tell your men that I am serious about using this bomb."

"But you have the boy with you. You'll never do it!"

"He's a guildsman. He's sworn the same oath as you and I: honour, duty or death." The captain raised the tip of his blade a little higher.

"No, Fitzroy," grinned Borelli. "You might have the guts to use it if you were alone, but not with Hamish and Elena's son standing beside you."

From Doug's sketchbook. (DMS 4/52)

"Hmm, you have me there, Borelli," considered the captain. "Have you met the Duchess?"

The animal bounded into the control room, flattening the Italian against the deck. She was huge in the confined space, and the crew backed and scrambled away.

"Captain, there's a lockable cage in the torpedo compartment big enough to hold them," shouted Doug as they followed behind the Duchess. "Borelli has the key."

The Duchess corralled the men forward into the torpedo compartment, unleashing roar after roar, her hackles raised as they cowered backwards. Borelli was at the centre, pushing the submarine skipper in front of him for protection. One crewman made a run for the hatch but was floored by the tiger before he was halfway to the ladder.

"Quiet now, Duchess. Borelli – the key to the cage, please. And which is your chief engineer?"

"This man. Do as MacKenzie tells you," muttered Borelli, handing over the key. The Duchess was stalking back and forth, her eyes fixed on him.

Captain MacKenzie's brow furrowed as the engineer stepped forward. "Any deviation from my orders and I'll send my tiger down there to sort you out. Understand?"

The engineer glanced at the Duchess and nodded. The captain let him pass and return to his station. "Slow ahead both. The rest of you, into the cage." The men filed in, thankful for the iron bars between them and the tiger. The captain booted the door shut. "The padlock, nephew, if you please."

Doug's hands were shaking so much he could hardly get the key in the lock.

Then his uncle saw the archive material and gasped. "These are Guild papers. What have you done, Borelli? Robbery as well?"

"The Guild is finished, Fitzroy. I'm sitting on its rotting remains. You cannot stop the Coterie. With or without me, it is the future."

The captain didn't answer. Instead he turned calmly to Doug. "Ever stood watch on a submarine, nephew?"

"Can't say I have."

"No time like the present."

The *Fighting Dragon* rode the swell. Becca motored the plane about a mile from the island and cut the engine. She found a first-aid kit in the nacelle and set about dressing Liberty's wound. She tied the bandage off as tightly as she could, but already the fabric was blooming red with fresh blood.

"Well, coz, we're in a fix. To put it simply, we'll both be killed if we go back to look for Doug and the skipper."

Becca turned away and busied herself with repacking the first-aid box, tears stinging her eyes.

"Hey now, he might have gotten out on a boat."

"Look at it," Becca blurted out. "Just look! How could he have survived that?"

Ton upon ton of pumice and rock was still blasting out of the volcano. Clouds of ash covered the island and smoke rose thousands of feet into the air. Huge rivers of lava poured down into what had been the compound.

Liberty took in the apocalyptic view. "Boisterous conditions, coz. Doesn't mean he's dead, though. Don't give up hope. Doug's a tenacious little terrier, and the skip's with him too. We'll make a couple of passes close to the island and see what we can make out."

Becca wiped away her tears. "Do you think you can fly now?"

"Jump on up and swing the airscrew. Let's get airborne."

The *Fighting Dragon* lifted off and Becca turned and scanned the island. She couldn't see anyone at all. They circled back for another pass, lower this time, but Doug still couldn't be seen.

"It's no good!" shouted Liberty. "I can't fly any closer. Let's get back to the *Expedient*. If they escaped, that's where they'd make for."

Liberty set a course back towards the channel between the islands. About halfway across, Becca saw a figure floating on a section of generator house roofing. She turned and pointed; Liberty immediately cut the engine speed and fixed the target.

"Is it Doug?" bellowed Liberty.

"Can't tell."

"I'll bring her in to land."

The plane touched down once more, and taxied towards the slumped figure.

"It's Charlie," Becca exclaimed as they ran up alongside. She climbed down onto the float, grabbed the wooden beam and manoeuvred him nearer. "Charlie? Charlie!"

"Is he alive?"

Charlie didn't regain consciousness as they struggled to pull him on board. Liberty's bandage dripped blood with the effort, but finally they lifted him into the forward cockpit. Becca kicked the roofing away and swung the airscrew once more.

CHAPTER NINETEEN

The battle on South Island had raged all through the night. Without Master Aa's leadership, the Sujing Quantou had still managed to stop three major assaults as Kalaxx miners poured onto the island. Chambois's trebuchet halted the first attack by delivering a deadly Sujing bomb. The second had been repelled by the cannon, which cut through the jungle leaves and found their targets easily. Some Kalaxx had also stumbled into the first line of explosive booby traps with devastating results. But the third attack had been the most dangerous. The Kalaxx had almost broken through to the ship, forcing the Sujing to give up the redoubt and retreat to the *Expedient*, which was still stuck on the beach. They had fought a vicious defence, using the ship like a castle.

The *Expedient*'s crew fought hard alongside them, firing the twelve-pounder gun with deadly accuracy. When the volcano erupted the fighting had lulled, but the Kalaxx on the peninsula hadn't moved – they lay waiting to spring their trap.

In the dawn light a large Kalaxx boot momentarily blocked Xu's view as one of the miners clambered stealthily over the boulder sheltering them. Three more Kalaxx followed. Xu and Xi held their breath. Master Aa picked up both his swords, but the miners' attention was fixed on the ship as they crawled forward and fanned out along the ledge below the Sujing's hiding place.

"The Kalaxx here on the peninsula are readying to rush the *Expedient,*" whispered Master Aa.

"If only we could warn them. Must we wait here any longer?" fretted Xi as he stared down at the stranded vessel. "Can't we join the fight?"

"We must protect *The 99 Elements,*" said Master Aa.

"We've been here all night, Master. I cannot sit here and watch as our friends battle for their lives!"

"Xi," murmured Master Aa, "there is no greater honour than protecting *The 99 Elements,* but my heart is also torn. It is painful for me as leader of the Sujing Quantou to watch my fighters, whom I have chosen and trained, in battle without me. Yet this box contains secrets that must not be lost, whatever the cost. This is everything the Order has ever fought for; everything we have striven to protect. You must put thoughts of our comrades from your mind."

"But our brothers and sisters will surely die—"

As Xi spoke, a detachment of Kalaxx broke cover from the direction of the graveyard and surged across the beach towards the ship. The men in front of Xu and Xi opened fire, raking the stern of *Expedient* and mortaring the beach. The twelve-pounder was trying to rotate as fast as it could, but the Kalaxx had the lead. Mortar bombs landed close to the rudder with deadened thuds, sending up storms of sand. Another Kalaxx detachment of thirty miners raced forward from the redoubt to support the new attack.

"The Kalaxx have made bamboo ladders." Xu's voice was just audible over the hard clatter of the machine gun twenty yards in front of them. "They are storming the ship. We *must* go and help them. Master Aa – please?"

The attackers waded into the water and positioned ladders

against the hull's side. The Sujing Quantou and ship's crew rushed to counter them, but the first few Kalaxx shimmied up and boarded the ship via the captain's stern gallery. Two Sujing warriors fought to push the ladder away, but were overwhelmed and forced to retreat into the ship as the Kalaxx pressed home their attack.

Moments later, dozens of Kalaxx were on the poop deck, and in a mêlée of hand-to-hand combat took control of the twelve-pounder gun. The early-morning sunlight glinted off whirling blades as they consolidated their position. The fighting was intense and savage as the two divided brotherhoods battled to redress age-old scores, screaming out ancient war cries which echoed up to the peninsula.

Another wave of Kalaxx stormed across the beach from the redoubt.

"We're losing the ship. We must be able to do something!" persisted Xi.

Xu grabbed his brother's arm and pointed towards the narrow channel as the menacing silhouette of the submarine slipped into the cove. "We'll never escape now."

Master Aa smiled. "All is not lost. Look who is in command."

"Doug? Doug is in command!" laughed Xi. "The Duchess stands at the bow like a figurehead."

"Sujing Cha!" chanted Xu.

Master Aa reassessed their position. "There may now be a chance to save *The 99 Elements*. Prepare to fight."

Doug took up a pair of watchkeeper's binoculars he'd found on the sub and picked out Mrs Ives lugging a pair

of ammunition boxes along the boat deck. "This is a very dangerous enterprise," he muttered to himself.

The sky was darkening as the morning sun was obscured by smoke and clouds of volcanic ash falling like dirty snow. He leant forward and called down the voice pipe to the control room. "We're in the cove now, Captain. *Expedient* is still on the beach. She's under attack!"

The captain's voice echoed back. "Douglas, check we are clear to turn."

Doug looked fore and aft. "Yes, Uncle – I mean Captain. All clear."

A lava bomb crashed into the water with a steaming fizz.

"Very well," barked the captain. "Send in Morse to the *Expedient*: PREPARE TO BE TAKEN IN TOW."

"Aye, Captain."

Doug picked up the signal lamp and aimed it at *Expedient*'s bridge. He clicked the button on the side and sent the message. The submarine began to turn.

The battle to retake the *Expedient*'s twelve-pounder gun had intensified, with a concerted counter-attack from the Sujing fighters and *Expedient*'s crew. Boat-hooks were being used to push the ladders away from the sides, the height of the ship playing to *Expedient*'s advantage. Doug instinctively ducked as machine-gun fire from the peninsula rattled and ricocheted off the pressure hull and conning tower. He yelled down the speaking tube: "Captain, we're under fire from the peninsula."

"A thousand curses. Keep your head down."

The submarine finished manoeuvring and stopped thirty yards off the *Expedient*'s bow. Captain MacKenzie climbed up through the hatch and surveyed the scene.

Four of *Expedient's* men dived from her bows and swam fast for the submarine. Ten Dinners clutched a messenger rope and once aboard the sub hoisted the towing warp over *Expedient's* bows and into the water. The others ran forward to the conning tower.

"Arrow, find some ammunition and put the submarine's deck gun to use. Sam, get to the control room and man the helm. Frankie – the engine room, and quick."

"Towing warps belayed!" shouted Ten Dinners.

"Very good. Join Sam in the control room. We must save our ship."

Xi was the first to spot the new threat: the Kalaxx who had evacuated the mining compound after the volcanic eruption were now approaching the hourglass beach in boats from the open sea.

"The Kalaxx are coming to rescue their brothers," said Xi. "They will storm the *Expedient*."

"We can escape if we reach the *Expedient* before they join the battle. Our moment is now."

"Yes, Master."

"The destiny of the Sujing Quantou is in our hands. These southern chapters of *The 99 Elements* must not fall to the Kalaxx. The honour of defending them will sharpen our reactions in battle and put the fire of victory into our blood."

Xu and Xi nodded eagerly.

"We will advance on the beach in fighting diamond formation."

Master Aa squeezed through the gap in the rocks and

broke cover; Xu, Xi and Ba'd Ak followed. Master Aa ran forward and dispatched the machine-gunners with two powerful sword strokes while Ba'd Ak silenced the mortar crew with a pair of metal throwing stars. They formed up into a diamond pattern and made for the track.

FIGHTING DIAMOND FORMATION

A Sujing fighting manoeuvre allowing a small group of warriors to defend themselves on all sides. One of 33 sacred battle formations.

"Tell Herr Schmidt to give her everything she's got," Captain MacKenzie yelled to the *Expedient*.

Laughing Boy waved acknowledgement and ducked inside the ship's wheelhouse. The submarine deck gun opened fire on the Kalaxx fighters on the peninsula. The captain leant forward and called down the voice pipe to the sub's control room. "Full ahead both."

A few seconds later, the diesels roared into life. The towing warp straightened, flicking up sea water as it stretched taut.

"More revs!" shouted the captain.

The submarine twisted and bucked as its propellers bit into the water. *Expedient's* partially covered propellers started to turn, much to the astonishment of the attacking Kalaxx at the stern of the ship.

Doug couldn't judge if the submarine was making any progress; the towing warp was bar taut, and the sub was crabbing to starboard. Beneath his feet he could feel the throb of the engines as Fast Frankie accelerated to full power. The water at the stern was thrashed into white foam and clouds of dirty fumes poured from the exhaust manifolds.

Suddenly there was a muffled explosion from deep within the *Expedient*. The stern of the vessel shuddered and kicked up; smoke poured from the scuttles in the after cabins. The port propeller slowed and stopped, but the ship began to move, and the submarine's stern pressed down as her propellers caught.

"She's afloat. Both slow ahead!" ordered the captain. "Hard a'port."

Both vessels glided out into the cove.

"Midships."

"What was that explosion?" asked Doug.

"Sounded like dynamite – in the propeller shaft by the look of things. The Kalaxx must have planted it. The shock of the explosion has broken the surface tension under the hull and released her."

FAST FRANKIE

Fast Frankie was born in Swift Current, Saskatchewan, Canada. He always referred to his home town by its local nickname "Speedy Creek", so the ship's crew naturally attributed this expeditious characteristic to Frankie himself.

Kalaxx miners were now jumping off the stern of the *Expedient* and swimming for the shore. The rest of them were retreating across the hourglass beach to the safety of their comrades' boats.

"We must get as far away from that volcano as we can. Starboard ten degrees."

From Doug's sketchbook: The Kalaxx jumping off the Expedient. (DMS 4/62)

Doug swung his binoculars around and up to the peninsula. Through the terrible visibility he caught the glint of a blade. He thought of Becca, and hoped and prayed that she was far away from the monstrous volcano, flying with Liberty to safety.

"I can't see a darned thing," bellowed Liberty, wiping her goggles. Ash was building up on the struts and wires of the *Fighting Dragon*, making her sluggish to fly.

"They must be down there."

The cove opened up through the gloomy monochrome scene a hundred feet below them. *Expedient*, under tow from the submarine, was halfway up the channel and making for the open sea. Liberty dived and flew overhead. Figures waved at them from the deck, and Becca saw her brother and uncle on the conning tower.

"Oh, Liberty, look! They made it. They're safe!"

"Didn't I tell you, coz? It's those darn socks, I swear it. We'll fly out and meet them in open water."

The plane banked around and climbed over the empty cove.

Becca looked down on the hourglass beach and saw the Kalaxx boats pushing off too. But then she saw four familiar figures fighting for their lives against twenty others who had surrounded them: Xu, Xi, Master Aa and Ba'd Ak. Liberty saw them too, and turned for another pass.

"We gotta help them," she shouted. "I'm gonna land. When I do, I want you to turn this kite around, then get back aboard in the pilot's seat and be ready to get us outta here. I'll leave her runnin'."

Liberty cut the power and dropped speed. She levelled out and touched down on the water covered in a scum of floating ash. She gunned the engine to give the plane enough revs to glide over to the beach, then jumped up, the freshly loaded blunderbuss hooked over her injured arm.

"She's all yours, Becca."

Liberty bounded ashore as the plane touched the beach, but was careful not to fire so near her friends. She let her first barrel loose into the air to get the Kalaxx fighters' attention. The Sujing gunpowder ignited in a shocking blue-white flame thirty feet long, sending her sprawling backwards into the sand. She sprang up and levelled the barrels at the Kalaxx.

"Liberty da Vine, pleased to meet y'all – and this here is my pal the Liberator," she said, patting the blunderbuss. "Kalaxx, Crozier's done fooled y'all. He's gone and left us here to burn under a pile of ash. This island's set to blow – get goin' while you still can."

A series of burning lava bombs slammed into the beach, striking one of the miners. With the threat of Liberty's blunderbuss and the worsening lava storm hailing down on them, there was an uneasy stand-off.

"Another time, Master Kuibyshev!" bellowed Master Aa.

The huge Kalaxx leader raised his sword in a sign of truce. They both bowed. Then Master Kuibyshev pulled the northern gyrolabe from inside his coat, his hard face cracking into a brittle smile. "After five centuries, we have reclaimed what is rightfully ours."

Master Aa hesitated. The gyrolabe from the captain's cabin was now in Kalaxx hands. But no battle could be fought in such conditions. To contest the issue would mean certain death for all.

"Hey, Mister Aa, move it!" yelled Liberty.

"To the aeroplane," he ordered.

Becca had worked hard to turn the plane around. The engine throbbed and stuttered at idle and she prayed it wouldn't stall as she scrambled back into the pilot's seat. She found the throttle and levelled the control column as Liberty and the others sprinted towards the plane.

The *Fighting Dragon* rocked as they all boarded the floats. Xu and Xi clambered on and grinned up at Becca. Master Aa and Ba'd Ak sheathed their swords and pushed the overloaded plane into deeper water.

"All aboard," yelled Liberty. "Your pilot today is Miss Becca MacKenzie, the world's newest aviatrix."

Only existing photograph of Master Kuibyshev.

MASTER KUIBYSHEV

The notorious Kuibyshev usurped the primacy of the Kalaxx order after fighting rival candidates to the death in unarmed hand-to-hand combat, as dictated by the bloody rites of Kalaxx tradition. As leader, he masterminded a ruthless campaign of diamond and gold extraction in Africa which brought the Kalaxx both enormous wealth and global condemnation as mercenary killers.

A South African newspaper was first to investigate the rumour that Kuibyshev had ordered the dynamiting of five African villages – complete with their inhabitants – in order to plunder a particularly rich seam of gold. The report profiled him as "a Russian giant at nearly eight feet tall, with pale, fish-cold eyes and an unflinching stare that strikes a note of hair-raising funk into anyone unfortunate enough to find themselves in his presence". Further records seem based on fanciful rumour and unsubstantiated hearsay. One newspaper suggested that Kuibyshev kept fifteen wives and drank ox blood for breakfast; another said that he never slept, and such was his mastery of the occult that he could "summon up ghouls as readily as a judge summons criminals".

Becca took a deep breath and nudged the throttle forward. The plane picked up speed but she knew that it could never take off. The water was covered with so much pumice that it looked as if it had frozen over. She set her jaw, pulled down her goggles and steered for the open sea.

CHAPTER TWENTY

Charlie

From Doug's sketchbook. (DMS 4/73)

Deep within the submarine, Charlie lay motionless on a bunk. Becca held his elegant hand, which hung cold and lifeless. "Charlie, squeeze my fingers if you can hear me."

Doug leant closer. "Charlie? Say something."

Mrs Ives bustled up with the captain. "Right, you two, out of the way. I don't know if he's alive or dead, Captain."

"Is he breathing?"

Mrs Ives held a feather to his nose. The merest movement could be detected.

"Yes, I do declare he is," she said with joy.

"Let him rest," the captain said softly.

"But why did he go to Sulphur Island? Why did he think Pembleton-Crozier would listen to him?" asked Becca.

"Because they are brothers. Despite everything, he cherished Julius. He thought he could make him see sense."

"Brothers?" exclaimed Doug. Suddenly it all fell into place. He thought back to their fishing trip in the cove. *That's the trouble with siblings. They can make you more exasperated than any other person alive.*

"Charles Pembleton-Crozier?" said Becca, looking at her uncle for confirmation. "Posh Charlie?"

He gave the briefest of nods. "He thought he might have a chance of stopping Julius. It is clear from what has gone on in this archipelago that it's far too late for that. I don't think Charlie finally realized until he saw the generator."

Mrs Ives tucked the blanket around him and switched off the bunk light. "Let him rest now. Bit of shut-eye will do him no end of good."

"Now to attend to another old friend. Rebecca, Douglas, come with me."

Outside on the conning tower the air was beautifully clear. They were in open water ten nautical miles from the volcano.

Expedient lay half a mile away, abandoned and stripped of everything useful or precious. She was down by the stern, and heeling over to starboard. The Kalaxx dynamite in the propeller shaft had exploded and flooded the engine room. After that there'd been no hope.

Doug focused his binoculars on the wallowing ship. The water had reached the level of his old cabin's scuttle and the captain's gallery; he pictured water flooding into his and Becca's cabins as the sea steadily claimed the ship. He felt a lump in his throat. He'd hoped to sail the seven oceans aboard the *Expedient*; that now seemed just another disappointed dream. He dropped the binoculars and turned away.

Crates of books and artefacts from the *'Pedie* were stacked on the submarine's deck ready for taking below. The *Fighting Dragon* lay alongside in the water, where Chambois was helping Fast Frankie to cover over the burn holes in the wings. Liberty was busy stowing fuel cans in the aircraft's nacelle. She saw the captain and called up, "Hey, Skip. Thanks for the plane and the chart."

"It's the least I could do, Miss da Vine. Where are you headed, if I might ask?"

"Ah, Manila, I suppose. Da Vine Oil has an exploration team based there. I've got fuel and a fair wind, so should make it in a couple of days. Mrs Ives has fixed me up pretty good, but I reckon my ol' daddy owes me some serious luxury treatment in Manila's finest hotel."

"That's it, Liberty," said Chambois, climbing across the float. "All the holes are patched. Are you sure you won't wait until morning?"

"Wait till mornin'? When I've got a plane, daylight and a big beautiful blue sky?"

"I just thought you might like…"

"What? To take a cruise with you on *that*?" Liberty pointed at the submarine and laughed. "Au revoir, Luc."

She swung up into the cockpit and pulled down her flying goggles. "See y'around, Skip. Hey, Becca, Doug. Take it easy. I might not be there to pull you out of trouble next time. Go to school or somethin'."

Fast Frankie flicked the blades of the airscrew and the engine fired into life. Liberty buttoned up her flying jacket and gunned the engine. Frankie jumped back aboard the submarine and pushed the plane's starboard float out. With a brief wave Liberty headed the plane into the wind and gave the engine maximum revs.

Liberty takes to the skies   DM. May 1920

From Doug's sketchbook. (DMS 4/78)

With heavy hearts, Becca and Doug waved goodbye. It wouldn't be the same without Liberty. The fuselage rocked and bounced across the sea until the fragile plane gained enough speed for the floats to lift clear of the water. She was airborne. She banked around and buzzed low over the submarine; something landed at Becca's feet – a pair of flying goggles. Liberty wobbled her wings, then turned and flew north into the vastness of the sky.

"An impossible woman to thank," remarked Captain MacKenzie. "Useful in a tricky situation, I must confess. Did she take that wretched blunderbuss with her?"

"Yes," said Becca.

"She might need it. It's a long way to Manila."

The distant volcano interrupted their thoughts as it vented another vengeful eruption. They all turned to look at the lava spewing from the caldera.

"One of the world's most remarkable sights, wouldn't you say?" said the captain.

"Yes, Uncle."

"Obliterating the Coterie's abomination. Nature is not to be toyed with. Not by the likes of Julius Pembleton-Crozier."

"Captain," called Chambois from the submarine's deck. "We will be safe at this distance."

Captain MacKenzie's reply was barely audible. "Very good, Monsieur Chambois." Then, straightening his spine, he turned slightly. "Mrs Cuthbert?" he called. "It's time."

Mrs Cuthbert strode on deck at the head of her dishevelled choral society and some of the other ransom hostages. She looked up expectantly. "Now, Captain? Any particular movement?"

The captain gazed back at the volcano, then, after some consideration, said with cold conviction, "*Dies Irae.*"

Mrs Cuthbert stepped forward, a breeze lifting her hair. She raised her head slightly, glancing from singer to singer until she was sure they were settled, then mouthed the count. The choir began to sing with shocking power, sending Mozart's requiem out into the silence. The forlorn harmonies drifted out across the water, reaching for the *Expedient* and wrapping her in a shroud of proud melancholy.

Captain MacKenzie leant forward to the speaking tube and gave the simple command. "Fire."

Two torpedoes launched from the submarine's bows and tore through the sea towards *Expedient*'s side, exploding in a blue flash as the zoridium warheads initiated. Her hull lifted from the water like a toy, breaking in half, as the choir finished their piece.

Doug watched dumbfounded as the *Expedient* crashed back into the sea. Both pieces of hull capsized with a gasp of escaping air, and began to sink. The last section to go under was the ram stem, which sank slowly like a shark's fin. The water bubbled and boiled for some time, then the surface calmed and smoothed until there was no evidence that the *Expedient* had ever existed.

For a while nobody spoke.

The captain pushed his cap back on his head, his gaze still fixed on the water. "A good ship. A fine friend. To have lost her and the gyrolabe in a single day..." His words trailed off.

Becca had never seen her uncle look so desolate. Then a thought occurred to her, and she whispered to Doug, "I thought you disconnected the sub's torpedo launch controls?"

"First thing I did after we took control was reconnect them. I thought I might be able to fire one of Sheng-Fat's torps at the Kalaxx. I was virtually in command of the submarine after all, sis."

Becca opened her mouth to put Doug in his place, but seemed to change her mind. "Course you were, Douglas," she smiled sadly. "Course you were."

Becca's diary: 12th May 1920
Aboard the submarine

I'm on deck, where there's a breeze. The submarine is an absolute mess below as everything is being stowed. There's hardly any room and it's humid, overcrowded and claustrophobic. There's nowhere to sit down either, although I've been allotted a bunk. The bad news is we'll have to sleep in shifts. When I'm not sleeping, Doug will be – at least that's the plan. "You'll have to climb into my stink when I go on watch," he said gleefully, shoving those filthy socks in my face. How can they have survived? Again? Reviewing the evidence of the last few weeks, I'm forced to confess that they may indeed be lucky.

I gave the code books and Mother's message to the captain immediately after the Expedient *had sunk, and explained the real reason for our trip to the island. The captain simply nodded and gave them to Sparkie. The truth is, of course, that we cannot crack the message without their help, and recent events have convinced us that the captain has our best interests at heart.*

I managed to discover more of the circumstances surrounding the loss of the northern gyrolabe. When the Kalaxx stormed the stern of the Expedient, *a vicious battle took place below decks in the captain's quarters. Fearful that the Kalaxx would set off charges or simply set the ship ablaze, Mr Ives and three Sujing fought hard to rescue the gyrolabe from its secret compartment in the day cabin. But the Kalaxx charges exploded deep within the ship, knocking the gyrolabe from Mr Ives's hand, and it was seized by a Kalaxx fighter as the coxswain lay dazed on the deck. The captain has praised* them for the audacity of their rescue attempt, but Mr Ives looks very low and angry with himself.

I've lost two things important to me today. Liberty and Expedient. *Both exceptional friends. Cabin number five is gone for ever. The ship felt like a second home, and now lies shattered on the seabed. I have gained one thing in exchange, however. A new passion to fly. I want to start lessons immediately. Flying the plane was terrifying, but I know deep inside, without even thinking about it, that I belong in the air.*

Once again our future seems uncertain. Ahead is open sea and an ocean of possibilities. Oh, but Liberty is right. Ships are slow. How I wish I could just fly away from here like her.

CHAPTER TWENTY-ONE

It was difficult to knock on the captain's door, as it was merely a velvet curtain. But Becca and Doug knew the Duchess was in there, and had learnt their lesson long ago.

"Captain?" said Doug tentatively. "You sent for us?"

"Yes, come in!" Their uncle was reading through the submarine's log, seemingly at ease in his new surroundings. The Duchess was stretched out on the bunk, eyes closed but ears twitching. "Sorry there's nowhere to sit. Duchess!" The tiger opened one eye. "Make some room. Go and get some air." With a strangled moan, the Duchess slunk off the bunk and sloped out, tail swishing. "Perch on the bunk. It's hardly *Expedient*'s day cabin…" The words stuck in his throat a little. After a pause he said, "How do you find our new boat? Rather cramped?"

"Ship, surely?" Doug said.

"No. Submarines are classed as boats. We've dropped down a nautical peg, in more ways than one."

Doug's eyes lit up. "Will we be diving? How deep does she go?"

"This class of boat is notoriously unreliable underwater, so I'm not keen to try. Safer on the surface. Our progress so far has been good."

"Progress where?" asked Becca.

"To Singapore. Now, this note from your mother." The captain opened the desk drawer and took out Sparkie's deciphered message.

"Was Pembleton-Crozier's translation accurate?"

"Yes … well, in essence. You did the right thing bringing it to me." The captain handed the deciphered message to Becca.

COTERIE RESURRECTED. HGS NOT TO BE TRUSTED EXCEPT FITZROY AND CREW. CONTACT HIM AT ONCE. HE MUST STOP COTERIE EXTRACTING DOS FROM TEMBLA MINES AT CELEBES SEA POSITION 03 DEG 05 MIN 10 SEC NORTH 125 DEG 10 MIN 40 SEC EAST.

WE GO TO SINKIANG VIA NEPAL TO FIND CAPULUS AND UR-CAN. ALSO AIM OF COTERIE. CAPULUS ALLIED WITH RUSSIAN COSSACK GENERAL PUGACHEV. HAVE LEFT FALSE TRAIL. WILL GET SUJING HELP AT KHOTAN.

H AND E

"Who is this Capulus?" she asked.

"A Russian, we think. Your father said he posed as a cinnabar ore trader from Samarkand."

"Father met him?"

"Oh yes, years ago. Back in 1912 he approached your parents with copies of Tembla hieroglyphics taken, so he said, from the walls of Ur-Can. He was offering them for sale."

"So Capulus knows the location of Ur-Can?" asked Becca.

"It is difficult to be certain. He revealed very little."

"Why did Capulus approach our parents?" Doug questioned.

"Because your mother is a renowned language scholar. Your parents bought them on behalf of the Guild. Your mother then devoted her time to trying to crack the meaning of the Tembla symbols. The work was painfully slow, I understand. From our correspondence I know she made some sort of breakthrough in the summer of 1915. She was bound by secrecy not to write specifics in a letter."

"All those symbols," Becca recalled. "I remember Mother working on them night and day."

"Did you ever see Mother's translation?"

Captain MacKenzie sighed. "No. I've been away from the centre of things for many years working on research projects of my own. The contents were regarded as so secret that the translation was kept in the Guild vaults at Firenze. I've not been to Italy for a good half-decade."

"Borelli. He'd have had access to the translation."

"Yes. Borelli read your mother's work on its arrival at Guild headquarters. Your parents had no idea... Indeed, I had no idea that Borelli was in league with Pembleton-Crozier. He's the head of scientific research for the Guild! The Coterie must have allied with the Kalaxx shortly after your mother had identified the archipelago as the site of the Tembla mines. With a new supply of zoridium, Borelli could begin his dangerous pursuit of scientific celebrity."

"Why did the Guild not launch their own expedition?" asked Doug.

"All research expeditions were suspended during the Great War. Pembleton-Crozier was free from the risk of discovery. My ship was the only vessel suitable for such a mission, and as you know, I was in the Antarctic."

Doug's face took on a scheming look. "So Capulus might know something of Mother and Father's whereabouts?"

"It's possible. Of course, Liberty had dealings with Capulus, and I presume Pembleton-Crozier was trying to buy information on Ur-Can from him. I wish I'd questioned Liberty more about their meeting."

"We must go to Samarkand and find him," Becca stated firmly.

Their uncle guffawed. "Samarkand? You two are going nowhere near Samarkand – or the Sinkiang. You've had enough adventures to last you a lifetime. Without the *Expedient*, I cannot fulfil our contract to educate you at sea. I'd been planning to send you to Firenze, Douglas, since you've sworn the oath, but I realize the board can no longer be trusted. I intend to go and search for your parents myself, but it is far too dangerous for you to join me. You have been lucky so far; in my experience, luck should not be pushed. You will have to return to San Francisco."

"No, please, Uncle. Not Aunt Margaret. Not after all we've been through."

"I have no choice. As Liberty said, you should try going to school. The matter is closed."

Xu and Xi tried to comfort Becca and Doug. They all sat cross-legged on deck watching the sun dip and touch the horizon. Doug looked tired and dejected.

"Didn't we do enough? Didn't we find the trireme, the gyrolabe and *The 99 Elements*?"

"That's not enough for the captain," said Becca angrily. "Seems the Guild has made good use of us, but we've nothing to show for it in return."

"We'll look out for your parents when we get to Sinkiang," said Xi.

"You're not going as well?" asked Doug in disbelief.

Xi looked away.

"Um, yes," Xu replied apologetically. "We are to take the Khotan challenges to become full Sujing Quantou fighters."

"So everyone's going apart from us two," muttered Doug.

It seemed to Becca that they were soon to lose two more friends and end up with Aunt Margaret as a consolation prize. "Oh great. So we're being dumped on a steamer at Singapore while you're all bound for China."

"Singapore?" said Xi. "You're being put ashore there?"

"Apparently. Along with Borelli. They're shipping him and his crew back to Italy under armed guard. Why?"

"You can get a ship to almost anywhere from Singapore, east or west."

"I know. We're going east, to America."

"Since when did you two start following orders?" said Xu with a wry smile.

Doug put his hand in his pocket and pulled out some of the slender gold bars he'd rescued from Sheng-Fat's junk at Wenzi Island. The warm amber of the sunset danced up and reflected on his face as he grinned broadly at his sister.

Captain MacKenzie and Master Aa were also enjoying the sunset from the conning tower.

"I dare not give Rebecca and Douglas false hope, but I've a mind to believe Hamish and Elena may still be alive," said the captain. "I'm certain the key to all of this lies with Capulus and this Russian General Pugachev mentioned in the cipher."

"General Pugachev has an army, Captain. An army of five

thousand. I suggest we make for Khotan and join forces with my western brothers and sisters before we begin our search for anyone."

As the submarine gathered speed, Master Aa and the captain shook hands.

"Our alliance continues, Master Aa."

On deck below, the Duchess paced forward past Xu, Xi, Becca and Doug and took up position at the submarine's bow, her nose already sniffing for the parched desert winds of the Sinkiang.

END OF BOOK II

Appendices

TYPHOON DAMAGE TO THE EXPEDIENT

Above: The Expedient *before the typhoon.*

Below: View aft from the fo'c'sle during the typhoon.

Top right: Flooding in the boiler room.

Bottom right: Vasto and Leaky repair the hull while beached on South Island.

(MA 556.208 EXP)

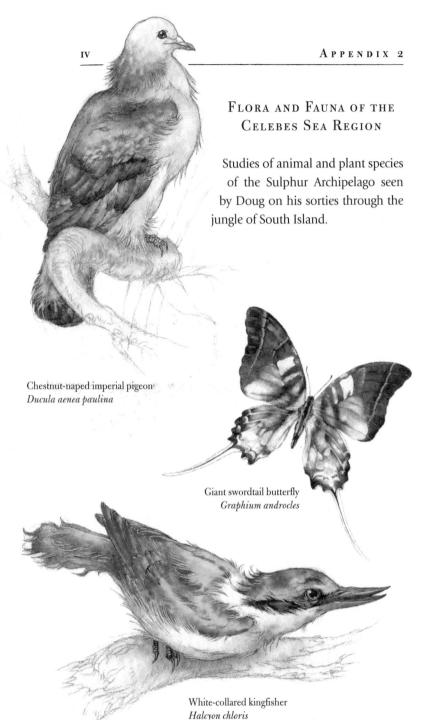

Flora and Fauna of the Celebes Sea Region

Studies of animal and plant species of the Sulphur Archipelago seen by Doug on his sorties through the jungle of South Island.

Chestnut-naped imperial pigeon
Ducula aenea paulina

Giant swordtail butterfly
Graphium androcles

White-collared kingfisher
Halcyon chloris

Reticulated python
Python reticulatus

Butterfly orchid "Mariposa"
Phalaenopsis amabilis

Pig-tailed macaque
Macaca nemestrina

THE ZORIDIUM GENERATOR

Borelli's zoridium generator was an exploitation of the gyro-labe's capacity to spin with extraordinary speed and power. Coterie scientists saw that if they could convert this mechanical rotation into electrical energy they would create an effective and economical power station. But the generator was essentially an enlargement of the gyrolabe, and unanswered questions relating to the ancient science behind the machines were magnified on a parallel scale. Although operating in this dangerous knowledge vacuum, Borelli's generator worked well, producing vast amounts of clean energy from minute quantities of zoridium. His revised design, incorporating Charlie's gravity shield revisions, was engineered and constructed by the Kalaxx, experts in early twentieth-century mining technology.

TRANSLATION OF RUSSIAN KEY TEXT ON THE GENERATOR BLUEPRINT

1. Foundations	16. Electricity generator 1
2. Steel roof frame	17. Electricity generator 2
3. Wooden roof	18. Radius arm 1 (upper)
4. Side columns	19. Radius arm 2 (upper)
5. Magnetic field shielding	20. Radius arm 3 (upper)
6. Copper plating	21. Radius arm 4 (lower)
7. Circular gallery	22. Radius arm 5 (lower)
8. Control platform	23. Radius arm 6 (lower)
9. Measuring apparatus	24. Alignment arm 1
10. Gravity shield (upper)	25. Alignment arm 2
11. Zoridium node (upper)	26. Alignment arm 3
12. Central sphere	27. Magnetic field intensifier
13. Zoridium node (lower)	28. Alignment machinery for
14. Gravity shield (lower)	gravity shield supports
15. Gravity shield support	29. Alignment control motor

Above and below: Expedient's *Number 5 Mark 1 theodolite/gun director. This served a dual purpose as a surveying instrument and a director for* Expedient's *guns. In its surveying role, it would have been used to create accurate maps or lay out engineering and construction projects. In its role as a gun director, it would have been taken ashore to plot targets for* Expedient's *guns to fire at with pinpoint precision.*

A History of the Gyrolabes

The four gyrolabes were discovered in India by Alexander the Great's army in 326 BC. References in Sujing Quantou texts suggest that these devices originate circa 4,000 BC. Found with the gyrolabes was *The 99 Elements*, in part a work of science and in part philosophy. It told of an incredible machine that could only be started using all four gyrolabes as a key.

By 326 BC Alexander's army was weary of war. Fearful that Alexander would exploit their find to further his military ambitions, his generals decided to keep their discovery from him. Rather than destroy *The 99 Elements* and the gyrolabes, they agreed to divide them up and conceal them in the furthest reaches of Asia. The finest of the reconnaissance troops – the prodromoi – were selected and split into four teams. Each was given a quarter of *The 99 Elements* and a gyrolabe. Each gyrolabe was engraved with an ancient symbol referring to one of the cardinal points; the troops accordingly carried them to the north, south, east and west.

Gyrolabe Timelines

All four gyrolabes

❖ *c.4,000 BC:* Believed to have been created by the Tembla civilization as the initiators to a machine located at Ur-Can.
❖ *326 BC:* Found by the army of Alexander the Great.

Northern gyrolabe

❖ *326 BC:* Hidden by the prodromoi in northern Asia.
❖ *14th cent. AD:* Lost by the northern chapter of the Sujing Quantou.
❖ *1533:* Came into the possession of Jean de Dinteville, who co-founded the HGS. Taken to Firenze.
❖ *1920:* On board the *Expedient* until the battle on South Island. Now in the hands of Master Kuibyshev, leader of the Kalaxx.

Southern gyrolabe

❖ *326 BC:* Taken to be hidden by the prodromoi in the south.
❖ *c.1720:* Found (with trireme) by Duncan MacKenzie, who was killed by Celebes Sea headhunters before he could reveal his discovery.
❖ *1920:* Found by Becca and Doug on South Island. Now in the hands of Julius Pembleton-Crozier.

EASTERN GYROLABE

❖ *326 BC:* Hidden by the prodromoi in the east.
❖ *1720:* Gifted to Duncan and Cameron MacKenzie for HGS research purposes by the eastern Sujing. Taken to Firenze by Cameron.
❖ *1920:* Stolen from HGS headquarters by Alfonso Borelli. Now in the hands of Julius Pembleton-Crozier.

WESTERN GYROLABE

❖ *326 BC:* Hidden by the prodromoi in the west.
❖ *1920:* Still under protection of the western Sujing chapter in Khotan.

THE SUJING QUANTOU

The four chapters of the Sujing were the direct descendants of Alexander the Great's reconnaissance troops who were entrusted with *The 99 Elements* and the four gyrolabes. Alexander, believing they had deserted, sentenced them to perpetual exile. Over the centuries they adopted Chinese ways and became known as the Order of the Sujing Quantou.

Realizing the magnitude of the knowledge the Tembla civilization had amassed, the Sujing dedicated their lives to guarding *The 99 Elements* and protecting the secrets of Daughter of the Sun. After centuries of searching, they concluded that neither Ur-Can nor the legendary machine existed. Nevertheless, the western chapter retained their gyrolabe to safeguard the Sujing stake should the machine ever be found.

The eastern chapter, based in Shanghai, researched the properties of Daughter of the Sun, creating spectacular fireworks as a by-product.

The western chapter guarded the Daughter of the Sun mine and refinery at Khotan, which had been documented by the Tembla in *The 99 Elements* and rediscovered by the western prodromoi.

The northern chapter allied with the Ha-Mi in 1719 in order to gain control of the Daughter of the Sun mine at Khotan. After the Ha-Mi Wars, they fled to Russia, where they remained until their expulsion 140 years later. Profiteering from the gold rushes of America and diamond mines of Africa, they became rich but notorious mercenaries (the Kalaxx).

The southern prodromoi were never heard of after 326 BC. It was rumoured that they had sailed in search of the Tembla mines detailed in their quarter of *The 99 Elements*, but this remained unproven until Becca and Doug found their ship in 1920.

ABOUT THE AUTHOR

Joshua Mowll lives in Pimlico, London. He studied design at Canterbury and Ipswich and has worked for a national newspaper as a graphic artist since 1994. Joshua spends much of his spare time curing leaks in his two British design classics: a Walker Tideway 12 clinker sailing dinghy and a canvas-topped Land Rover nicknamed the Lady Godiva. Operation Typhoon Shore *is the second book in the Guild Trilogy.*

ACKNOWLEDGEMENTS: I would like to thank: my agent, Clare Conville, for her steadfast dedication to the trilogy; Gill Evans for her expert captaincy; Ben Norland for his enthusiasm and design flair; Anne Finnis, Lucy Earley and Georgina Hookings for making it all happen, page by page; Andrea Tompa for her involvement at Candlewick Press; Linda Morgan for exquisite production; Julek Heller and Niroot Puttapipat for their consistently excellent illustrations.

I would also like to thank: Emma Lidbury, Emil Fortune, Alison Morrison, Jo Humphreys-Davies, Rebecca Linsley, Caroline Muir, Michael Jordan, Gavin Stannard, the Reverend William Mowll, Benjamin Mowll, Steve Wood, Timothy Smith, James Del Mar; and a special thank you to Martin Northrop for his technical assistance in reconstructing the *Powder Monkey*.

First published 2006 by
Walker Books Ltd, 87 Vauxhall Walk,
London SE11 5HJ

First edition

Text © 2006 Joshua Mowll

All illustrations © 2006 Joshua Mowll except:

All Doug MacKenzie sketches
© 2006 Julek Heller

Illustrations p.20, p.81, p.85 foldout
(Kalaxx miner only), p.97 (hand-lettering
only), p.153, p.256, Appendix 2
© 2006 Niroot Puttapipat

Sujing warrior icon © 2006
Benjamin Mowll and used
under licence

Photo permissions:
p.124: dagger illustration
created using photograph by
Roger Doonan and the pupils of St
Mark's Primary School, Bournemouth.
Breathing helmet and signalling lamp
(Appendix 4) used by kind permission of
the Lowestoft Maritime Museum.

Joshua Mowll has asserted his moral rights

This book has been typeset in Giovanni and
Bulmer MT

Printed in China

British Library Cataloguing in Publication Data:
a catalogue record for this book is available
from the British Library

ISBN-13: 978-1-84428-646-1
ISBN-10: 1-84428-646-0

www.walkerbooks.co.uk